THE DOG
WHO
DANCED

THE DOG WHO DANCED

SUSAN WILSON

St. Martin's Paperbacks

This is a work of fiction. All of the characters, organizations, and events portrayed in this novel are either products of the author's imagination or are used fictitiously.

Published in the United States by St. Martin's Paperbacks, an imprint of St. Martin's Publishing Group.

THE DOG WHO DANCED

For information, address St. Martin's Publishing Group, 120 Broadway, New York, NY 10271.

www.stmartins.com

Library of Congress Catalog Card Number: 2011041345

ISBN: 978-1-250-25872-4

Our books may be purchased in bulk for promotional, educational, or business use. Please contact your local bookseller or the Macmillan Corporate and Premium Sales Department at 1-800-221-7945, ext. 5442, or by email at MacmillanSpecialMarkets@macmillan.com.

Printed in the United States of America

St. Martin's Press hardcover edition / March 2012
St. Martin's Griffin edition / June 2013
St. Martin's Paperbacks edition / March 2020

10 9 8 7 6 5 4 3 2 1

Dedicated with love to our mothers,
Dorothy Geer Hidler and Claire Darling Gibson

PART I

PROLOGUE

Nothing was ever handed to me. My old man taught me the value of never expecting kindness. My stepmother taught me that the only way you get to be first in life is to stand alone. I've managed. I've never gone hungry, or worn anything I was ashamed of because it was threadbare, at least not since I left home at seventeen and a half. I've never sold myself in order to eat; I've met women like that. It's true I've had living arrangements that might be looked at as nearly that bad, but that's only if you're looking in. I have done some things I'm not proud of, but each one was the result of wanting something I was willing to make a hard choice to get. And, yes, I've made those "bad" choices along the way. Even if you don't grow up with religion, you still know right from wrong, and the difference between good and not so good.

My name is Justine Meade, and in my forty-three years, there have only been a handful of people I have loved. No, that's an exaggeration. Two. Two whom I lost because of stupidity and selfishness. One was my son. The other was my dog.

CHAPTER 1

"You gonna finish that?" Artie stubs a blunt finger in the direction of my English muffin. We're sitting in a Travel America rest stop, one of the several that we've visited on this west-to-east run. He likes to keep on schedule; I like to pause for an hour and get the blood flowing in my legs again after hours in the cab of the eighteen-wheeler, inhaling Artie's cigarette smoke and drinking warm, flat Coke. TAs are little shopping centers, catering to folks who live on the road, modern Gypsies, with anything you can think of for your vehicle from oil to mud flaps to little bobblehead dashboard figures of football players and Jesus. The restaurants offer big man's meals, all-you-can-eats—chicken-fried steak, biscuits, apple pie. How hungry can a man be who has sat in a rig all day, keeping busy with radio and Red Bull?

"No. Take it." Unlike the majority of the people jammed into the booths and bellied up to the counter, I have no appetite, no desire to heap my plate with eggs and sausages. The good hot coffee is enough for me. I'm

hoping that Artie will stay put long enough for me to
visit the ladies' shower room.

I'm riding shotgun with Artie Schmidt because I need
to get back to the East Coast. He comes into my bar
pretty regularly when he's not on the road. It was Candy's
idea, hitching the ride instead of flying. She knew that
round-trip airfare would make me have to choose between rent and food; and a one-way ticket might mean
that she would have to find another girl. Besides, this way
I could take Mack with me. The idea of being in my stepmother's presence without an ally was unthinkable. Going with Artie meant that I could take my dog with me,
and there is no way I'd subject my Sheltie to being cargo.

Frankly, it was Candy who convinced me that I had to
go east in the first place. My stepmother didn't reach out
often, or at all, so when she called to say my father was
failing, it was almost impossible to get past the fact that
it was Adele on the phone, rather than take in the fact of
my father's dying. Wicked stepmothers are only in fairy
stories, right? I'm here to tell you that Cinderella had it
good compared to what that woman put me through. But
Candy said I should go, that it was important. Family is
important. Right. Despite my better instincts, I set my
course eastward and signed on with Artie Schmidt. Mack,
my blue merle Sheltie, right alongside me. The boyfriend
who gave Mack to me is long gone, but my little man stays,
keeping his long, pointy nose at my heels wherever I go.

Candy Kane—and that's her real name—runs a decent tavern just outside the city limits of Seattle. I've
lived pretty much everywhere. Starting when I walked
out of the house the day after high school graduation,
getting as far as Somerville, where I bunked in with a
pair of roommates I found on a message board in a coffee shop. Then down Interstate 95 to Brooklyn, where

I might have stayed; then Florida, then Louisiana and Texas. I have made my way as far west as California, and as far north as Washington State, where I've stayed put longer than anywhere else. When I look at a map of the United States, touch all those big cities and little towns that I've spent time in, I see that I've been moving in a slow clockwise circle around the country. When we're getting the place ready to open, before the first happy-hour customers come in and want to watch ESPN or CNN, Candy calls me over when *Jeopardy* is on; I can nail the geography questions.

My point was never to return to my starting place, New Bedford, Massachusetts. I'm like the old-time whalers, seeking my fortune far from home. Instead of the ocean, I travel along major highways. Instead of ships, I own clunkers good for only a few thousand miles. Instead of whales, I'm not sure what I'm seeking. Ahab had revenge in mind. I just haven't found the one place that will hold me still. When I was young, I thought that there would be a man to tie me down, but it never worked out that way. And no job was ever lifelong interesting; not one has ever gotten me to sign on for the retirement plan.

You might think that having a kid would have kept me in one place, or at least slowed me down, but even that failed to root me. Every time I pulled up stakes, I told my son that no matter where we were, we were at home as long as we were together. For a long time, that was true, but then, well, it wasn't.

So, here I am, circling back to my starting point in a direct run down Interstate 90, New Bedford–bound.

"I'd like a shower."

"And I'd like to keep on schedule. You've already slowed me down with twice as many pee breaks as I take."

"You pee in a bottle."

Artie pulls off his greasy Tractor Supply cap and runs his fingers through his stringy hair, resettles the cap, and drags a long breath. "Five minutes, or I swear to God I'll leave without you."

Artie has said this before. I smile and grab my duffel bag, which nestles at my feet. It contains everything I need and nothing that I don't. That bag and I have a longer relationship than most married couples. I pull a couple of dollars out of my back pocket and drop them on the check. "Give me seven and I'll meet you at the truck. Go buy yourself a pack of gum."

"Justine. I mean it. I come in late with this load and I'm fucked."

"Then don't hold me up talking to me." I shoulder my duffel and stride off to the showers.

Once Artie figured out that I meant it, that I was paying him three hundred bucks to let me ride east with him, and that didn't include any physical stuff, he'd turned sullen. It's funny how the barroom personality can be so different from that of the real person. Mr. How's My Girl quickly became Mr. Cranky. Tough. I'm not taking this ride for the company. I keep Mack between us, and get out of the cab while Artie catches a few hours' sleep—walking Mack around quiet parking lots, sitting at empty picnic tables and sipping cold coffee—then unroll my sleeping bag and crawl into Artie's man-smelly bunk to catch my own z's. Artie doesn't want Mack in his bed, but that's okay. The dog curls up on my seat, his little ears twisted in my direction, so I know he's not really sleeping. On guard. Shelties, miniature collies, are guard dogs by breeding. His instincts are to watch the hills for wolves. Artie is on notice every time Mack stares at him with his eagle eyes.

* * *

There are three shower stalls. One is broken, and the other two are in use. I should forget about it. I wash my face and brush my teeth. Whoever those two women are, they are flipping taking a long time. I floss. I wait. I know that Artie is getting pissed. Finally, the shower turns off. Now I have to wait for Miss America to dry off and get dressed. "People waiting out here!" I shove my washcloth and toothbrush back into my bag.

No answer. The second shower shuts off. The room is suddenly quiet except for the sound of towel against skin. I look at my watch. My time is done. I pick up my duffel, and, miraculously, Shower Queen exits the booth. I can do this in one minute. I can't stand the feeling of dirty hair. I hate that I smell like day-old sweat and Artie's cigarettes. I can get in and under and out in two minutes, tops. I won't dry my hair.

Artie will be pissed, but I'm confident that he'll just bitch, not leave. I strip.

Five minutes later—it can't have been more than five minutes—I emerge from the shower room, wet towel rolled up under my arm, duffel over my shoulder, and my hair, wet and unstyled, hanging to my shoulders. I'm in the second of three T-shirts I've brought and the same jeans I started out with. But I feel better. I'll finish the job in the truck, put on the mascara and finger-wave my hair.

As I promised, and only a couple of minutes late, I head out the automatic doors, making straight for the truck lot. Maybe thirty semis are lined up in rows, Roadway, Bemis, UPS, Mayflower Movers, and independents with family names on the cabs and unmarked trailers behind. Rigs with full berths above, rigs with shiny red and chrome, fancy lettering, rigs with more lights than a carnival midway. And campers. Campers snuggled up between the big guys, tagalongs and fifth wheels; double-axle motor homes. Four-wheel-drive trucks with engines that rival those powering the big rigs.

I don't see Artie's truck. I look to the diesel pumps and then the line for the truck wash, but he's not there. I start to trot down the lane between trucks. His rig isn't distinctive, a plain dull green. He's hand-lettered his name, Arthur B. Schmidt, on the driver's door in an uneven attempt at block letters—the Schmidt is narrower than the Arthur. He's hauling a trailer that he was hired to haul. Nothing to distinguish it from the others. But I can't have missed it. It's been my home for the past two days.

"Artie, for God's sake, stop teasing." I say this under my breath, but the panic is rising, a sour taste in my freshly brushed mouth, the taste of trouble. I stop looking for Artie. I know that he's gone. The mean SOB has called my bluff. He's taken my three hundred bucks and abandoned me in Ohio.

Then it hits me, like someone has punched me in the stomach. Mack was in the cab. My dog was in the truck, where I'd left him after giving him a quick walk in the doggy rest area. He's been waiting for us to come out and give him a little treat of Artie's leftovers, a bowl of fresh water. I can't believe that Artie would have driven off with him. There's no chance Artie would keep him. He's dumped him into the middle of this parking lot of bulls.

I call and whistle. Mack won't know where I am, and he'll be frantic. *I* am frantic as I begin to run, my wet towel lost on the pavement, my duffel banging against my back. "Mack! Mack! Come, boy. Mack!" My mouth dries out and I can't whistle anymore.

Mack is obedient; if he hears me, he'll come like a shot. He's not the type of dog that would wander around; he'll be looking for me, his nose to the ground, maybe heedless of the danger of being in this active parking lot. All of a sudden, it seems like every truck in this parking lot starts its motor in a cacophony of diesel. Mack can't hear me over the noise; I bend to peer beneath the behemoths, looking and looking for the flash of white and gray that will be Mack. I can't find him. I stop dead in the path of a moving truck. The driver slides a hand out his window, waving me across the lane.

Okay. If Mack isn't here, then Artie still has him. I circle the TA building. Artie's yanking my chain. If he's still got Mack, then Artie hasn't gone anywhere. He's not going to do that. He's got to be here. If he's back on the road, there's no way he's going to turn around and come back; the time he'd lose in playing me would be too precious.

But there are no trucks on the other side of the building, just family cars, a horse trailer, and a Harley with a one-legged rider parked in a handicapped spot.

"Have you seen a dog? A Sheltie? Gray with black streaks. White ruff? One blue eye and one brown eye?" I keep talking, as if adding to the description will make the answer become yes.

The one-legged rider shakes his head, which is swathed in a filthy red bandanna. "Nope. Sorry. This is a tough place to lose a dog." Like a lot of the rugged men I meet, he has a sympathetic voice, which does not match his tough appearance.

I collapse onto a bench in front of the building, all the strength in my legs gone, my heart thumping with a disconcerting loudness. I fight back the tears. In my experience, tears have never been useful, neither relieving pain nor offering comfort once shed. What I need is a plan. I need to stop Artie.

Artie has driven off with Mack.

Mack sleeps with his brushy tail curled up over his pointy nose. Tucked up like this, he's a small package of dog, burrowed into the sleeping bag Justine has left unrolled on the bunk behind the driver's seat. He's quite pleased to wait, dozing, waking, dozing, for the people to return to the truck. There might be a taste of something good as a reward for being quiet and patient.

This mobile living is a bit boring, but he is satisfied with the almost constant presence of his Justine. Usually he has to doze, wake, doze for a long time every day until Justine comes back from her day away from him, smelling of beer and fried food. He loves that smell; once, when she took him with her to work, just to pick up her check, he immediately recognized the place as where she went during the day. The lovely odors defining her away time and making it comprehensible to him. Who wouldn't want to be in a place that smelled like burgers?

When only Artie got back into the cab, Mack merely opened one eye. He isn't a big fan of the guy, but that's mostly because of the stink of his cigarettes and the fact that the man ignores him. Mack is more accustomed to having Justine's males be friendly, sometimes even presenting offerings. Good stuff, like rawhide chews and squeaky toys. This guy just talks and smokes and, once in a while, gets too close to Justine. That's when Mack will find a reason to squeeze himself onto Justine's lap. No need to show teeth, just be there, a reminder that he is in charge, that she is his person.

Artie lights up another cigarette, not even rolling the window down to release the smoke. Mack tucks his nose deeper under his tail, his jack-in-the-pulpit ears turning like miniature radar detectors to catch the sound of Justine's feet on the pavement. Artie drums on the steering wheel, fidgets with the arrangement of knickknacks on the dashboard, cranks down his window, and ejects the butt of his cigarette. "Goddamn. She's pushin' me."

Mack keeps still. He wishes Artie would be quiet so that he can listen better for Justine. The dog lifts his head to sniff the air as the window goes down, but the cigarette stink is an impenetrable barrier, obscuring even the fresh air outside, and Artie's head blocks his view. She'll come. Justine will be back. She always comes back.

The first day that he lived with Justine, he learned that lesson. A mere baby, a pup of few weeks, he'd been taken away from his mother, his littermates, and the only human hands he'd ever known. He was boxed and carried to Justine. When she took him up and rubbed her inadequate human nose against his pointy one, he fell in love. And then she left him, putting him back in the box that would be his cave, his home, until he outgrew it. Then she came back and let him out. Fed him, cuddled him on the couch, named him. He never worried about her absence again.

Mack is startled back into full awareness as Artie hollers a stream of tongue language that Mack doesn't recognize word for word, but he gets the meaning. The man is angry. There is no one here for him to be angry at, unless he's angry at him, so Mack shrinks even more into the dim closet of a bunk. Suddenly, Artie starts the truck, and the rumbling vibration of the big engine fills the air. The gears grind and the truck moves forward. Justine isn't here. Maybe Artie is going to find her. Mack's soft whine is shadowed by the sound of the diesel engine. They pull away from the other trucks and shoot down the TA access road. In a minute, they are back on the highway. Justine is not there.

CHAPTER 2

"You don't have his plate number? I can't have every truck with a green cab stopped before it leaves Ohio. I'm sorry about your dog. If the guy gets pulled over, we can maybe get the dog."

I hang up before the state trooper can give me any more bad news. They can't, or won't, help track down Artie. I've called Artie's cell eighteen times, but he won't answer. If he did, I wouldn't ask him to do anything but leave Mack where I can pick him up, maybe at another TA, or a vet not far off the road. But Artie sees my number and ignores me. I don't exist for him anymore.

I need a ride. I need to catch up with Artie. Feeling like a tramp, I start talking to the truckers arrayed around the counter like piglets on a sow. "No can do." "Against the rules of my company." "Back off; I'm a family man."

Soon enough, I attract the attention of the center's manager, who gives me the look. I hold my hands up in the universal sign of "no harm" and move away from the truckers.

Families are tucking into the all-you-can-eat brunch. I sit alone at a table a mere three feet from a likely-looking group: mom and dad, two chunky preschoolers, and a grandma. "Nice day. Where you headed?" Nice, ordinary midwestern friendliness, nothing scary here.

"We're headed down to Disney."

That's east enough for me. Maybe they can get me as far as New York before they head south down 95.

"What'll you have?" The waitress is looming over me. The seventeen-inch-tall multipage plastic menu is still flat on the table.

Hungry I'm not, but I need to look like a customer. I order two eggs and bacon, white toast, coffee. I think that I'm going to hurl. I smile at the family beside me. "I'm heading east, too. Any chance you've got room for a passenger? I'll pay your gas."

The father twitches his mustache-covered lip like an old-time movie Lothario. His wife's eyes open in that wifely "Don't you dare" look I've seen on the wives who sometimes come looking for their husbands in my bar. He holds his hands palm up. "I don't think so. We're pretty full." Grandma, intent on her biscuits, suddenly gets what's going on. From her corner of the table, she sets an eye on me, and I nod and go back to playing with the sugar packets in their little white box on my table.

Before my food can arrive, I drop a dollar on the table and leave the building.

"You need some help?" It's the one-legged Harley rider. He leans on a single crutch, resting on a leg that ends in a traditional motorcycle boot, the leather beneath his left knee vacant, moving slightly in the Ohio air.

"I guess I do."

"Your boyfriend dump you?"

"No. My ride east abandoned me. But, worse"—I swallow to gain control of my voice—"he's got my dog. He took off with my dog."

"Bastard."

"I need to catch up with him." I hate that my voice cracks.

"Where's he headed?"

With those few words, I feel a flicker of hope, as tiny as the flame on a Bic, but a flicker nonetheless. "Boston."

"No stops on the way?"

"No. Nonstop."

"Down Ninety?"

"Yeah. He'll keep going straight through. He can do twenty hours with enough Red Bull."

"I can get you to Erie."

"That'll help."

"Climb on board." My one-legged Harley rider slips his crutch into a special hanger and slings his bad leg over the saddle. "There's a helmet in the pannier, and a headset. Put it on and we'll be able to talk."

I find both, a turtle-shell helmet that scarcely looks like it would protect me, and only if I fell directly on my head, and the headset. I stow my duffel in the pannier, fishing out my sunglasses first. I slide onto the seat behind him, careful not to kick him.

Using his one good leg, my new friend backs the Harley out of the space, then carefully removes the handicapped placard from the handlebars and places it in his jacket pocket. "I'm Mitch." His voice in my ear startles me.

I bring the mouthpiece up. "Justine Meade." As I'm about to embrace this stranger for the better part of the day, I offer him my hand.

He takes my hand in his leather-gloved mitt, an oyster in a black shell, then brings my hands around his middle. "Hang on tight. We'll catch that son of a bitch."

Mack doesn't know how long they have been going. He only knows that it is time for dinner. His dinner. His kibble, which he can see in its plastic bag on the floor of the side of the cab where Justine should be, is tantalizingly out of reach. It would be nice to have a lap of water. His Shetland sheepdog ancestors knew about privation as they rounded up sheep on the rocky hillside, but he's a domestic house dog and quite used to routine. Dinner at six. Water all day long. If he were any other dog, he might take himself down from the bunk and go help himself, ripping into the flimsy plastic with sharp teeth. But Mack is not just any other dog. He is a well-trained dog. One of his first lessons was in *don'touch*. Stare at that kibble in the bowl all you want, but *don'touch* it until given the word. *Don'touch* the garbage pail, despite its temptations. Justine once left a package of cold cuts on the kitchen table, an easy reach from his back legs, but he disdained touching it, although he spent the day staring at it in futile hope that it would fall off the table and become fair game. Justine hadn't said *don'touch*, but he'd never reach for anything on a table anyway.

Artie keeps staring at his cell. Mack knows that it's called *cell* because Justine has taught him to fetch it when she's in one room and the cell is singing in another. Artie's cell doesn't sing; it makes a sound like a miniature truck horn: *blat blat blat; blat blat blat.* Artie thumbs it quiet. He doesn't speak to it. But each time it honks, Artie looks at it.

CHAPTER 3

We've been on the road for twenty minutes. My only thoughts are the calculation between a fast-moving semi and a faster-moving Harley. It's like one of those math problems in junior high that I could never wrap my mind around: If vehicle A is traveling at sixty-five mph and vehicle B is traveling at seventy-five mph, how long will it take for vehicle B to catch up to vehicle A, and will Artie even stop in Erie? Mitch pulls me out of my mathematical reverie. "So where are you from?"

"I've been living in Washington."

"State or D.C.?"

"State. Seattle."

Our conversation is bulleted, quick phrases spoken through tiny mouthpieces directly into ears. A weird intimacy. Can he hear my breath in his ear? Once, I was a telemarketer for a male-enhancement product. We were encouraged to be breathy.

"Where you from?" I'm not sure what I'm expecting.

He has the look of a man who might not be from anywhere.

"Cleveland Heights."

"So you were just starting out on your trip?" The
travel center is only a few miles from Cleveland Heights.

"Not going anywhere. I was just buying coffee. Taking the bike out for a spin."

I feel a little flush of embarrassment. "Look, I'll pay
for your gas when we stop."

"Not to worry. I was looking for an excuse to take a
good ride."

"Don't Harley riders tend to ride in packs?"

"Only on weekends." His chuckle actually tickles my
ear.

We drive in silence for a few more miles. Even though
I know we're traveling over the speed limit, it feels too
slow. The scenery flowing past seems too distinct, as if it
should be a blur, a mass of green and brown and white.
Instead, I can pick out individual trees and houses and
farms that take forever to move behind us. I want to tap
Mitch on the shoulder and beg him to go faster. I am secure behind him, his body protecting me against the cold
slipstream. Billboards advertising attractions one hundred miles away tick off the miles in tortoise slowness.
Annie's Café one hundred miles. Annie's Café ninety
miles. Eighty miles. Will we never reach Annie's Café?

The road trips of my childhood in the memory of another person might come across as a good thing. Dad,
stepmother, stepbrother and me, looking for all the world
like the average family. Dad married the wicked one
six months after Mom died. Six months in the life of a
fourth grader isn't the length of time it is to an infant, or
a toddler. I was still moving around like a zombie, waiting for someone to come along who could explain to me

why this had happened and tell me that I would someday be okay. Instead, Dad married our divorced next-door-neighbor, Adele Rose.

Adele had aggressively courted Dad, supplying us with casseroles long after my mother was in her winter grave and the daffodils were coming up in the backyard. She had him going next door to fix things—lightbulbs, loose hinges, the clock on her microwave after a power outage. The first time I heard my father laugh after my mother's death was in the company of Mrs. Rose. Even a nine-year-old could figure out what was happening.

It wasn't enough that Dad married her; in some bizarre decision, he moved us into her house. We lived on a typical New Bedford street of three-deckers, built in the heyday of small manufacturing, as the whaling industry petered out and the textile industry grew. As owners, we lived on the first floor and rented out the other two three-bedroom flats. Mrs. Rose lived in the only single-family house on the block, a modern ranch house built on an empty lot where once there had been a three-family that had burned down in the sixties. Dad rented out our flat, and I was literally given a tiny closet of a room, the walk-in closet they'd turned into my bedroom by moving the door. It came with one rectangular window placed so high that all I could see was sky. Living in a closet, I didn't have one, so my clothes were stored in a series of cheap cardboard storage boxes piled one on top of the other in order of the prevailing season. My bed and bureau from our old house occupied most of the floor space. When Adele screamed at me to clean my room, it took barely four sweeps of the vacuum.

My new stepbrother, Paul Scott Rose, Jr., exactly two years older than me, slept in the real second bedroom of this two-bedroom ranch house. A room that was filled with his stuff—model airplanes, hockey equipment, stinky clothes.

Paul, as it turned out, could do no wrong, not just in his mother's eye but also in my father's. He was the son he'd never had, a reprieve from being the father of an only daughter. Paul, bright and precocious, was the sun around which this pair revolved, and woe was me if I didn't see Paul in that light. Paul was mean. Paul set me up for trouble. When Paul lied, I was the one who got punished. The more I protested, the worse it got. I was no longer Daddy's little girl; I was a stepchild. I had inherited my mother's Portuguese coloring, brown eyes and a unibrow; my only Meade quality was that my hair wasn't dark brown, but dirty blond. Adele never avoided an opportunity to remind me of my Azorean heritage: "Don't dress like that; you look like a little Portagee." A slur that puzzled me until I understood that Adele had been brought up to think that any vivid color combination was somehow low-class. And, from her lofty position as a WASP, everyone who had been baptized in the Catholic Church was low-class. I was an adult when it finally occurred to me that she lived in New Bedford, too. What made her so high-and-mighty? Her first husband, a nice-enough guy, smart enough to bail on Adele, was Portuguese, which made Paul as Portuguese as I was, but somehow that didn't sully him as it did me. A Rose in New Bedford, by any other name, is Portuguese.

Once a year, we traveled to some exotic location: Atlantic City, Myrtle Beach, Kennebunkport, in that peculiar way of seaboard people who always venture to someone else's coast to enjoy themselves. When I was fourteen and Paul sixteen, we made the pilgrimage to Disney World. Which meant two days in the backseat of the Chevy Citation with Paul. Two days for him to torture me with farting and shoving. Adele and my father would trade driving in five-hour increments. We spent one night in South Carolina before forging on to Orlando in a manic race against the clock. Getting there late meant losing out on one of our three days in this mecca of American fun.

While Paul wasn't particularly interested in Disney, I was excited to be going. We had both reached that chill of adolescence that didn't allow enthusiasm for anything faintly resembling family togetherness, but I couldn't hide my excitement about going to the place where so many of my peers had already been. If only my mother had been the woman in the front seat, and a real brother, a younger one, beside me, it would have been perfect. But Adele was in the front, Paul beside me, and a curiously quiet father in the driver's seat. Adele talked. It was her thing, her right, and her most killing attribute. The woman never shut up.

She had recently taken to expecting me to become a slut. What I remember most about that family trip to Florida was Adele's reaction when I came out of the hotel bathroom with my eyebrows plucked. I had found her tweezers and gone to town, weeding through the thicket that was my most embarrassing feature. Following the recommendations in a teen magazine, I had spent an hour "shaping" my unruly brows. They had gone from overhang to slender silkworms poised over my suddenly enhanced brown eyes. It was like raising a shade to a sunny day.

Needing no further evidence of my inevitable downslide into slutdom, Adele punished me in the way she saw as the most convenient. I spent the entire vacation in the hotel room, the television my only entertainment. My father didn't make a single protest. Not once did he assert himself and overrule Adele. Not then, and certainly not later, when the stakes were so much higher.

When I left home at seventeen, a stolen fifty-dollar bill tucked in my pocket and an overstuffed suitcase dragging behind me, I wasn't leaving because of Adele's miserable treatment; I was leaving because my father had finally proved that he didn't love me.

The daylight in the cab has faded; the late-September sun behind them slips away into a pale sunset. Artie has mostly stopped his muttering. The cell has also stopped honking. Justine has not appeared, and Mack is less certain that she will be able to. The forward motion of the truck has been steady except for those places where Artie brakes and dances on the pedals and they slow down through little doorways where men or women stand and wave at them. Mack lifts his head at each of these, with the fleeting hope that Justine will be there, waving from one of those little doors. Waiting for them to find her.

From his nest in the bunk, Mack decides that he is hungry enough to mention it to Artie. As a dog used to long stretches of waiting, he has an internal clock that is on Greenwich dog time. He's well past his usual dinnertime; he is well past his usual outside time. He knows this and has allowed that these couple of days on the road have changed his routine significantly. But he was still getting fed and walked at regular intervals. If he could tell time, he'd know that it had been nearly seven hours without a break. If he could read an odometer, he'd know that there were about five hundred miles between himself and Justine. If he could read a map, he'd know that he was in New York State, bearing down on Albany. The only thing Mack can read is his hunger and his thirst.

Mack stands and stretches, loosening the limbs that

have been curled up all day. He yawns, a long jaw loosening to settle his anxiety. Artie is unaware of him, eyes on the road, cigarette burning between fingers gripped on the wheel. He's turned on the radio, and a man's voice is barely audible above the engine noise. The cell suddenly commences its honking again. Mack sits down, waiting until Artie attends to the object's needs. Once again, Artie silences the cell without speaking at it. He lets loose with a stream of volatile tongue language. Mack decides he can wait a little while longer before asking for dinner. Artie's voice sounds like a kick in the ribs.

CHAPTER 4

"What takes you east?" Mitch's voice in my ear yanks me out of my reverie.

"Sick father. Duty call."

"How far east?"

"New Bedford, Massachusetts."

"Far enough. Whaling capital, right?"

"That's what the sign says." I try not to shout, even though I can barely hear my own voice over the slip of the wind. I know that I can whisper over this mic and Mitch will hear me, but I still feel the temptation to shout. "What about you? What takes you on the road on a Wednesday?" Because I can't see his face, I don't register that this might be a rude question until it takes him a minute or two to answer. I've been embracing this stranger for the better part of an hour, the scent of his leather jacket so deep into my nose that I could pick it out of a crowd, the age-softened leather like chamois beneath my fingers. I don't even know his last name and I've trusted him to take me across a state line. "How come you're free?" Maybe my question isn't about why he's free on a weekday to ride his Harley, but why he's free to help me pursue Artie.

"Felt like taking a day off."

"What do you do?"

"Tap dancer."

I don't know whether to laugh or not, sort of like laughing at an off-color joke, but it was his joke, so I do. "Really? Tap dancer."

"I wear a peg."

"Okay. I believe you." I'm willing to let him keep himself to himself. I get it.

"Actually, I'm a musician." This makes sense, I can see him behind a guitar.

"In a band?"

"Symphony orchestra. Cleveland SO."

This is one of those moments that makes me nervous. Is he still joking around, or could this rather large, un- shaven, but not in a good way, Harley rider really be telling me the truth? I decide to let myself be strung along. "What do you play?"

"Violin. First chair."

This is so specific that it sounds plausible. "You must have to practice a lot."

"That's what I'm taking the day off from. I'm skip- ping out on rehearsal. Being rebellious."

"You look the part for that."

"Thanks. I've cultivated the look."

"A Harley-riding violinist. That's a first for me." Ahead of us, for the tenth time, is a semi that might be Artie's. I tap Mitch on the shoulder and point. He speeds up, overtaking the truck easily. It's not Artie. A skinny guy in a Raiders cap salutes from the driver's seat.

"Here's the thing—I've got to be back for tonight's performance."

If I had any hope that he'd be my knight until we caught up to Artie, this shatters it. We'll go to Erie and he'll turn around and go back, transform himself from shaggy Hell's Angel into this longhair classical musician and forget about the woman he let ride on his bike, whispering over his microphone, urging him to catch up with the rat who stole her dog.

"So why take me to Erie?"

"Like I said, nothing better to do. Wanted to feel a little wind on my face."

"Well, I appreciate it. Maybe Erie will be far enough."

"Do you think he'll stop so soon? It's less than a hundred miles."

One hundred miles doesn't sound like a lot. Not after two days of making five or six or even seven hundred miles. Back in the day, when I was more of a rambler, I could do that much all by myself. But I'm out of practice. I'm not hopeful that Artie will stop at all, not without me beside him, reminding him that Mack needs to get out and stretch, or I need to pee. Besides, where he might stop is an open question. There's no TA near Erie, no Interstate 90 rest stop anywhere near Erie. I want Mitch to just keep going all the way to Boston, but that's not going to happen. I wonder if I have enough credit on my card to rent a car.

"Maybe you should just drop me at a car-rental place. There's no telling where Artie might stop, or even if he will stop."

"There's a gas station popular with truckers just off the highway. We can check there first; then I'll find you an Enterprise or an Avis."

"Thank you, Mitch. I really do appreciate what you've done for me." I fight the urge to rest my forehead against that soft leather jacket. I'm pretty sure I've maxed out my credit card. I have no idea what I'm going to do.

It is such a familiar place, this pennilessness, this hopelessness. I have been so often on the edge of out of control that it has a bizarre comfort to it.

Abruptly, the truck swings off the highway and into a rest stop. Artie jumps out of the cab, slamming the heavy door behind him. Alone again in the cab, Mack stands and shakes, stretching himself fore and aft, yawning. Relief starts his tail wagging. Justine will be here. In a minute, she'll come and let him out, then give him what he is beginning to need desperately—water. Then dinner. Then she'll climb up and let him sit on her lap, running his brushy tail through her fingers. She'll apologize for being gone, whispering little words in his ears so that it tickles. He'll give her a forgiving lick of his tongue. He's not like some dogs, perpetually trying to lap a human's face, but once in a while he'll give her a quick reminder that she belongs to him.

As abruptly as he'd left the truck, Artie reappears, holding a bag of food, which he tosses onto the empty seat beside him. A rich amalgam of meat and cheese, grease, and salt filters out of the bag, making Mack, patiently waiting on the bunk, salivate. He whines, but the sound of the engine turning over veils the noise. He considers pressing his nose into the back of Artie's neck, but the idea of touching this man is repellent to him and he sits down. Justine will be along, and she'd be plenty unhappy with him if he was to be caught begging like some common cur.

But Justine doesn't come. Artie wheels the rig out of the parking lot and, stuffing a cheeseburger into his mouth, where it dangles like a kill in a cat's jaws, strong-arms the truck back onto the highway.

The cell honks again. This time, Artie doesn't even bother to shut it off. Eventually, the honking ceases and the cab is filled only with the sound of the radio voice and the undertone of the engine.

Mack curls up on the sleeping bag without further consideration of food. Sometimes it's just best to sleep, to let hunger and thirst be forgotten. Suppressing his discomfort, Mack lets the sanctuary of sleep press him deeper into the folds of Justine's sleeping bag, where he takes a deep breath of her scent. Maybe Justine will be there when he wakes up.

CHAPTER 5

"Answer, you bastard." I have been calling Artie's cell once every five minutes since Mitch and I landed safely at the Crossroads Convenience Mart. My behind is numb from the hour and a half spent riding pillion. Mitch had to grab my hand as I dismounted. With a grace I wouldn't have expected, Mitch was off the bike and into the store ahead of me. By the time I'd phoned Artie the first time, Mitch was in line, a travel mug with the Harley-Davison insignia on it in one hand and a packet of peanut butter crackers in the other.

"I should buy you a meal."

"I'll have dinner at home."

"Then let me get your snack. And your gas."

"What, and cheat me out of being a gentleman? No. I was going to be doing this or something like it today anyway."

"Artie isn't answering his phone."

"Let me try."

"What do you mean?"

"He won't recognize the number."

I hold my phone steady while Mitch reads Artie's number off the contact list. He pulls off his right glove, punches in the number. "Voice mail." Artie has shut his phone off. "Schmidt, if you don't want some serious trouble, get off the road and get the dog back to Justine Meade. If you don't, you'll be looking in your rearview mirror for the rest of your life." My soft-voiced violin player has become a Hell's Angel. "You see a Harley, you'd better hope your life insurance is paid up." Mitch snaps his phone shut with a flourish. "Sorry, that's the best I can do. Empty threats."

"Thanks for trying."

The look on my face is pretty telling, because he pats my shoulder with a hand that is improbably large for a man who fingers violin strings for a living.

"You weren't playing hooky, were you?"

"I was thinking about it. Then you came along and I gave in to temptation. I just wish I could help you further, but I can't. I have to go back pretty soon. This is as far as I can take you. I'm really sorry."

"I can't thank you enough." I thrust a couple of dollars at the cashier, blocking Mitch's attempt to pay for his coffee.

Mitch propels himself back outside, sitting sidesaddle on the Harley while I hunt down a phone book to find a nearby car-rental agent.

I know that this is going to prove an exercise in futility. I have maybe a couple hundred bucks available on my credit card, probably not enough to rent a car to take out of state. I'm not one of those spendthrift people. I haven't run my credit card up on the temptation of using it for day-to-day living. I don't own a flat-screen TV. I don't even own a decent pair of shoes. No one had to teach me that using credit cards willy-nilly was bad. I didn't go to college, so I wasn't one of those kids who got handed a card at freshman orientation, then jacked it up, confident that Mom and Dad would cover the bill. I have lived by a pay-as-you-go policy all my life. Until Mack got sick.

It doesn't take much to run up a vet bill. A simple well-care visit can set me back half a paycheck. But when Mack needed emergency surgery for an intestinal blockage, I never hesitated. The credit card was always for emergencies, and this one was a big one. I've been paying it down for a long time, but the balance remains stubbornly high. It was scary enough to have a $2,500-plus balance on a $2,500-limit card. It didn't help that my day job at the health center ended when they lost funding and I was left to living on my job at the tavern. I've only been able to chip away at a little of that bill, a fact that sits on my shoulders like a ten-ton dollar sign. It colors every decision I make, even the one that has cost me my dog. I should have said no. I should have said I couldn't afford to fly, I couldn't get there. I should never have taken Artie up on his offer of a cheap ride to Boston.

I don't regret the expense of that surgery. Mack is more than a dog to me. He's my partner. We dance.

From the very beginning, Mack was easy to train. We aced puppy training and quickly got into obedience. But all that *sit-stay, down-stay* just didn't showcase my Sheltie's personality. Agility was more his style. Here's the thing. I'm not a joiner; I'm not a performer. I'm the woman behind the desk, or the cash register. I've been so transient that I've never felt that belonging to anything made sense. A year here, a few months there. The need to keep moving is like an itch. Usually, I feel that

urge after a breakup, or if a job has just gotten too an-
noying. My résumé, if I had one, would be a long list of
short-term jobs. I've thought about training as a dental
hygienist. Or a nurse's aide. I like the health-care field.
I've even taken a few courses as an EMT, but never finished. But we joined the Agility Club, and that is what's
held me in Washington for longer than any other place
I've lived. And when Saundra Livingbrook introduced
me to canine freestyle, I knew that Mack and I had found
our game. Canine freestyle, dog dancing, is not obedience or field trials; it's not a beauty pageant. It is egali-
tarian, open to all dogs, regardless of breed. The beauty
comes from the enthusiasm of the dog for its work. All
dogs that show a devotion to work and are easily trained
are welcome. Trained, not like dogs, but like balleri-
nas. The talent coaxed out with hand signals and repeti-
tion, praise and bits of bacon. Lots of hard work. Mack
took to it like the natural athlete he is. I could make my
signals as subtle as could be and he'd see them. Those
herd-dog eyes, mismatched though they are—one blue
and one brown—catching my slightest movement. Hand
up, palm out, spin; hand up palm out, one finger cocked,
back up. Depending on the music, those movements look
like a waltz or a rumba, like we are dancing, when, in
fact, I am giving him signals, his eyes on me with such
focus, the world could drop away. Mack never tires of it.

*Mack waits for me to fasten his little tuxedo front on.
His little white feet dance in place, happy that we're getting ready to strut our stuff. He shakes himself from the
tip of his little black nose down through his magnificent
white ruff, along his silver-and-black body to the tip of
his plumed tail tipped in white. He's ready; he's got his*

game face on. I adjust my own costume, a white jumpsuit embellished with silver sequins, a white top hat finishing the look for "Puttin' on the Ritz." There we were, in this high school gymnasium in Seattle, costumes on, Saundra doing a last-minute adjustment to the straps of my jumpsuit, my blue merle Shetland sheepdog already pumped to get out there. An announcer speaking our names: "Please welcome Justine Meade and her dog Maksim." The spotlight is on us.

Mitch finishes his coffee and watches me as I write down the number of the only car-rental agency in this area. "They'll pick me up; that's what it says. You can head back now."

"That's okay. Let me drop you off."

I really don't want him to. I'm that certain that I'm not going to be renting a car, and I don't want him to be a witness to it. My alternate plan is to get one of these truckers to take my last hundred dollars and let me ride with him. I'm trying not to think of how poorly that plan had worked before.

"I'm fine, Mitch. You need to get back home."

Mitch swings his bad leg over the saddle but makes no move to start the motor. "I really don't like just leaving you here." I can't see his eyes behind the aviator-style sunglasses he's wearing. His red bandanna has slipped forward over his forehead. He looks tough, and can sound tough, but I know that he's not. He didn't have to tell me that he was a musician; he could have kept the Hell's Angel persona, stuck with the impression he seems to want to make. We exchange cell numbers, carefully punching in the digits and saving, as if we're going to stay in touch.

"Don't you worry. I'll be fine." I step away from the motorcycle, give him space to maneuver.

He starts the engine, which comes to life with a heavy rumble, deafening beneath the gas station canopy. "Let me know what happens."

"I will." He's got the bike pointed back the way we came.

"Wait." I almost have to shout to be heard over the sound of the motorcycle's roar.

Mitch wheels around to come back to my side.

"What happened? Your leg, I mean." I'm not usually this rude, but given the circumstances of our meeting, this seems like a fact I should know about him, something as personal to him as the raw facts I've given him about myself are to me.

He doesn't say anything at first, and I wonder if I've offended him with my sudden curiosity, or if he's trying to come up with some smart remark like he's done before.

"Nothing terribly interesting. Bone cancer. I was fifteen."

"I'm sorry."

"Don't be. If I'd been able to play football, I probably wouldn't have played violin. Things happen. Things happen for a reason."

"I guess." But to me, losing a leg seems a harsh price to pay for discovering a musical talent. I don't add that I can't see the reason for my particular situation, because it seems childish to compare losing a dog to losing a leg, but it's what I'm thinking.

Impulsively, I hug him, and then he's gone.

Mack and I step into the spotlight. The music begins. I tap my cane against the floor and Mack rises to his hind legs and, in perfect time with the music, turns in a clockwise circle, then extends his right front paw to me and I take it, bowing to him. By the time he leaps into my arms three minutes later, the crowd is clapping wildly.

CHAPTER 6

It's worth a try, calling the car-rental agency, so I do. Get a nice young man to pick me up, just as promised. He takes me back to the office, and as soon as he runs the card through, I know that I'm cooked. As I feared, they want a lot of money to take a car one-way out of state. More than is available on my abused credit card. He looks at me with a sheepish face. "Sorry, ma'am. I can give you a car for the day."

"No. Thank you anyway." I shoulder my duffel, jam the offended credit card into my back pocket, and walk out of there with as much dignity as I can muster.

I have no idea where I am. There is a bench outside of the rental place, and I sit on it. No sense walking off into the unknown. I should go in and ask the nice young man for directions. But to where? To what? The ride from the Crossroads Convenience Mart wasn't long or complicated. I'll walk back there and go back to plan B. Surely some nice trucker with Mass. plates will want a quiet rider.

"Ma'am?" The nice young man, really not so young—
he's old enough to have a day job and not be in school—is
standing beside me.

"Yes?"

"The bus station is about half a mile from here. I bet
you can get one to Boston."

I am touched by his concern. "That's a good idea."

"I'll take you."

Twice in one day, I've been rescued by unlikely heroes. I want to find my dog, but I know that a bus to Boston is really my only hope of getting where I'm going. In
all of this, I've forgotten that I have a destination.

I don't let him see that I have been defeated. I shake
my head against that thought. Oh no, I'm not giving up
hope of catching up with Artie. This is just a better way
to find him. When I get to Boston, I'll locate Artie easily. I know I will; I'm certain I'll remember where he
was going with his cargo. Once I catch up, I know that
I'll find him. He won't turn around and head back immediately. He said something about a relative. I try to
think back on Artie's conversations. Mostly, I had tuned
them out, since they were the kind of brash manly-man
nonsense so many men like to think they impress me
with. But I'm sure, mixed in with the hero-in-his-own-
life stories, that he'd mentioned a sister or a cousin he
would see when in Boston. I'll find him. I have to.

Artie has my dog.

"That would be nice."

The young man spins a key ring around his forefinger
like a gunslinger. "We can take this one." He holds the
passenger door open for me, a gesture that makes me feel
old, or at least old enough that he sees me as requiring
courtly behavior. He's got to be around twenty-one or
twenty-two, about the same age as my son. Which makes

me think, as I am actually old enough to be his mother, that's how this young man sees me.

"What's your name?"

"Tyler. Tyler Schmidt." This boy still has that adolescent gawk about him that will diminish as age thickens his neck and bulks up his skinny chest.

"Justine Meade."

We don't shake hands. "You said Schmidt?" Artie is Schmidt.

"Uh-huh."

"I'm trying to find a guy named Schmidt. I guess it's a common-enough name."

"Millions of us. Some related, most not. Where's your guy from?"

"I have no idea. I met him in Washington State, but he's got relatives in Massachusetts, I think." This is a silly conversation, like asking if all the Smiths in the world are related. "Arthur Schmidt."

"Doesn't ring a bell. Why are you looking for him? You a bounty hunter?"

I catch the look in his eye; this entry-level boy has a sense of humor. "Something like that. He's got my dog and I want him back."

"Isn't dognapping against the law? Can you get him arrested?"

"I'd like to try."

The bus station is nothing more than a convenience store. Tyler pulls up into a bus lane and hops out as if he's my taxi driver and is going to repeat his chivalry of a few minutes ago, but I swing the door open and we end up facing each other on the cracked sidewalk. He is just the height of my son, and I resist the urge to give him a quick hug good-bye, if only for the feeling of holding a son, in my arms again, even if not my particular son. It has been a very long time since I've had that privilege.

"Thank you, Tyler." I try to give him a couple of bucks.

He quickly forces the folded-up dollars back into my hand. "It's part of the service."

I feel the chill sweat of embarrassment dampen my shirt. This boy has me pegged. He knows I need every penny I have on me. "Do you have a card?"

Tyler fishes a company card out of his wallet, hands it to me as if he, too, believes that I might rent a car from him someday. I'm just thinking that I'll send him a nice note he can have put in his personnel folder—service above and beyond, rescuing maidens. Then I wonder if he'll get in trouble for being my taxi. Then I do hug him. And, strangely enough, he hugs me back.

"I hope you find your dog."

"Me, too."

He drives off, leaving me standing on the filthy sidewalk, thinking about my son.

I was so young when he was born. Not unreasonably so—plenty of girls have babies at twenty. But then choosing to raise him alone, without help, comes back to me now as the sort of reckless hubris of the very young. I named him Anthony, like his father and grandfather, but called him "Tony" from the moment he was born. Every mother thinks her baby is the most beautiful, but Tony really was: curly dark hair still wet against his tiny skull, murky dark eyes that would become chocolate brown in a few weeks. Starfish hands reaching out for me.

What girl doesn't believe that the guy who is her first real lover is the one who will remain the love of her life? At least back then. Not like now, when girls take up partners as if they're making sandwiches. Two bites and you're done. Move on. Meaningless. Anthony wasn't meaningless to me.

Every girl who worked at Marcone's Grill had a crush on him, the youngest son of the Marcone family. I was working there, taking courses at the local community college, and definitely not interested in complicating my life—at the tender age of twenty—by falling in love. It's probably because I didn't pursue him that Anthony began to pay attention to me. Long talks as we closed the place up for the night, then coffee in the all-night diner that was their nearest competition. Very platonic, very sweet, and this sweet, unthreatening attention made me fall in love with him.

But, in the end, I was meaningless to him. He married me because he had to, but he never loved me. Not the way a woman wants to be loved.

"Anthony, I can't do this anymore." I face my husband of three and a half years. His face is a mask of indifference, which is how he is treating me, with indifference. He goes out every night with his friends; he rarely plays with his son. The sweet, gentle nature of our friendship has become silence and avoidance. I no longer delight in his physical beauty; I cannot see it anymore. His fastidiousness has gone from endearing to unbearable; his loyalty to his friends undermines our marriage. Our marriage, clearly, is not important to him. Maybe even abhorrent. "I can't stay if things keep on the way they have."

Anthony shrugs, as if his wife's telling him she's leaving is of no consequence. I wonder if he's calling my bluff, but the relief in his eyes is clear. I have been the braver partner; he's been waiting for me to pull the plug so he won't have to. "So go."

When I left his father, Tony was almost three, just young enough to think this was a normal life; just old enough to ask, every now and then, where Daddy was.

"When's Daddy coming?"
    "He's not coming, baby. He lives in Brooklyn."
    "Why don't we live in Brooklyn?"
    I have no answer for that. How do you tell a little boy that his father won't love his mother?

If I thought that Tony would keep me tied to one spot, I was wrong. But he did give me a different reason for moving on: I was pursuing the better life for him, one that didn't mean living in a motel by the week or taking a shit job just because it came with some benefits. I wanted to give him a home, one he could be proud of. I always told him that the next place would be better, bigger, cleaner, safer. The next place we lived would be where he could play with kids in the neighborhood, ride his bike. Heck, own a bike. The next town or the next city, the next state, would be better. What I didn't realize was that in order to have a stable home, there must be some permanence. It isn't enough to have a loving mother. You need a place to call home.

I'm a little puzzled by the seeming lack of a bus station, until I figure out that this is a stop, not a station. The storefront has high windows, plastered with beer advertisements and lottery signs. To the left of the Budweiser ad is a smallish placard stating the place's secondary function as a bus agency. Outside the place is a single bench, occupied by a large black man wearing an old-fashioned fedora. Inside, the place is tiny, tight, with too closely arranged displays of potato chips and lager beer. It smells like spilled beer; it smells a little like my bar. The wood floor is littered with a healthy scattering of abandoned lottery tickets.

I wait in line to buy a ticket to Boston from a cashier who may be Pakistani or Sri Lankan. On the counter, tucked between Slim Jims and condoms, is a cardboard box with bus schedules in it. I grab one and stand aside to let the line move forward. The lottery must be big to-night. The line keeps forming, filled with quiet people, fruitless dreams of a new life playing behind down-turned eyes.

The next bus from Erie is at 8:40 tonight. It will take thirteen-plus hours to make it to Boston.

"One way to Boston, please." I fish out my credit card and hand it to him.

"No credit card. Cash only."

"You have a terminal, so why won't you take credit cards?"

"Not for bus. Store policy." He doesn't even have the good grace to look sorry. "You go to Erie to use credit card."

"I thought I was in Erie."

This does get me a crooked smile, like the kind you'd expect from somebody who enjoys other people's troubles because they make him feel momentarily superior. "No. You have to go to Erie."

Suddenly, the logic of a bus ride fails me. By the time I limp into Boston, Artie will surely have turned around and headed home. I wonder if there's a cheap flight, one of those thirty-nine-dollar specials. If I could fly, I might even beat him there.

My cashier friend offers no help, just shrugs and waits with a feigned patience for me to decide what to do. I move out of line again. The sun is setting as I sit beside the old black man on the bench outside the store. I hold my duffel on my lap and fight the urge to rest my head on it. In the fading September light, the shadows pool at my feet.

"Nice evening." My bench companion says this quietly, as if afraid to mention it.

"Yeah. I guess so."

"Don't sound convinced."

"How far is the Erie bus station?"

"You're in Conneautville. Erie's thirty miles away."

"Then I guess I'm not walking there."

"That's why there's buses."

I know that I'm going to have to go back into the store, use some of my dwindling cash reserve to buy a ticket for a bus to get to a bus. I suddenly feel the lack of food and the exhaustion of defeat. I want to lie down. Mitch has failed me; he didn't get as far as Erie. I'm in Erie County. I've been fooled by the same generalization that people from Boston suburbs use when they say they're from Boston.

"Going home?"

"No. Well, my father's home."

"Not your home?"

"Hasn't been for a long time."

"But you don't live around here."

"No. I just found myself here. A long story."

We sit quietly for a time, watching the gradual lengthening of those shadows. I study the bus schedule as if it's tea leaves. I look in vain for a faster, cheaper, more convenient bus that will magically transport me to Boston.

"So, where is home?" His voice is still just above a

whisper, making his question seem far more philosophical than the simple words would suggest.

And then it hits me. Why not just go back? Turn around and wait for Artie to come back to town and show up at the bar. And then I will kill him. The logic of this is breathtaking. In the next breath, I realize that the chance that Artie will show up in that bar without my dog is a chance I do not want to take. No, I've got to catch up with him.

I finally answer the old man. "Where my dog is."

"I had a good dog once. Saw me through a lot of years of hard times. Never once complained."

"They rarely do." I shoulder my duffel and go back into the store. When I come out, the old man is gone.

I hunker down in the bus seat, sitting toward the rear, left side, against the window, which is streaked with the dried paths of raindrops from some past storm. I am bone-tired. My dinner of microwaved burrito is sitting uncomfortably mid-belly. I've smuggled a can of Coke onto the bus to wash away the metallic taste of prepackaged food. Thirty miles is far enough to catch a quick nap, and I close my eyes. But the image of my dog rests behind them and all I see is his little silver-and-white face, with the dollops of black eyebrows over those mismatched eyes. I named him Maksim after that ballroom dancer on *Dancing with the Stars*. I am an unabashed fan of that show, although the only ballroom dancing I ever did was in junior high when the phys ed teachers made us all learn the box step, even though disco was the rage. Everyone thinks I named him that because we dance together, but the truth is, canine freestyle came well after I'd named my puppy.

Rodney Parris gave me the puppy. He was a nice

guy with an unfortunate handicap—he was married. I didn't know that, of course. I've never dated married men, and have been cautious around those who claim to be "separated." But he was married, and that was a very disappointing fact to me, because I really liked him. He was the first guy in a long time to make me glad he was around. Having discovered the wife—or rather, she discovered me—I told him good-bye. I shut the door in his face, turned my back to it, and slid to the floor. I've broken up too many times to forget that the pain does go away, but in that moment I was crushed. My little puppy, maybe four months old at this point, dashed over to where I sat on the floor and dropped his teddy bear in my lap. I burst into tears, me, a noncrier, and he looked at me with such worry. Sniffing back the momentary deluge, I hugged him and swore then that he was all the man I'd ever need.

And, so far, he has been.

I feel that long-ago dammed-up deluge working its way up from just above where that burrito is sitting. I bunch my fists up under my closed eyes, hoping that no one sits next to me, that no one hears me sniffle like some brokenhearted teenager. Stifling the urge to cry, I pull my phone out of my pocket.

My cell has only a tiny percent of battery left. I close the cover, praying that Artie will call me before I run out of juice. I have no idea when I'll be able to recharge it.

By the time the bus pulls into the bus station in Erie, it's full dark. I have a long night ahead of me.

CHAPTER 7

I manage to recharge my cell phone while waiting for the 8:40 bus to leave from Erie—the city, not the county. I'm leaning against the wet counter in the ladies' room, my charger plugged into a random outlet beside the hand dryer, when the phone rings with my "Puttin' on the Ritz" ringtone, startling the bejesus out of me as the music bounces off the tile walls of the hollow room. My hand literally shakes as I flip the phone open, praying that Artie's number is on the display. It isn't.

"Where are you?" My stepmother doesn't even begin by saying hello.

"Erie. Waiting for a bus."

"I don't know how much time you think you have to get here, but you should hurry up. This isn't a drill. I thought you'd be here by now."

"It's a long story."

"It always is with you."

"I'll be there tomorrow."

"Why didn't you fly? You could have been here two days ago. I could use the help."

"You know why."

"Because you had to bring that dog?" Adele smacks the word *dog*.

"No. Because I couldn't afford it." I say this loudly enough in the echoing rest room that my voice is amplified and the woman just shaking the wet off her hands and hunting for the dryer that I'm blocking stops and walks out of the room, wiping her hands on her pants.

"It's not that expensive. You should have just done it." Good old Adele. Wanting something and not being able to have it just isn't part of her world. I find it slightly curious that she doesn't even suggest that they might have helped me get home, not even as an afterthought.

"I'll be there tomorrow." I would like nothing better than to hang up, but I don't. I wait. I listen. When the silence builds, I finally ask what she should have been offering. "How is he?"

"Dying. How else do you think he is?" Adele sounds royally pissed off that she's going to be a widow.

"Please don't."

Adele finally drops the outdated angry-stepmother role. "He had a good night last night. The pain is manageable with the morphine, but he's not very talkative."

I bite back the obvious jab—that she never let him talk anyway, so why should he start now. "Can you still keep him home?" I'll give her that; she hasn't opted out for hospitalization or a nursing home. Last spring, when my father was diagnosed with prostate cancer, no one seemed overly concerned; it was treatable and I didn't get the feeling that there was a time bomb ticking. So when it metastasized into his bones, it was a complete surprise to me. Adele's call last week to say I should come home really did come out of the blue. She didn't bother me with "details," as she liked to say. She waited until it was almost too late to have me come. But he was still at home.

There is another silence. I lean toward the wall, press the charger cord deeper into the phone. Wait.

"I hope so. That's why I need you here."

I fled that house as soon as I could, bitter and heartbroken. And yet I am going back, dutiful daughter to a man who turned his back on me when I needed him most.

"Tomorrow. I get into Boston at about nine-thirty. I'll grab the first bus to New Bedford I can and be there maybe around noontime."

"Good." She never says hello and she certainly doesn't say good-bye.

It doesn't escape me that I am faced with making a choice. My desire is to find my dog. My self-imposed obligation is to go to my father. In both situations, timing is going to be everything. I could abandon my journey to New Bedford and focus on finding Mack, except that I hold on to a childish hope that, in showing up, in facing my father, I might get an apology, an acknowledgment that what he did to me when I was seventeen was wrong. I'm not sure if I want him to have the opportunity to clear his conscience; or is it more that I want the opportunity to forgive him? Ever since Adele called, I have run little dramatic scenes in my head. Deathbed handholding, my father begging my forgiveness for betraying me so long ago. My saying something that would bring us both peace. Some might call it a desire for closure. I guess so. You can't live most of your life with anger your primary emotion.

I pull the phone-charger cord out of the wall and coil it around the plug. I have a half-full battery now, so at the very least I can keep dialing Artie. By this time, he must be close to his destination. It's been over seven hours since he abandoned me and stole my dog. Without stops, going seventy—my math fails me again and I can only imagine that the distance between us is growing minute by minute and a thirteen-hour bus ride will never catch me up to him.

Fully armed with a recharged phone, I dial Candy. When she answers in her usual businesslike "Candy's Place, proprietress speaking," I almost burst into tears. With Candy, you always get the feeling she'll fix the problem, whether it's the leak under the sink or a customer complaint, a staff member's broken heart or the need to get an ordinance against sticking advertising flyers under windshield wipers voted in. "Oh Candy, I'm in a fix."

She listens without interruption. There's a pause before she weighs in, a gentle, thoughtful pause. "Okay. Let's see what we can do." I lean back against the wet apron of the sink and allow a flutter of relief. "I'll make a call or two, see if I can find out where Artie is going. You get on that bus and keep your phone on. Once we know where he's going, we can call and have him held up there."

"Do you think you can find out? I've been with him for two days and I can't remember what he said or even what he was hauling. I'm not sure if he ever said, just told me Boston." Which, if my recent experience of Erie is any indicator, could mean anywhere in the vicinity.

"I can't make any promises. But I'll do my best. Just get on the bus. I'll call you later."

Unlike my stepmother, Candy leaves me with a "Good-bye" and a softly spoken "God bless."

Candy Kane is maybe ten years older than I am, but that doesn't stop her from treating me like she does all the women who work for her—as her child. Not *like* a child, but with the same care and concern that a good parent shows a daughter. I sound mushy, and I don't mean to. It's just that her quick call to arms has me emotional. Maybe it's just that her instinctive mothering skills have always left me jealous. Lacking a good example, I turned out not to be such a good one myself. In my experience, mothers either died or preferred other children. Having grown up pitted against two people who saw me as an inconvenience, I swore I'd be a better mother to my son. I wanted to lavish attention on him, but, young, single, and poor, I'm not sure I lavished the right kind. Late at night while he slept, I would crawl into his bed and press my weary body around his, sorry that when he was awake, I was more stressed than loving, more impatient than playful—the daily fear of not being able to keep him in sneakers and cereal making me short-tempered and unable to take pleasure in him. I wanted to make him feel as though he was the most important thing in my life, but that was harder than it sounds.

Tony sits very still on the daybed that I convert from my bed back into the couch in the living room of the efficiency apartment. He clutches his special pillow, the one that ensures that wherever he sleeps, he has his own pillow with its singular Donald Duck motif. A sitter is coming in a minute, but she's late and I'm beginning to get nervous that then I'll be late. Late again, and I might not get the extra shifts at the restaurant where I've waitressed for the past six months.

Tony has already spent the entire week in day care, and he is so stoic about being left again so that I can work a Saturday shift. He never gives me fits about leaving; he understands, even at four years old, that I have to do whatever it takes to keep him in juice boxes. I never promise to bring him treats; I never make promises I can't keep. But the juice boxes, little individual servings of grape or apple or mixed-berry juice, are his special treat for his lunch box. Just like all the other kids have.

The sitter finally arrives, a scrawny teenage girl with braces that look like they could tune in Mars. I bend down to give Tony a kiss good-bye. "Be good for . . ."

"Molly." The girl has the good grace not to roll her eyes at me. All these Mollies and Shannons and Morgans blend together, an unending supply, courtesy of the local high school.

"Mom?"

"What, sweetie? Mommy has to go; I'm late."

"I don't need juice boxes."

I still have a few minutes before boarding the bus bound for Boston, so I thumb the number for my pal Saundra Livingbrook. Saundra is the one who got me involved in canine freestyle, and she is the sole support of six dogs, all rescues. I can hear them in the background as she answers my call, sounding like children clamoring for mom's attention when she's on the phone.

"He is chipped, isn't he?" Saundra is talking about the microchip embedded beneath the skin between Mack's shoulders that identifies him as my dog to anyone with a reader.

"He is." I take small comfort from that fact. He's with Artie, and who knows what Artie will do with him. If Mack is picked up by a dog officer or dropped with a vet, then I have hope. But I simply can't imagine that Artie will do anything thoughtful like that.

"Let's think about this. I'll post the story on my Facebook page and get the word out to as many rescues as I can. It'll be like putting up posters all over the country. He's a Sheltie, so I'll make sure that Sheltie rescues have his information." Saundra has to control a pack of dogs, so she's no stranger to getting things done.

"If you could do that, it would be great. Candy is trying to find out specifically where Artie is going and see if she can get help at that end. I'm boarding a bus and won't get to Boston till tomorrow morning. And I've got my father to deal with."

"How is he?"

"If my stepmother is to be believed, on death's doorstep."

Saundra has known me long enough that I've let her in on some of my history. I don't do that too often; usually, I speak of my past in safe generalities. It's not that my story is particularly interesting or rare, but I don't really want to think about it. I prefer talking about the now. The past is like a series of black curtains; each one covers the essential scenes of a life that only in the last half decade has become less damaged. A tough childhood, single motherhood. Bad choices and better ones. Just like everyone else. So, I keep myself to myself except with certain people, friends like Saundra, whose life hasn't been that famous bowl of cherries, either.

Mack awakens from his wolf sleep with a jolt. The truck is moving; there is no light but the stars that flee past in the night sky. They are climbing, and Artie shifts the lumbering vehicle to gain more power. The cab is fetid with the miasma of greasy, farting man and cigarettes; the driver's window is down a crack, not enough to let in sufficient fresh air, only a vague trickle of breeze. Then the truck levels off and almost immediately noses down the long incline they have just climbed. Just as Mack feels the truck speed up, Artie downshifts to slow the pace.

Artie lights another cigarette, inhales deeply, then blows the smoke out of the side of his mouth into the moving air, which catches it, pushing the drift of smoke into the bunk.

Mack sneezes.

"What the . . ." Artie's head swivels and dog and man look each other in the eye. "Shit."

Mack braces himself against the sudden lurch of the truck, shakes from head to tail, and jumps into the passenger seat, where he fixes his eye on Artie, giving him his best I'm-a-good-dog look. This is more like it; now things will improve. A quick glance at the bag of kibble on the floor, just to remind Artie that dinner is late. A soft whine to emphasize the need to go out.

Artie grabs his mute cell phone and scrambles his fingers over its face to find the right buttons to listen to his messages. "Nothin' but trouble. I need this like a hole in the head. Goddamned bitch. I knew this was a bad idea. Freakin' dog. Twenty-seven unheard messages!"

Artie keeps up the tongue language and Mack sits confidently in the seat, where Justine's scent lingers on the cracked plastic. He should have come down sooner; he just didn't believe that Artie hadn't known he was there. How can a man not scent a dog lying close by? Now that the man knows he's here, things must improve. Anytime that Justine has left him, which is rare, the person he's left with knows about the basics: food, water, toys, go-out. It is inconceivable to him that Artie doesn't speak enough dog to get those basics attended to. But the man just keeps yakking and flailing the cell around. The truck is picking up speed, and if the dog could see over the hood, he would notice that they are too close to the little car in front of them.

The truck banks left, then right as Artie drops the phone and pays attention to the road. He's still grumbling, tossing sideways glances at Mack every now and then. He rubs his sandpaper chin with rough hands, making a whiskery sound. Mack sits in the passenger seat, never taking his eyes off of Artie. Artie hasn't used any tongue language to let Mack know where Justine is. He's only used the more subtle but highly legible body language of a man powerfully annoyed. There was a dog in agility class with the same pissed-off demeanor. No one wanted to be near him, always afraid that the next growl would be followed by a bite. Everybody else loved the free playtime they were given after class, chasing each other, wrestling, or simply standing side by side. Not this guy. He left as soon as the class was over, his human keeping his leash in both hands.

Artie holds the cell in front of him, resting it on the steering wheel. Mack hears the distorted sound of Justine's voice emanating from the tiny rectangle as Artie listens to the stream of messages. One word is recognizable: *Mack*. He wags the tip of his tail at the sound of it. Yawns and swallows to show Artie that he knows that word. If he can hear that word, and recognize Justine's voice, she must be close by. Just out of sight.

Then there is the sound of another voice leaking out of the tiny speaker.

"Shit." Artie glances at his side mirror with the expression of a squirrel being chased. "Goddamn it." Artie pitches the cell phone into the back, where it lands with a silent thud in Justine's vacant sleeping bag. "Freakin' A. Hell's Angels?" He guns the motor and picks up speed.

Artie continues to mutter. Mack remains upright on the seat that bears so much of Justine's scent. He gives Artie sideways glances, the tenor of that voice keeping him alert and wary. He won't go back to sleep. Not now. Mack will stay alert until Justine comes back.

The dog knows that it is deep night, the time of day when a good dog is tucked into his bed, nose under tail. A good dog who sleeps only lightly, one part of him always at the ready to defend the house against intruders. Skunks. Possum. Nightmares. One of Mack's jobs is to comfort Justine when she wakes at night.

Artie downshifts and brakes, the truck slowly coming to a halt. Mack wags his tail. At last! He even whines, just a little, to let Artie know he's happy. Artie has stopped talking. The truck idles and Artie sits still. Mack peers at the window but sees nothing.

This wasn't like any of the places where they'd stopped before. This was just the side of the road. The cars zoom past them, the headlights streaming together like something liquid; other semis rush by, making even the weight of the truck vibrate a little.

Artie pushes open his door and drops to the ground. He comes around to the passenger side. The door swings open and man and dog are face-to-face. "Get the fuck out." Artie grabs for Mack's ruff. The dog instinctively pulls back and the man is left holding the dog's collar, not the dog. He makes another lunge and this time gets a fistful of fur and skin. Artie drags Mack across the seat, yanking him out the open door so hard that the dog falls to the ground before he can get his feet under him, landing hard on his side, pushing the air out in an audible *whuff.* Mack gets up, shakes, and waits. Artie is on the ground now, feet planted, hands in fists. "Get out of here. Go on, git."

Mack growls; this is too much. Even a well-behaved dog has limits. Artie steps closer. Mack pins his ears back and lowers his head, but he doesn't growl again. He knows that this man is his last connection to Justine. He keeps his head down, his eyes pinned on Artie's eyes, like his sheep-herding forebears.

"They can't prove nothing, if you ain't here." The flashers are beating a hectic rhythm against the dark. Artie swings a leg over the guardrail. "Come here, boy." His voice is all sweetness, a gooey sound that doesn't fool the dog.

Mack keeps to his side of the metal rail. Artie pats his knee. "Come on."

Mack is still skeptical, but the man is his only connection to Justine. Then Artie utters the magic words. "Let's go find Justine."

At once, Mack leaps over the rail as if it's one of his agility obstacles and lands at Artie's feet. Artie is taking him to Justine. Finally!

Then one well-aimed kick sends him down the steep grade. Stones and twigs catch in his coat as he rolls out of control and lands at the bottom of the slope, his breath knocked out of him. By the time Mack is back on his feet and up the embankment, the truck is gone.

CHAPTER 8

I am wide-awake to Buffalo, drowsy by Rochester, and sound asleep by Syracuse. I miss Albany altogether. I wake cotton-mouthed and cramped in a window seat. I need to pee, and the person beside me has stretched out her legs and sleeps with her cheek propped up against her hand. If I try to slip out, I know I'll step on her. We haven't spoken and I can't remember when she got on; the bus has gone on and off the highway so many times, I can't remember each little town or hole-in-the-wall bus stop we've pulled up in. The whole of New York State is a tangle of sodium-lighted pauses along the way, each one a delay in my pursuit, and I try not to think about how much longer this ride is taking than if I could have rented a car. I would have been there by now. I would have found Artie by now.

I guess I can hold on for a little while longer. I'd like to go back to sleep myself, but now I am wide-awake. The dim interior light of the bus turns everything a vague green and I feel like I'm underwater. Outside, the pinpricks of light from houses unfortunate enough to be located along a highway remind me that I am not home, tucked beneath the patchwork quilt that I have moved with me everywhere I have been. The quilt that Tony peed on as a baby, and that Mack inevitably chooses to lie on when he's wet. This quilt that is the only possession I have that came from my mother, who, by being blessed by sudden death, is forever my ideal of motherhood. An ideal I was never able to achieve. I've sorted through my memories of her, and keep only those that appeal to me. Each of my recollections corresponds to one of the four pictures I have of her: Easter morning, Christmas morning, my fourth birthday where she bends over me helping me to blow out candles, and the random photograph that isn't of her, but of my father. She is caught in the background, but it is the only one of her pregnant. In each photo she is idealized and that's how I like to keep it.

The house lights move by and the bus moves back into deep countryside. I have no idea where I am.

Dawn creeps up on me. Maybe I've slept again, because suddenly the trees and fences, the barns, and the cattle standing in the fields are distinct. Color eases its way into the landscape. I still don't know where I am, but it's pretty. I'm on the wrong side of the bus to read the signs that might let me know how much farther I have to go.

The woman beside me suddenly startles herself awake with a violent jerk of her legs and hands. "Oh!" She looks at me sheepishly and wipes the drool from her chin with the back of her hand. "Where are we?"

"Don't know. Not there yet." I excuse myself, climb over her, and make for the stinky rest room.

When I get back, my seat companion stands up to

let me climb back into my place. She's a large woman, in her fifties, if I was to guess. She wears a loose dress clearly chosen for its traveling comfort and not the fact that it makes her look nine times bigger than she is. She fumbles around in a cloth grocery bag until she extracts a can of Coke and a banana. "I got more. Want one?"

I'm not proud. I'm really thirsty, so I say yes. The Coke is sweet and hardly my morning drink of choice, but it burns through the cotton in my mouth and makes me feel less gross.

"I'm heading for Springfield, going to see my grand-kids. Where you heading?"

We haven't even exchanged names, but the rules of the road are clear: story time.

"New Bedford."

"Never been there. Went to the Cape once. But mostly we go to Canada for vacation." My companion needs nothing further from me. She chatters happily on and on. I wonder how close we are to Springfield. I wonder if this is her normal way, or whether she's quiet at home, keeping to herself, baking those pies for the church sup-per, minding her own business. But traveling by herself to visit kids she probably rarely sees opens something up in her and the floodgates of talk gush open. Kids, grandkids, little Mikey's First Communion. I'm not even listening when she tires of herself and asks me the inevi-table woman-to-woman question: "You got kids?"

The question is a normal one. She's handed the deck to me. My turn to deal story now. "A son. He's grown." I don't say grown and gone. He was gone and then grown. "Tony."

"Where's your boy now?"

This is a hard question. Before I have to answer with some tepid reply, my phone plays its little tune and I fish it out of my pocket, that little compulsive prayer that it be Artie singing along with the tune: Let it be Art-tie. Please be Art-tie. I don't even look at the display to see who it is. The woman beside me presses back against her seat, as if that gives me privacy.

"He's going to a warehouse to leave the trailer." Candy gives me the address, and I know Boston well enough to recognize a street along the harbor, near or even in Southie. Not terribly far from South Station. A cab ride, a good walk. I thank her and promise to keep her posted. I can't find any paper in my duffel, so I write the address down on the palm of my hand. The bus schedule I have doesn't tell me anything about buses from Boston to New Bedford, but I know they must be fairly frequent. We're entering Springfield now. Boston is at most two hours away. At the least, Artie got there at night and may still be asleep in his cab. I press a hand to my chest to feel the impulsive beating of my racing heart. I feel like this is that TV show, *The Amazing Race*. I'm closing in. Maybe I'll catch him. Maybe this will all fade to a bad dream in a few hours. I'll have my boy back. My Mack. He'll jump into my arms like he does at the end of our performances, overjoyed. A furry bundle of wiggles and kisses.

"Are you okay?"

Funny how so many people have asked me that question in one form or another in the past twenty-four hours. I look at my companion, who is gathering up her Coke cans and bundles of presents for the grandkids. We're at the Springfield station, her stop.

"Yeah, I'm fine. You enjoy your family."

She looks at me for a long moment. Her chubby face doesn't hide the fact that she has beautiful eyes. I expect that it was those eyes that drew her husband to her, those eyes that have kept him despite the baby weight that didn't disappear, but settled in; despite the years of caring for children, caring for his house, settling for a life lived in terms of vacations to Canada and First Communions. "You, too."

She struggles to make her way down the narrow bus aisle. I can see a woman who must be her daughter, a little kid clasped by one hand. Simultaneously, they both open their arms to the woman as she lumbers down the bus steps.

Yeah, I'll be enjoying my family all right.

The points of the compass are not nominal values, but instinctive. Standing on the verge of the highway, he raises his muzzle to the air, orients himself, and begins to walk. Cars bullet past him, flattening his coat by the force of their passing. He keeps to a westerly course but moves into the protection of the tree line, keeping up a businesslike trot despite the ache in his ribs. This takes him under the highway and into a culvert that has only a sluggish trickle of water running through it. Inside the culvert is the scent of ground animal, possum or raccoon. Mack is fiercely thirsty and laps gratefully at the shallow stream as if he could lap it dry.

As he emerges from the culvert, Mack pauses, listens. Justine must be somewhere. He heard her voice. He's not ignorant enough to believe that she was trapped in the cell, but he has a vague idea that if he could hear her voice, she can't be far off. If he wanders too far, she won't find him. Even so, he keeps moving, instinct telling him that she won't find him here in this wild place.

The highway is a distant susurration; the slow passing of cars on a back road is closer. One at a time, slow enough that he can discern the sound of their radios, smell

the waft of cigarette smoke exhaled through cracked
windows, the voices of couples arguing late at night.

Justine will expect him to wait for her someplace. He
needs to find that place. In their life together, she often
tells him *down-stay,* leaving him waiting outside doors,
or gates, or on sidewalks. He needs to find a place where
Justine might ask him to down-stay. And then wait for her.

PART II

CHAPTER 9

Alice spots the dog first.

She mentions to Edward that she noticed this furry little dog sitting quietly between the twin painted brick pillars of the cemetery. "I thought about stopping." Alice Parmalee pulls a can of tuna out of the carrier bag, studies it for a moment. "I sort of wish I had. I hope he doesn't get hit by a car."

Edward grunts, shakes his newspaper in half, peers at her over his glasses. "Best not to approach strange dogs. He'll go home."

"I don't think he had a collar." Alice doesn't know why she says this; the dog has a thick ruff, which certainly would obscure any collar. "He was just sitting there, like he was waiting."

"He probably was. Maybe his owners were tourists looking for ancestors." Ed slides his glasses back up onto the bridge of his nose, the box scores regaining his full attention.

Alice finishes emptying the green cloth grocery sacks,

lining her cupboards with the same cans of peas, corn, and Campbell's Chunky soup, the same boxes of cereal that she replenishes every few weeks from the Big Y. For the most part, she shops at Potter's General Store—150 years and still going strong—which offers basics like milk and bread, eggs if she wants to make omelettes for dinner, as well as things Ed calls "gourmet," although she buys nothing more exotic than guacamole. Anything with a pretty label and Ed scoffs that she's paying for packaging.

Alice can no longer raise any enthusiasm for cooking. Edward is happy with "plain fare," and it isn't any fun to have a new recipe consumed with the same unappreciative haste as a meal of hot dogs and beans. Alice doesn't mind, not really. It's easier, in some respects, not to have to think about meals, not to have to care.

Once upon a time, she imagined that in her middle years she'd take up tai chi or go back to college and finish her degree. That was when she thought her life would travel along a smoother road. She also expected to have children while still in her twenties. She never expected that it would take a miracle to have the one child in her fortieth year. She certainly never expected that, as hard as it was to get her, it would be so easy to lose her.

When Stacy was born, the folks at the plant chipped in and bought Ed and Alice a video camera. Ed got quite adept at using it, and for years they filmed every significant moment of Stacy's life, from crawling to tap dancing; from T-ball to her first day of high school. She was used to it, although as she got older she tended toward foolish faces and rude gestures whenever Ed fired up the recorder. They almost never watched those videos, not then, and certainly not now. Then, they were too busy raising her; now it is out of the question.

Stored in sleeves, labeled carefully with years and events, the rows of boxes remain untouched. A video collection of Anastasia Marie Parmalee's life. They could have her back at any point in her short life, relive the moments preserved on VHS tape, but they never open the glass doors of the breakfront, never do more than run a dust cloth over the labels. Neither Ed nor Alice can allow the emotion that lives just beneath the surface to get out. They dealt with it then, and opening the doors now would only serve to start the process over again. They aren't like the other families they met at grief counseling, scrapbooks and albums opened and reopened so many times that the bindings were worn; grief-stricken parents making you look at the faces of lost children, acting like those children weren't lost, but just out of sight. Talking about their children, as if whatever tragedy had taken them was merely a part of growing up—cancer, car wrecks. Iraq.

Ed and Alice closed the doors and kept the evidence of Stacy's short, active life inside that cupboard. They never speak of what might have been, nor of what is past.

Alice keeps busy with her little cutting garden, her yoga classes, and her part-time job at the library. She fills her days up with housework and chores enough for any woman. Who has time for anything more?

The dog had looked so forlorn. Maybe *forlorn* wasn't the right word. The way it looked at her car as she drove slowly out of the cemetery, ears pricked in her direction, and then lowered, as if, well, as if it was disappointed. Maybe after dinner she'll go see if it's still hanging around the cemetery. Besides, she should check on the russet and gold chrysanthemums she planted earlier today to see if they need a little more water.

CHAPTER 10

Edward Parmalee sees the dog as he heads out in the morning to gas up the Cutlass. Can't miss it. The dog is sitting just where Alice saw it, between the cemetery gates. It carefully studies Ed's car as he slowly drives by. He probably belongs to some neighbor who lets his dog loose to roam the countryside. Don't see much of that nowadays, not like when he was a kid and everyone knew everyone else's dogs because they were allowed to wander—as were the kids. You didn't worry about leash laws or child molesters in those days. Didn't neuter male dogs, and bike helmets hadn't been invented. Ed rolls his window down, slows enough to lock eyes with the dog. "Go home!" Didn't worry about drugs and AIDS and terrorists. Well, maybe they worried about the Russians, but by and large, they didn't worry about the things that he and Alice had to worry about with Stacy, the dangers of perverts lurking in malls or poisoned Halloween candy. Not wearing a seat belt, or easy access to drugs.

"Go home!" Ed stares at the dog that sits outside the

cemetery gates. No. It's always been tough to raise kids. His parents had to cope with potentially fatal childhood diseases that they were lucky enough to have vaccines for by the time Stacy arrived.

But sometimes the threat isn't external at all. It doesn't come from outside, but from the inside.

The dog doesn't move.

Like Alice said, no visible collar, but that doesn't mean anything; he might have slipped it, or maybe it's buried beneath the fur of its ruff. If Moodyville had a dog officer, he'd probably get a call. Lacking one, what can be done?

It's unlikely that the resident state trooper will come by and collect it. He barely responded that time the gas station alarm went off. Meandered over from the MassPike half an hour after Tooley figured out it was a bird that had gotten caught in the garage, its panicked fluttering in the bay triggering the motion alarms that the tire distributor had insisted Tooley install if he was to sell that brand of tire. Goddamned statie took so long that a tire thief could have taken the whole inventory and been all the way to Hartford by the time he showed up. It's a different guy now; the former trooper, the one they knew, had moved on.

Ed cranks the car window back up, thinking, He'll find his way home. Thinking that he'll mention the dog to the guys at Lil's, where he's going after he gasses up the Cutlass. It isn't a planned thing, this coffee with Joe and Chuck nearly every morning. Joe calls it "the early retirees club." Stupid, really. They barely knew one another at the plant, and now, forced into retirement five years earlier than any of them planned, they meet like a clutch of old hens to knock politics and weather around, tell bad jokes, talk about their wives as if the women are really the tough old bats they make them out to be. *My old lady.* Christ, they sound like yokels or, worse, toughs. But it is the time of day Ed Parmalee looks forward to the most. He says it gives Alice time to vacuum without having to make him pick up his feet. It means a little time out of each other's hair. Out of the silence. Maybe it's the only thing he looks forward to these days.

Being cut loose from his job of thirty-five years has left Edward Parmalee rootless. He lives in this town only because of the job. He met Alice because of the job. His daughter grew up with dozens of other kids, attending the annual holiday party, sitting on Santa's lap in the evergreen and construction-paper chain–decorated cafeteria. The "old man" of the plant, the owner himself, ho-ho-hoing and handing over the bubble makers and coloring books as each child perched on his knee, along with a big candy cane, which would later show up under the seat of the car or end up sticky on the kitchen counter. Then the old man sold up, caved in to progress. And then some fucking Japanese company swooped in and everything was about efficiency and function, the bottom line. Pride and longevity were no longer hallmarks. The old man is living in Florida now; word is that he found himself a new young wife.

So now Ed looks forward to killing some time with the guys at the diner. Killing time.

Ed does a Uie from the gas station driveway, going across Route 146, which serves as Moodyville's main street, and directly into an angled parking space in front of Lil's. He gets out and nods to Chuck, who is pointing his remote key lock at his 2007 Tundra. "How ya doin', pal?"

"Can't complain."

"Won't help."

Same old greeting, more like code words than sentiment. Friend or enemy? The Lil's Coffee Shop Secret Society.

Joe has claimed the counter, his big butt drooping over the old-fashioned canister-style stool, the tumor of his overstuffed wallet protruding from his back pocket. Ed and Chuck flank him, nod, and simultaneously reach for the folded sections of the *Boston Globe* in front of him. Ed scores the sports page; Chuck is left with the "Styles" section. Lil pours coffee into the thick ceramic mugs in front of them and walks away. This is most likely all any of them will order. Ed is perfectly aware that, arrayed along the counter, these three don't have to face one another, look one another in the eye. All conversation can be spoken out of the side of the mouth. "Sox are going to be out of it."

"Maybe. They can still get the wild card if they pull it together." Chuck positions the sugar dispenser over his mug and lets it pour freely.

"Remember the pools?" Ed sips his black coffee, winces at the temperature, and sets it back down. If he were at home, he'd blow into it, but here he just pretends he's taking his time.

"Office pools?" Joe hands the front-page section to Chuck.

"Yeah, the betting that we'd do on the Sox or the Pats."

"I remember the year we got to betting on the pregnant women. Remember, there were three of them at once?" Joe swallows the last of his coffee and holds his mug out to Lil.

"Hey, Ed, didn't you win one of them?" Setting the sugar dispenser down, Chuck pours half-and-half from the little metal pitcher.

"Fifty bucks." Ed makes another attempt at drinking

his coffee. He doesn't add that he gave the money to the new mother, one of the secretaries. Or that he never told Alice he was betting on delivery dates and baby weights. That was the bet; You had to get two out of three—date, time, and weight. He'd managed to pick the right time and weight, and was only a day off on the trifecta. It was when they were still trying to get pregnant. Alice was in a weepy stage and any mention of someone else's success sent her into a funk.

"Good times," Joe says, his lumpy hands embracing the curve of the mug.

"Yeah." Ed's coffee is finally cool enough to drink. He handed the cash to the new mother, who had come into the plant to show off the baby. He put the fifty bucks in her hand, admired the child, and told himself that it didn't matter, them not being parents, that it just wasn't meant to be. You couldn't dwell on it. You couldn't let it ruin your life.

The dog is still waiting by the cemetery gates. Once again, its eyes follow him as he slows down. Ed won't stop, won't turn into the cemetery road. Not for this dog, not ever. But he slows down enough to see that the dog's eyes are two different color—one blue, one brown. "Go home."

The dog merely cocks his ears at Ed's words, unimpressed.

It's a fanciful notion, but Ed thinks that the dog is waiting for someone.

Mack positions himself at the cemetery gates. In his mind, this seems like the likeliest spot for Justine to find him. His scent won't be mingled with that of other dogs. Besides, it looks like the place near home where they go when Justine decides that walking isn't enough exercise. It's not the park. It's like the park, but not the park. She puts him into a down-stay position at a spot that looks like this one, stone pillars that cast enough shade that it's a comfortable wait while she runs. So Mack decides that if he stays here, Justine will come back for him.

He's found the brook that runs alongside the western perimeter of the graveyard, so he is no longer thirsty. He's discovered acorns and roots beneath the massive oak trees that border this little plot of grass and stones. They crunch in his mouth, unappealing, but are a little something to put in his belly, although he throws them up a little while later. There are field mice; he can hear them in the tangle of briars and in the grass, but he has yet to capture one. He imagines snapping his jaws down on the fragile bones of the rodents, savoring the wild meat, being true to his distant ancestors, but the field mice are too quick even for a dog that dances. That's the word that Justine uses: *dance*. "Want to dance, little man?" He always keeps his eagle eye on Justine's face and hands, watching for the subtle signals of weave and bow, prance and spin. And, finally, his favorite—leap into her arms as she laughs and cuddles him close, proud and pleased with their performance. He has learned to like applause.

CHAPTER 11

The second time she sees the dog, still at his post between the cemetery gates, Alice pulls her fifteen-year-old Dodge Caravan to the narrow shoulder of the road, a few yards from where the dog waits. "Here, boy." She clucks at him from the safety of her car. A half a pound of sliced roast beef is in the sack beside her on the seat, Ed's lunch. The dog stands up, then sits again, but his eyes remain on her, odd eyes, one blue and one brown, clearly skeptical. Why should he trust her? Alice climbs out of the van. The dog watches with interest as Alice pulls the meat out of the plastic deli bag. Ed won't miss one slice. The dog does not approach her, nor does he move away; the unmatched eyes focus on what's in her hand. The skeptical look has become that of wishful thinking. Gingerly holding the floppy piece of roast beef where it stains her fingers pink, she proffers it. "Come on, boy. It's okay."

Suddenly, the dog trots over, as if he's made his mind up about her, that she is trustworthy, and all hesitation is gone. She holds out the meat and he takes it from her fingertips with surprising gentleness, swallowing the slice without chewing. He licks his muzzle, cocks his head with its jack-in-the-pulpit-shaped ears, and waits for more.

"Oh, what the heck." Alice takes another slice of roast beef out of the deli bag. Now the dog's tail end wriggles from side to side, his eyes on her hand, and his tongue, pink and narrow, appears. She can't just leave him here on the side of the road, now, can she? He's been here long enough that she knows he must be homeless. Just waiting outside the cemetery gates like that Scottish dog, Greyfriar's Bobby, keeping his dead master company. Maybe the dog belongs to someone recently deceased. Alice can't think of anyone who's recently passed. Mrs. Fontaine died a couple of weeks ago, but she was in a nursing home, so this can't be her pet. Besides, nowadays most everyone gets planted in the new cemetery, closer to town. In an old-fashioned way, this place is still called "the graveyard." No one but those with old Moodyville names buried here. Moody, Thompson, Pierce. Her family names, dating back to when her great-great-grandfather came from England with a young bride, bringing his skills as a metal smith to the new factory.

Four generations of Alice's family before her. And one after. Their daughter. All here.

Alice thinks of Ed's warning about approaching strange dogs. This one isn't so strange, except for his eyes. He is now fully engaged in rump wagging and whining for more roast beef. He prances on tiny Muppet paws, making little chuffing noises of hope. His plumy tail gracefully waves in the warm September air. He's an unusual color, deep gray, with a white ruff and black streaks here and there in his coat, like someone with a

wet paint brush got too close. He looks like a miniature
Lassie painted all the wrong colors.

"Ed'll kill me for sure." Using the last piece of beef,
Alice entices the dog to the sliding door on the passenger side of the van and opens it up. "Get in." As if he
expected nothing less, the dog hops right onto the middle bench, turns around three times, and curls up. Alice
slams the door shut and goes around to the driver's side.
A car passes her, slowing down to see if she needs help.
It's their next-door neighbor, Mr. Fry. Alice waves him
on. No problem here.

Not yet.

The woman gives him meat. From her fingers. He wants
a slice of the cheese he can smell in its plastic wrapper,
but she doesn't offer him that. As a dog, he seldom gets
to choose. Usually, things are just the way they are. Out
now. Eat then. If offered meat and cheese, take both.
Maybe there is choosing in where to bed down for the
night—in his bed or in Justine's. Snooze on the couch or
in front of the sliding glass door where the sun beats in
at noon on cold days. But other than that, Mack has never
made a deliberate, meaningful choice in his life. Even
living with Justine wasn't a choice. It wasn't his choice
that she disappeared.

When the woman talks to him, Mack feels soothed, a
little of the anxiety smoothed over by a woman's voice.
He is lonely. He's never spent more than a few hours
alone. No one is here to tell him what to do, and he is
nervous. Justine hasn't come, and he's been here, in this
down-stay spot, for what even a dog knows is a long
time. So when this woman speaks sweetly to him, calling him "doggy," Mack knows that he has a real choice.
If he jumps into the van, he is leaving Justine behind.

She won't be able to follow his scent. But if he stays here, waiting for her to find him, he will die.

He stands at the open door, nerves making him yawn.

"Go on, then, hop in." The woman's voice is gentle. Maybe she knows where Justine is and is taking him there. With that thought, Mack leaps into the car.

CHAPTER 12

"Alice, this is not a good idea." Ed leans over to place both palms on the kitchen table, pressing his weight against the surface. The dog stands in the center of the room, tongue lolling out, almond-shaped eyes focused firmly on Ed's face. Ed can't decide if the gaze is friendly or judgmental; the odd eyes study him, minute flickers of movement at Ed's changes of expression, as if they're having a subtle conversation without words. When Ed straightens up, the dog's muzzle lifts, his blue-and-brown focus penetrating. Little smudgy circles of black against the silvery fur of his forehead act like tiny eyebrows, giving him a quizzical expression that is very nearly human.

"He's been standing outside the cemetery gates since yesterday, and he's starved." Alice has made tuna fish sandwiches for Ed's lunch. "You should have seen him drinking the water I gave him, like he was parched. If anybody has lost him, they aren't looking for him very hard." Ed Parmalee has been married long enough that he knows when to sit down and eat his sandwich and put the conversation aside. Alice has always been a tough fighter for things she wants—a new couch, when he knew the old one had years of life left in it; a deck on the back of the house, when he couldn't see the point of sitting outside slapping mosquitoes and staring out over the neighbor's backyard. Theirs was the first development carved out of cheap farmland when the plant was running at full capacity and new people were coming into the area, swelling the class size at the elementary school. Now half the houses on their street are up for sale and no one wants these little raised ranches with one and a half baths on half an acre of lawn, and the student population has diminished so much, teacher layoffs have been threatened.

He watches as Alice places the plastic bowl back down, the fresh water swirling a little but somehow not slopping over the edge. The dog waits patiently until she straightens up, then laps politely at the new water, clearly sated, but willing to be grateful. Alice trails a hand down the length of the dog's body, picking out bits of leaf and twig. She is smiling, and she reminds Ed suddenly of her younger self, the one who smiled down on the baby as she nursed, holding to herself a singularly female satisfaction in having this ability. As if the child belonged more fully to her.

"Well, don't get any ideas about keeping him. We don't want a dog."

"I never said anything about keeping him." Alice turns her back to him, busying herself with cleaning up the counter. "If this one-horse town had a dog officer, I'd have called. What else can we do until someone claims him?"

"How long do you expect that's going to take? We don't need the bother of a dog. You don't need the extra work. And what if we want to travel?" Ed fists half of the tuna sandwich, taking a large bite.

Alice laughs, a sharp, humorless laugh. "Ed Parmalee, when was the last time we traveled anywhere but to my sister's for Christmas?"

"It would be that much harder if we had a dog."

"I never said I wanted him." Alice holds out the empty tuna can for the dog to lick. He does so daintily, his facile tongue sliding along the smooth interior of the can. "But please don't make travel an argument against it."

Once upon a time, travel was the grail at the end of child rearing and mortgage payments. Once Stacy was launched, they dreamed of Europe or a Caribbean island. Looking back now, the only travel they ever did of a recreational nature were the trips they took to Disney World and camping in the White Mountains. The occasional weekends they spent in Boston with Ed's relatives, wanting to give Stacy some culture: the BSO, the MFA, Faneuil Hall and Quincy Market. Once Stacy had gotten busy with Girl Scouts and sports, ballet lessons and band concerts, they had a hard time finding a free weekend. Eventually, they traveled east only for the day, paid their duty call, and came home. Now with Ed's parents gone and his siblings scattered as far away as Poughkeepsie, they haven't been east in years. The idea of a European vacation or the winter visit to a warm island has been not so much abandoned as simply forgotten.

Can cleaned, the dog goes back to sitting in the middle of the kitchen, as if he's waiting for something, some action on their part.

Ed gets up from the table with his empty plate in hand. He has to pass the dog as he goes to the sink. A pat on the head is only a pat on the head. Not capitulation. The fur beneath his hand is as soft as down. The dog presses his skull up into Ed's palm. The eyebrow spots lift, making Ed think of Stacy when she saw him coming home from one of his rare trips, maybe a union gathering in Springfield or training on a new machine out in the Midwest. The eager anticipation of *presents* writ large on her face, the hope for a new board game or the next book in The Baby-sitter's Club series, nothing exotic.

Ed looks down on the dog. "What do you want, fella?"

The dog suddenly yawns, his sharp muzzle widening, his tongue curling up in a lingual arc. He emits an elastic vocalization that ends in a sound that could have been words: *Home-home-home.*

Ed and Alice Parmalee laugh simultaneously. They keep their eyes on the dog, where he absorbs their surprise at the sound of it.

He watches these two new people carefully. Food, water, and gentle touches are very welcome, but what he really wants is for them to take him home. He's tried to tell them, but, like most humans, they are single-language speakers. For now, though, this is all right. He is satisfied with his decision. He is safe, fed, and watered. The woman has tidied up his coat. There is a tension in the man, not like Artie and his solid hostility, but a withholding. Like some dogs who refuse to sniff and get acquainted. That's okay; Mack can handle aloofness, even respect it. He also enjoys a challenge. Just accepting the man's grudging pat on the head is a start.

The woman takes him outside at night, fastening a length of clothesline around his neck, walking him around the grass until he squats. He keeps to his training, staying close to her side until he needs to do his business, which she picks up with a plastic bag and a squeamish look on her face. She praises him with words he knows: *good boy*.

He is Maksim, although Justine mostly calls him Mack. This person just calls him "boy." He's been called that before; it's okay. If she calls, he'll come to it.

The important thing is that maybe they will know how to find Justine.

CHAPTER 13

This morning, after coffee with the guys, Ed Parmalee points the Cutlass toward Aubuchon Hardware. He's out of 3-in-One oil and could use some shop rags. The towel bar in the bathroom is pulling away from the Sheetrock. Maybe he should pick up molly bolts. Oh, and he should get some poster board, too; start tacking up FOUND DOG posters in the area. It's starting to sound like a Wal-Mart run, so if he can't get what he needs at Aubuchon, he'll keep going. Alice won't miss him till lunchtime, if then.

He knows that he drives her crazy. Alice never says anything, but it's there, this annoyance, evident in the angle of her chin when she wipes the counter after he makes a sandwich, or when she has to ask him to move his feet so she can vacuum. It hasn't always been there, this perpetual annoyance; it's something that has evolved out of the long period when they didn't know what to say to each other, or what they might have said would have been too toxic for their marriage to survive.

Ed doesn't imagine for a minute that Alice would

worry about him if he didn't show up at noon. She'd put his sandwich in the fridge and keep moving. She might scold him about not using the cell phone to say he was going to be late, but she'd never complain that he was. It's as if she longs for time by herself. Too much time alone, Ed knows, was a problem back then, back in those hard days when she'd become inert, as unmoving as a portrait, just the artist's imitation of light, illuminating the idea of movement. The stillness eventually gave way to the movement of chores and purpose, but it was always under the surface, always a possibility that someday he'd come home and find her frozen in place again.

His answer to those black days had been to throw himself into work, returning to the double shifts of his youth, expending his energy in walking the floor of the machine shop, monitoring the workers whose job he once did, approving, chiding, goading, joshing the men and women, most of whom spoke little English, feeling like a shark, the reputed need to keep moving the only way for him to stay alive. When Ed realized that Alice wasn't moving, he stopped working as much. Now he isn't sure anymore if that helped, or if she just had to move out of that fugue state on her own schedule. He knows of some couples whose troubles have made them closer. Theirs haven't. They both know it and have no idea what to do about it. So they go on with their day-to-day lives, living in tandem but not in companionship.

Ed squeezes the Cutlass between a Prius and a Volvo. It's strange, this going to the hardware store on a weekday. Typically, it was the favorite errand of chore-filled Saturdays, scheduled after the dump and before the barbershop; now he just goes whenever he thinks of something he needs. It's the result of having all this unoccupied time, time he should be putting to better use, but he hasn't found anything that interests him enough to commit to. He isn't keen to volunteer at the regional hospital or join the group of retired volunteers that do people's taxes, or substitute-teach at the high school. Maybe he suffers from his own kind of inertia, which is contradictory to the fact that, in being retired so early, he still has plenty of energy. Ed reads the want ads every week, but nothing ever appears that attracts him. He doesn't want to end up behind the counter at a McDonald's, although he knows a couple of guys who have and seem to like it well enough. Management is management, they say. Product is product. Instead, he fills the middle of his days with made-up errands.

Ed wanders the aisles, sliding his readers on and off as he examines the molly bolts; ponders the wisdom of the larger can of 3-in-One. Even so, it takes only minutes to find everything he needs. As he heads between aisles to get to the register, he spots the pet supplies.

There are fluorescent collars, nylon collars in pink, purple, blue, and black; varying widths of collars, choke chains, and something that looks like a tiny halter. They've been using a length of clothesline to walk the dog, but maybe they should at least buy him a collar and leash. He's going to be with them only until his rightful people are found, but still, a proper leash and collar wouldn't suggest that if they *don't* find his people, he's staying.

Ed stands long enough over the selection of leashes and collars that a salesperson finally takes notice. "Do you need help?" The clerk says this with the same voice she likely uses on her kids when they reach for the cereal. This is probably her job while they're in school. Mother's hours. Where are the men? When did hardware stores become a woman's domain?

"No. I'm good."

There are collars with gingham patterns, collars with little paw prints. Whatever happened to simple leather collars adorned with metal buttons? Here there are spike collars, thick macho ones.

"Are you looking for a training collar, or just something to hang his tags on?" The clerk, persistent, strums her fingers along the array of collars hanging by plastic hooks. They move like a rainbow-colored curtain.

"We've got him only until his owner is found. I guess I won't be hanging any tags on him, but I'm sure not going to be training him, either. I just need something we can use to walk him."

The saleswoman taps a finger to her lips, then pulls down a flat red nylon collar. "This'll do, and it's cheap. And the chain leashes are a bargain." With that, she walks away to greet a woman gripping a list.

Ed looks at the collars for another minute, puts the red one back and picks out a black collar with a rolled edge. He finds a matching black nylon leash. The dog, wherever he came from, isn't a red collar kind of dog. Then Ed pulls a dog brush off the rack. This one says it's meant for longhaired, double-coated breeds. Alice has been brushing the mats out of the dog's coat with an old hairbrush of hers. She still wears her hair bundled in a twist, a light fringe of bangs framing her face. In that way of random thoughts, Ed thinks of the nights when Alice pulled the pins out of her hair and let it fall like it did when they courted, curtaining them as they kissed. That stopped happening a long time ago.

As an afterthought, Ed selects a squeaky toy shaped like a hydrant.

His route home takes him along the Moody River, but Ed'll turn off before coming to the old pistol factory, where a two-hundred-year-old dam holds back the

Moody River, at one time forcing it into powering the old factory. Alice's great-great-grandfather came from England to work in that factory. Just like Ed migrated west from Boston to work in the screw-machine plant 150 years later. This late in the year, a day or so before the autumn equinox, the stream is shallow and hardly looks to be moving. It bifurcates around rocks littering the streambed. In the spring, the river is high with snow-melt and the rushing water can be dangerous even when the fishing is the best. In a moment, Ed sees the ruins of the old factory and signals his turn.

Mack thinks about going, leaving the comfort of this way station; pointing his nose in the direction from which they came and walking home. Justine must be there. He has only two places he can picture her: here and home. But he's not been given an opportunity to choose to do that. Every moment he's been with these people, Alice and Ed, he's been in their charge.

They don't understand his basic request. All Mack wants is for them to open the door and let Justine in. Each time he goes to the door, they tie a piece of rope around his neck and walk him around the perimeter of the house. Every time Ed leaves the house and Mack whines to follow, the woman calls him back to sit with her. When she's busy with her tasks, he stares out the sliding door into the empty backyard, glimpses of the local cat prowling the hedges the only entertainment. It isn't his house, so he doesn't bother sending up the alarm. He's not here to protect their territory. He is a guest and he will behave like one. Grateful for the rather tasteless kibble poured into a bowl, happy to be allowed on the couch to sleep beside the woman. She isn't Justine, but she is generous with the belly rubs.

She talks to him when the man isn't there. Tells him all sorts of tongue-language things that Mack doesn't interpret as particularly meaningful. Her language has some of the nuances of Justine's, although the words are unfamiliar. The pitch is the same as when Justine chats to him, higher and softer than when people talk to other humans. Humans have this need to express themselves through their mouths, and he supposes that this is because they are so poor with their noses.

There was that moment when he followed her into a bedroom that did not hold much human scent in it; an overlay of cleaner like Justine used on her furniture, almost, but not quite, masking a vestigial odor of some other person. Not so much the scent of a human as of the objects belonging to that human, an old scent lingering beneath the chemical. If she'd opened the drawers, he could have gotten a clearer picture of the room's absent human.

That's when she said the only meaningful thing, when he followed her in there. She said it clearly and in words he understood: "Get out."

CHAPTER 14

"Let's see how this fits." Ed holds the collar out with both hands. The dog trots over to take a good sniff. "Can you sit?" The dog sits. Ed fastens the black collar.

"Make sure that it isn't too tight, or too loose. We don't know if he'll walk without pulling, or if he'll try to pull out of the collar. Clearly, he's escaped once. How foolish would we look if he takes off on me?" Alice takes the new brush and smoothes the dog's ruff over the collar so that it doesn't show. "Let's see the leash."

Ed hands his wife the leash with the tiniest reluctance. Alice snaps the clip onto the ring. Ed takes it out of her hand. "I'll take him out."

Alice takes the leash back. "No. I will." She doesn't even make it sound like she's doing him a favor. "I'm going to take him for a proper walk."

"Where?"

"I should take a plastic bag, I guess. I don't think I want him soiling the neighbors' yards."

Ed snags a plastic grocery bag out of the calico sleeve

they stuff them into. "Guess we'd better stop using the green bags at the store for a while."

The dog is dancing on his little front feet, his tail swinging in anticipation of a walk. He looks from one to the other, a little furry linesman.

"He might be a little strong on that leash. You don't want him pulling you down the street."

"I'll be fine." Alice gathers the leash in her hands.

"Be careful on the road. It's getting dark earlier."

"I won't be long."

Ed asks again, "Where are you going?"

Alice knows what he's driving at. He's holding her up, questioning her decision-making abilities. "To the old path."

The old path is an ancient way that begins at the end of their dead-end road, which takes its name, Old Path Road, from it. It wends through the woods for a mile or so, to the rocky banks of the Moody River. The path meanders along the top of the escarpment, following the river, until it ends at the ruins of the old pistol factory. A set of steps lead down the steep grade to the quarter-acre millpond, where the Moody River was once harnessed for power. Alice and Ed courted along that path, holding hands, dreaming their future, walking to the place where there once was a footbridge, now a pair of stone abutments facing each other, separated by the river water that cascades over the dam in the spring. The slippery rocks are the perfect place to fish for the trout that the conservation commission stock in the millpond of dammed water. It was the place where Ed taught Stacy how to fish. They practiced mostly catch and release. Like him, Stacy preferred the hunt to the kill, and frankly, nobody in the house really liked freshwater fish all that much. In late summer, after dinner, he and Stacy would grab the poles and walk the path to the south abutment, where they would drop in their lines and call it fishing. That time of year, the Moody River no longer cascaded over the edge of the dam, escaping gently through the ancient sluice gates, so they might walk single file along the narrow lip of the dam to get to the north-side abutment, where the big trout were rumored to live, Ed holding Stacy's shoulder in front of him. Stacy was warned over and over never to go there alone. Ever.

Because the path also branches off to Alice's mother's house, they used to let Stacy use it to go to her grandmother's, because she wouldn't have to cross any roads. She wouldn't be in danger.

"Where else can I take him?"

"But why there?"

"Anywhere else, I'll have to drive to, and that's just silly. Besides, I'm not going all the way." Not going all the way to the millpond, she means. Not there.

It's been seven years. And still the thought of the old path hurts. Ed drops into the kitchen chair, the stony weight of his memory bearing down on him.

Ed runs the length of the old path, uselessly calling out Stacy's name, hearing his own voice echo against the newly leafed trees ringing the still surface of the still pond. There is no sign of her, and the relief is pounding in his chest. He runs home, believing that she must have gone to her grandmother's house, not come this way after all.

The dog, giving up hope that the leash means anything, rests his head on Ed's knee. "I guess he deserves a good walk." Ed turns away from Alice, but she sees that he has hurt himself with remembering. He strokes the dog's head, keeping his face from her.

Alice hands Ed the leash. "Do you want to take him?"

Ed shakes his head. "I forgot to get the poster board. For the 'Found' signs."

"That's all right. There's no hurry, is there?"

"His people could be looking for him. Panicked, don't you think?"

"If he's meant to be found, he will be."

This place reminds Mack of go-to-the-park. The tall squirrel-bearing trees, the enticing bolt-holes of ground vermin, the twitter of bird life above his head. The scents. Oh, the scents of a primeval wood on the nose of a dog long removed from his ancestral purpose. Justine would encourage him with a whispered: "Get it!" and then laugh when he couldn't. They never tired of the game.

Today, his new female, Alice, has linked him to the leash and led him to this equally glorious patch of nature. Above the scent of rodents lies the even more welcome scent of other dogs. He breathes in the calling cards of a variety of canines, all of which indicate they thought this was their territory. He covers their marks with his own. The only spoiler to this perfect outing is the fact that this Alice does not let him run off leash. She clings tenaciously to the other end, keeping up a soft patter of tongue language that Mack interprets as a request not to pull her off her feet. As if he'd ever do such a thing. From birth, Mack has known better than to pull on the leash. From earliest training, he has kept to the side of his person, his long nose just at the crook of the knee. Justine believes that he has genius. He may have, but he also has a Sheltie's proclivity for obedience, as well as a superior sense of dignity. He has always prided himself on being a perfect gentleman. So he lets this new woman, Alice, keep him close without argument. He accepts her restraint with equanimity. He listens to her voice as she speaks of what a good boy he is and cheerfully looks up at her, his herd-dog eyes locked on hers. In catching her eye as a good sheepdog does, he gets a glimpse of her own intelligence. She doesn't look away from his gaze; she looks deeper into it. And with that look comes a thin line of connection, of partnership. Alice strokes his muzzle and lifts it to her face. Just like Justine sometimes has on her face, this woman has tears streaming. Clearly, Alice, like Justine, needs him. He licks at the salty tears.

CHAPTER 15

I feel like a whaler reaching port after a four-year voyage as my feet hit the pavement in Boston. The morning commotion of traffic, and the pedestrians all vying for dominance as they stream toward office buildings and shops, catches me by surprise as I come out of the bus terminal. I have a ticket to New Bedford in my back pocket and exactly forty-five minutes to find the warehouse and Artie. And if not Artie himself, at least another clue as to where he might be. I have decided that he is still here. That there's no way he'd simply turn around and head back west. He'll need another job, another truck loaded with something needed west of the Mississippi. And surely that will take time, time enough for me to catch up with him.

I go in the opposite direction of the human current, heading away from downtown and toward the street where the warehouse is located. I'm lucky; it really is fairly close to South Station. But not that close. I still have a good walk ahead of me, over a bridge, down an unpopulated side street flanked by windowless warehouses. From the bridge, I can see the interstate highway with its thrombosis of cars working their way into the tunnel beneath the city. Overhead, a near-constant stream of jets coming in and taking off from Logan. A traffic helicopter makes a wide swing over the scene, hunting for accidents. I've lived in cities all over: Brooklyn, Louisville, Los Angeles, but I always think of Boston as the best. I guess everyone who grows up in eastern Massachusetts thinks that way. I shove my duffel behind me and pick up the pace. My nostalgia is costing me time.

By the time I actually reach the street where the warehouses are, I've got about fifteen minutes to locate Artie. Two long warehouses opposite each other have at least a dozen trailers backed up to loading docks. Men driving forklifts and other men watching them crowd the open bays. The trailers are in such perfect alignment, if I stand in the right position, it looks like there is only one. But there are no trucks attached to these trailers. I need to find the truck lot to find Artie's dull green cab. I don't have time to do this; I'm running out of time if I'm going to catch the bus to New Bedford this morning as I promised. But I have to find Artie. The urgency literally squeezes my heart.

"You lost?"

I turn to see a big black guy wearing a gray uniform, a yellow and black security badge sewn onto the right breast pocket of his shirt. He has a nightstick holstered in a belt that squeezes him so that he plumps up over it and below it. He has the look of a guy who has found a legitimate way to be a badass.

"I'm looking for someone."

"You need to check in at the office."

"I didn't see an office."

He slides the nightstick out of its loop and uses it like a professor using a pointer, as if his forefinger wouldn't be enough. "Over there, three doors down. Big sign. Somebody will help you."

"Thanks. I appreciate it."

"No problem."

I am aware of him watching me as I jog toward my destination. I assume it's to make sure I get there and don't cause some daytime mayhem on the way. Maybe it's that he's appreciating my ass. Either way, I'm glad when I reach the open office door, where, predictably, there is no one just sitting there waiting to help me.

I scan the company names printed over each of the bay doors, an array with a few familiar names, but mostly names of companies I've never heard of. I struggle to make Ra-Mar or De-Light-ly the name of the company Artie was hauling for. He was hauling a load of seed; that much I finally remember. Maybe one of the more floral-sounding names is where he backed up the truck. Or agricultural. Are there any farmers here? My mind is racing as the moments slip by and with them my chance to track down Artie. I start walking along the apron, skipping past skids loaded with shrink-wrapped goods. I look for any trailer that might have Colorado, Washington, or Iowa plates. I ask every worker there if he knows Artie Schmidt. "Did a guy driving from Washington State pull in last night?" They call into cavernous spaces, consult with one another, shift their yellow hard hats, but none of them has heard of Artie Schmidt. And no one has seen a dog.

I get down the length of one of the warehouses and realize that each building is two-sided; another whole lineup of trailers is backed up on the other side. As I

reach the end of the line, I see my friend the guard. He is
not smiling at me.

"You find the boss?" The guard is on the ground,
looking up at me as I stand on the loading dock.

"No, and I don't have time to wait."

"Then come back when you can. Only authorized
visitors can be here." Viewed from above, he's a little
less scary.

"Do I look like I'm going to run off with a load of
machine parts?" I've really had enough. The frustration
of the past day and night feels like an elastic band in
my gut. It is wound as tight as it can go and in the next
second it could snap, and I won't be responsible for the
outcome. The big guy needs to back off. "I'm looking for
Artie Schmidt. He's the thief. He's stolen my dog. I have
to find him now."

The guard is older than he looked to be at first. There
is a little round bald spot that is clearly visible as he
drops his gaze to the ground. He looks up at me. "You
want to file a report?"

"How long will that take? I have to catch a bus for
New Bedford in . . ." I look at my watch and the elastic
band in my gut takes one more twist. "In fifteen minutes."

"Ten minutes. I'll get someone to take you to South
Station."

In my life, I have come to the realization that time really doesn't stand still and that there is no way I'll make
that bus if I stop to fill out a report on a man who will
never be found. I don't know if the bus ticket is transfer-
able to another time, but I do know that if I don't show up
at noon, I will endure the wrath of Adele. "Will filing a
report help catch him?"

The guard shrugs. "It's a start. It's the only thing I can do."

"Okay." I walk down the cement steps to the ground. The guard now towers over me, and I feel like a captive as we head toward his little office. As we walk, I tell him my story. About being left, about Artie driving off with my dog. About trying to get to New Bedford before my father dies. About wanting my dog back and Artie drawn and quartered. He listens, and once inside, he's quick to call a cab to whisk me back to South Station even before he pulls out a form.

"Name, address, cell number or number where we can reach you." He's moving as fast as he can. "Theft of dog valued at?"

How can you put a value on Mack? What he means to me. He may be a puppy-mill dog, but he is everything to me. "Ten thousand dollars." What I mean is, priceless. I wouldn't take a million for him. But if I don't exaggerate his value in terms that mean something to a guy sitting in a guard's booth all day, can I trust that he'll take me seriously?

The guard looks me in the eye, weighing my exaggeration. "Have you gotten a ransom note?"

"No." I start to explain that I don't think Artie would think of that and then stop. If it's a clear case of dognapping, then maybe the authorities will do something. "I've been on the road, so how could he send a ransom note?"

"Okay. His name? Address? Make of truck? Rig?" The guard peppers me with questions I cannot answer. I sound like a jerk. I can tell him that the guy likes Camels, that he drinks Red Bull like it's orange juice, that he prefers redheads to blondes, and that when he's not on the road, he hangs out at Candy Kane's bar, bragging about his string of ex-wives. No, I don't know who his agent is. If I did, I'd know how to find Artie. I think this but don't say it. I need this guy. Getting snippy now won't do me any good.

The cab pulls up. I dig into my pocket to find my last ten. "You have my number. Please don't hesitate to call me, even if you don't think it matters."

"I can do one more thing. I'll talk to the drivers. They may know something, and they may be able to help. They talk to each other over the CB all day long. If they spot him, they can stop him."

The elastic in my belly snaps. Why didn't I ask a trucker to do that before? Artie was on the CB constantly. If I'd just used my head. "He has a name, a handle. When he talks to other drivers, he calls himself 'Rockin' Roadie.'" I am almost embarrassed at saying that out loud. Artie wouldn't tell me how he acquired such a nickname, just leered at me, implying a suggestive origin.

"That will help."

I have three minutes to make my bus.

This time, I am alone, no curious seatmate to ask me innocuous but challenging questions about my life.

When I left Anthony, I really thought that he would come after me, apologize, make things better. But he didn't, proving that he was relieved with my decision. At the very least, I thought that he would demand that I bring back his son. Instead, he was relieved to have dodged the responsibility of parenthood at age twenty-three. Maybe it was an accidental conception, but one I never regretted. Maybe ours was a forced marriage—a self-fulfilling prophesy, in my stepmother's eyes—but one I intended to make perfect. But when lovelessness becomes betrayal, the answer for me is to move on.

When I left home, I had fifty bucks and a suitcase. When I left Anthony, I had a thousand dollars and our car. I drove off with Tony, a suitcase full of his little clothes and a duffel bag with my essentials.

Tony and I sang songs all the way down Route 95. *Sesame Street* songs, Raffi songs, silly made-up songs, just to keep him from asking questions. We were on the road, on an adventure. Another chapter in the story of me.

"Where's Daddy?" Tony is in the back, in his car seat, playing with a magnetic puzzle that I've found in a rest stop convenience store.

I have rehearsed an answer for this inevitable question. "Daddy has sent us on a voyage like the old-time whalers. We're out to make our fortune."

"What's a fortune?" He lisps the word, making it sound like four-thune. I laugh, a bubbling sensation forcing its way up into my mouth. I'm laughing because if I don't, I'll cry.

CHAPTER 16

When I was a kid doing homework at the kitchen table, Adele would come up behind me and press one finger into my neck at the place where skull and vertebrae meet, forcing me to look down at my papers.

"Are you going to pass that mess in?"

I'd look at the math work sheet with the gray smears across the work space from the too-hard eraser at the end of my stubby pencil, testimony to my struggles with the subject.

"Use scrap paper if you can't do it neatly."

She never offered to help me figure out the arithmetic.

I often wonder where my father was when she was jabbing me with a finger or shoving me ahead of her to my room. Or chastising me for not closing the peanut butter jar tight enough or the bread wrapper secure enough. Or slapping me because she interpreted my response to some demand or question as impertinent. "I will not have impertinence." I thought impertinence was a venal sin. I would have confessed it had she ever taken

me to confession. I'm not making it up, remembering it
wrong, when I believe that Paul never suffered any of
these physical and verbal assaults. He fluttered in and out
of the kitchen, on his way to a practice or a game, or to
meet up with friends, leaving the jars open and the bread
hanging out of the wrapper like a tongue. He wasn't expected to sit at the kitchen table to do his homework; his
homework was done in the privacy of his room. A gentle knock and reminder not to stay up too late, the only
words his mother ever said to him on the subject. I know
for a fact he wasn't burning the candle on his homework. He was doing other things, things that I could hear
through the thin wall of my former walk-in closet.

I wonder if Paul will be there today. As the Bonanza
bus nears the transportation center in New Bedford,
I notice that my hands are shaking in a barely visible
tremor. Nerves. I haven't seen any of these people, my
family, in years. I might not even recognize Paul. The
last time I saw him was maybe ten years ago. I really
can't recall. I came back for his wedding. I had received
an invitation and I have no doubt that it was the subject
of great debate, whether or not to waste an invitation on
me. I was long gone. Paul and I had never kept in touch.
I knew that it was a courtesy invitation, probably sent
because the poor bride had foolishly insisted that I get
one, harboring some prebridal expectation that she'd be
able to heal family rifts out of kindness. I was just con-
trary enough to tick off "Yes, I will attend" on the tiny
RSVP card. I mailed it to the bride's mother, wondering if she had any idea who Justine Meade was. I'd gone
back to my maiden name a couple of years after leaving
Anthony. In a further act of defiance, I changed Tony's
name to Meade, too. He was young enough that changing his name seemed like a normal thing to do. Another

new school, another new neighborhood. Another name. Simple.

Maybe it was more like eighteen years ago. Time has a way of zipping by, the mile markers racking up so fast, whole decades disappear from sight in the rearview mirror.

Having spent my last ten bucks on the Boston cab, I sling my duffel over my shoulders and begin to walk. I have to climb Johnnycake Hill, New Bedford's best-known street, with its cobbles and whaling museum, and work my way under route 195 to the other side of town, where the double- and triple-deckers, built back when the city had industry, line residential streets. It is a perfect September day, warm and dry, with a high thin veil of cloud in the southwest, portending lousy weather in the next twenty-four hours. It's a nice day for a walk. If I had my dog with me, he'd be hoping that we would come to a park, where I could slip off his leash and toss the tennis ball for him. I actually have a tennis ball in my duffel. I brought one with me, as if they might not have them in New Bedford. I have the ball but not the dog. The hope that I had when the guard, Troy, told me about the CBs and how the drivers would put the word out is already fading into the more familiar sense of despair. I'm not a child, too easily inclined to hope for magic. I'm an adult whose life has pretty much been magic-free. The idea of a convoy of truck drivers caring enough to help find Artie is pretty far-fetched. Why should a group of anonymous drivers moving from one side of the country to the other care about my stolen dog? I wipe the "cavalry to the rescue" image out of my head.

I am at the corner of Lawton and Green. The house that I grew up in is half a block away. I can see the triple-decker that still belongs to my father looming over the ranch-style single family house that we crammed into for the eight years I lived there. It must suit Adele and my father so much better now. It's really a house meant for two. Before I make that final turn, I pull out my phone and call Saundra.

It is ominously quiet behind Saundra's voice. No barking. "I've got it posted online and I've contacted all the Sheltie rescues I can find from Cincinnati to Boston. Any word at all? Where are you?"

"No word. And I'm almost to the house."

"You need to focus on your dad. We'll keep going here. Do you need anything?"

"Just to find Mack."

"We're praying for you." And just like that, the background is filled with Saundra's pack barking joyously at being let in.

No one, to my knowledge, has ever prayed for me before. Tears prick at my eyes, but I don't let them fall. I can't let them start, because they might never end.

Swallowing against the lump in my throat, I march myself to the middle of the block and face my childhood home. It is the same vinyl white that it has always been, grimy now with decades of street dust. A pair of plastic shutters flank the picture window that looks out on the street and the neighbors' houses, no view worth such a large window, and one that had to have custom-made drapes to keep those neighbors from looking in. The foundation plantings have grown from shrubs into bushes and need a good trimming. *Unkempt*—that's the word that comes to mind, and I am a little surprised. Adele is a house-proud woman. This place doesn't look like anyone has taken care of more than getting the grass cut in years. I wonder how long my father has been sick.

I don't know which door to use. Should I mount the

three cement steps to the front door and ring the doorbell like a guest? Should I go through the one-car carport and open the side door and call out: "I'm home!" like a family member? As it turns out, Adele spots me and opens the front door, pushes wide the complaining screen door and stares at me. "It took you long enough. Come on in."

Now I know I'm home.

CHAPTER 17

"Wipe your feet. I've just had the rugs cleaned." The front door opens directly into the living room. It's different from my memory of white walls and fake Colonial-style furniture. Three of the walls are a pale pink and the fourth—the narrowest, at the far end of the room—is the designated accent wall, as it's painted a weird persimmon color. The furniture is modern; the couch and chairs have huge soft cushions that could swallow a child. The only thing in this room that I recognize is the antique oak sideboard, which is too big for the dining area in this house, but which once fit perfectly in the dining room in my mother's house. It's placed against the persimmon wall, with a collection of photographs in chunky frames displayed on it. Even from a distance I can see that all of the pictures are of Paul's kids. It looks like he has a dozen, but I realize that they're the same two, replicated over and over at different stages of their lives—as infants, as toddlers, in grade school photos, in middle school graduation pictures. There's no picture of Tony. Perhaps I've never sent one.

Adele is standing in the archway that leads into the kitchen, waiting for me.

"Shall I put my stuff in my room?"

Adele looks at me like I've asked for money. "I assumed you'd be staying in a hotel. We don't have room here. I never suggested . . ."

"I can't afford a hotel."

She doesn't answer me.

I drop my duffel bag, travel-worn and grubby, right on her cream-colored sofa. I want to ask why I can't use Paul's room. I know that the closet that was my space has long since been retrofitted into the walk-in closet it originally was designed to be. I decide to drop the subject for the moment. There are far more important questions to ask. "Where's Dad?"

My stepmother pins a look on me. "Paul's in with him now. When he comes out, you can go in."

"I'll go in now. I just came two thousand miles to see him."

"You will wait here."

I've been through the tortures of the damned to get here to see my father and this woman is going to prevent me with four words? "Give me one good reason I can't go in. He's my father."

"He gets upset if too many people are in there."

"You mean that you do." I turn around and go through the living room to the short hallway that leads to the two bedrooms. As provoked as I am, I hesitate before entering the hallway. I stand in the archway and listen to the voices coming from one of the bedrooms. I realize that my father isn't in his bedroom at all, but in what was once Paul's. The voices aren't live; they're coming from a television show. The canned laughter gives it away. I listen harder. If Paul is in there, he isn't saying anything. Then I hear a pair of chuckles, a shared amusement at whatever's on the screen, and I have a flash of childish jealousy.

Why should this stepson be there in the first place? Oh, yeah. I know why. Because his stepfather always treated him like a son—apple of his eye if not child of his loins. If Paul had been a wolf cub and my father the pack leader, Dad would have made sure Paul got the best chunks of the kill. If there was one life preserver in the boat and we were sinking, I know who would have gotten it. It wasn't normal. Weren't young men supposed to hate their stepfathers? I guess when the stepfather in question is treating you like the son he never had, you don't have to hate him. The laughter again. I march down the hallway and push open the bedroom door.

Because the television is on the same wall as the door, they are facing me as I enter the room. I am shocked at the sight of both of them. I know I should have been anticipating seeing my father as a dying man, but I am more shocked at the sight of Paul. He is huge, bald, and dressed in a Bridgewater State College sweatshirt that has seen better days. There is one brief, crystal moment when all three of us stare at one another, trying hard to reconcile this version of ourselves to those of our memories.

My father speaks first. "Justine? You're here." It almost sounds like a question.

"I got here a few minutes ago." I can't get near to him because Paul's bulk takes up the space beside the twin bed, which is shoved up against the wall and the bureau. "Didn't Adele tell you I was coming?"

"No. I guess she wanted it to be a surprise."

More like she didn't want him disappointed if I failed to show up. I sort of respect that.

"Well, I'm here now." I take a step toward the bed and Paul gets the message. He rises and squeezes himself out of the alley formed by the bed and the bureau.

"Hey, Justy, it's good to see you." He opens his arms wide and scoops me into an embrace I'm not looking for. The nickname reminds me of his taunting me with "Busty Justy" when puberty hit me like an invasion of the body snatchers. I've grown into them, but the girls are still worth a glance.

"Yeah, you, too." I hope that it doesn't show on my face just how startled I am by him, but he knows.

"My wife's a great cook." He's obviously had to explain before how he was a star athlete turned blimp.

Once Paul leaves the bedroom, I am alone with my father for the first time in decades. We are both silent for a moment, taking it in, figuring it out. Not just about the fact that I'm here only because he's dying but by the larger gorilla of our history—his failure to love me. His failure to make me an equal in an unequal house. His failure to stand up to that woman when I most needed him to, if only that once. I step to the side of the bed. He is sitting up, the thin blanket spread neatly over his lower half, with the top of his *Father Knows Best* pajamas buttoned right up to the top button. A glass of water is on the nightstand, a newspaper folded up neatly beside it. The television is blaring out a commercial for adult diapers, and my father points to it. "That's me. How about that? Just like a baby."

I wonder what I want from him, this desiccated remnant of the father who bowed to every opinion Adele voiced. I sit in the chair beside the bed and wait for him to say something of worth to me. What do I want? A deathbed confession of wrongdoing? I want him to tell me that he was wrong not to take my side. Wrong to be sucked into the lie that I had made the whole thing up. Isn't blood thicker than water?

I am trembling with the desire to hear his confession. Get an apology.

My father says nothing. He is attached to a morphine drip, and I excuse him again for his silence.

CHAPTER 18

Adele is sitting in a kitchen chair. Paul is gone. She says nothing to me, so that the silence of the sickroom and the silence of the kitchen make me think that no one will speak in this house until I go away. But I'm not going anywhere. She asked me to come, I'm here, and she'd damn well better like it. I've lost my dog because of this, so giving me the silent treatment is not acceptable.

I've lost my dog, my Mack. The thought keeps returning to me, fresh in its intensity each time.

"Got any tuna?" I suddenly realize that I'm really hungry and I'm not going to wait for an invitation.

Adele looks up from studying the pattern in the old tablecloth. "Yes. In the cupboard."

I don't move for a moment, just look at her. I'm having trouble recognizing this stranger as the same person who tortured me enough that I bolted from home as a girl; the one who gave me no choice but to strike out on my own as soon as I could. She traces the pattern of the flowers with her sharp nail and sighs. Should I feel sorry for her? She's remained my father's wife, taken care of him. Presumably loved him in some way. She doesn't look at me, doesn't tell me anything, and I don't know if she's expecting me to ask her questions or if she is so absorbed in her thoughts that she's forgotten I'm standing here. I look at Adele and see her as she really is, an old woman facing widowhood. The upright posture and the Wicked Witch of the West scrawniness have melted into a dowager's hump and a midriff roundness. Her hair is the yellowy white of faded blondes and the skin on her hands looks like paper that's been crumpled and then flattened. I try to think how old she is and am shocked to think that she's at least seventy-five. She's been a part of my life for over thirty years. I think that when I was a kid, I held out some hope that eventually she'd go away, or that my father would come to his senses and we'd go away.

Now she looks at me. "Well, are you going to stand there or are you going make us some lunch?"

I laugh out loud. The relief is amazing. She's still Adele.

She directs my making of the tuna sandwiches from the amount of mayonnaise to the way I cut the sandwiches. I ignore her and make it my way, lots of pepper. I plate the sandwiches, find an open bag of chips, and wrench open the antique avocado-colored refrigerator to hunt down something to drink. The first shelf is filled with some sort of protein drink, chocolate- or vanilla-flavored. Something intended to supply calories to a person with no appetite. I slam the door shut and fill two glasses with tap water.

How do you make small talk with someone who has always seen you as a burden, a pain in the neck, an unfortunate price to pay for happiness? Am I such an outcast that she can't bring herself to talk to me? Then I wonder if it is simply hard for her to talk about my father, to tell me what's been going on. She called me, called me here. But now she has nothing to say to me?

It's up to me to get things started. "How long will he sleep?"

"I don't know"

"Is he in pain?"

"Sometimes." She looks at me as if I have asked the most personal of questions. The hostility coming from this withered apple doll is less frightening than it was when she would focus her pale eyes on me when I was a teenager. Those looks were sharp and hurt as much as it did when she grabbed me by the bare arm and dug her fingernails into my flesh. "The morphine helps."

That's about as much conversation as either of us wants. So we eat in relative silence, politely passing the chip bag back and forth.

My cell rings. The sound of it startles both of us. A quick glance at an unfamiliar number and my heart starts to beat. It's a 617 area code. Boston. It's Troy.

"No one has seen a dog, but a couple of the guys recognize the Rockin' Roadie handle." Troy has been as good as his word. He's talked to truckers from all over, asking about the dog with Arthur Schmidt. I have to be satisfied that Artie or his road moniker is at least known, even if no one has seen Mack.

"Thanks for trying." I'm certain that the disappointment shows in my voice.

"Truckers do not take kindly to men who mistreat women or animals. No they don't. Word gets out, he's a dead man." He sounds vaguely like a cowboy, and I kind of think that he's not correct in this estimation. I can hardly believe that these hardworking drivers are that interested in my problem.

But I do appreciate what he's saying and tell him so, wondering why this stranger is doing this for me. I wonder enough to ask him.

"I have a dog, ma'am. If anyone ever stole her I'd kill the fucker. Pardon my French."

"No apology necessary. It's what I intend to do if I ever catch up with Artie."

We both laugh a little—that humorless chuckle people give when the next sound might be a cry.

I clear off the lunch plates while Adele goes into my father's room to check on him. They are the same Corelle plates that served as our everyday ware back when I was a kid. I am a little surprised that they have survived all these years. Why is it that a visit to a childhood home turns common objects into jarring memory? The sight of a white glass plate with a seventies orange pattern has the power to drag me into my childhood. Sitting here in Adele's kitchen, I am thrust backward in time. I have been gone so long, it should have changed utterly, but instead I see the same plates, the familiar cookie jar with the very same chip out of the lid. The clock on the wall is a three-dimensional memory, bringing me back to the hours spent watching it as I struggled through homework or sat there, being forced to consume some hard green vegetable left on my plate. Or to the night that I waited while my father and Adele argued over the story that I was telling them; argued over whether or not to act. I waited for them to do something the night I came home from my date with Paul's best friend. Waited for them to finally decide that I was being a big baby and order me to take a shower and go to bed. Nothing had happened that didn't happen on a date with a college boy, a grown man.

A man with a good upbringing. A man whose father was my father's employer.

I pull myself out of this self-indulgent funk. The clock becomes just a clock. I wash and dry the plates and put them away, noting that they are the last two of the set. That's all they need anyway. They have managed to grow old together, my father and our neighbor. They have more than doubled the number of years that my father was with my mother.

It was as if my mother vanished. One moment, we were sitting in our kitchen; the next, she was on the floor. I can't remember anything more except the way the ambulance driver took me by the shoulder and made me sit on the kitchen chair, out of the way. We'd been baking cookies; it was almost Christmas and my mother was trying out a recipe for a new kind. I don't know who called the ambulance. I don't remember my father's being there, but I guess he was. It is a seamless memory, going from hoping my mother would let me have the left-over cookie dough to standing in a line at the funeral home.

I flop onto that creamy white couch beside my grubby duffel bag and listen to the soft murmur of conversation coming from Paul's old room. I'm here, but who cares? Adele demanded that I come, and now she acts like I've invaded her home. Again. For the first time, I wonder whose idea it was for me to be here. Who convinced Adele and my father that I should be a member of the club that will witness his slow slide into death when I haven't been a meaningful part of their lives in years? I'm clearly an unwanted guest, and my father has nothing to say to me.

Mack would love this couch. If he were here, as he should be, I could tuck his body up close to mine. I would tuck his body up close and rest my head on the fine triangle of his skull. He would sigh and be happy to be held. I press a hand against my chest, where I can feel my heart squeeze down on itself each time I realize that Mack could be anywhere and that I may never find him. Or nowhere and that there's no point in searching for him. I can't think that way. I just can't.

I flip my phone open, hoping that by some quirk I have missed the call that will tell me where my dog is. No missed calls. No voice mails. No answers.

I hear the murmuring and the sound of a toilet flushing, then the click-roll of a walker being pushed down the short hallway. My father always prided himself on his height and his posture, but the glimpse I have of him now is that of a hunched-over old man who is gripping the handles of the walker and eking his way down the threadbare wall-to-wall carpet of the hall. This disease has reduced him to an old man even though I know he's not more than seventy. Isn't seventy the new fifty? It's what I tell myself when I think of going over the crest of forty-five, the short descent to fifty. If Adele, five years older than my father, looks her age, my father looks like someone else's idea of an old man.

There is a moment of suspension as the pair of them, father and stepmother, simultaneously look at me without smiling and then continue on their way down the narrow hall.

"Do you need my help?" I call out to them as I push off the couch.

"No." Adele, as always, answers for both of them.

Did I mistake the desire for my presence with what was only a courtesy call? Fulfilling the social expectation that a daughter be notified of her father's impending death? Was the truth of it that I risked everything on what amounted to manners? Or that Adele was calling my bluff?

The air in this living room is stifling, close. The windows are closed against the mild September day. Suddenly, I can't breathe in here. I bolt out of the front door and stand on the chipped front step, sucking in breath after breath. I can't make myself go back in there. I have come all this way, and sacrificed the being I love best next to my absent son—for what? To be revisited by every bad memory I've worked so hard to grow beyond? This is a haunted house, and I don't have to be here.

CHAPTER 19

I have no place to go, so I sit on the front steps and wish that I smoked, so that it would look at least like I'm outside for a purpose. I pick at the weeds that are growing at the base of the steps. Ugly, unwanted things, more green than the summer-burned grass. Hardy fools. Thinking that they are welcome.

I can call Candy and see if she'll buy me a plane ticket home. I know that she will, but I also know that she'll try and talk me out of leaving. I guess I haven't been as honest with her as I might have been. She just thinks that our family suffered the normal range of conflict. She thinks, like good people do, that a tearful and heartfelt make-up session will occur before my father's last breath and I will feel better, or relieved or something, so that this trip will help "heal" me. I know. I've seen her pull that Oprah shit on other friends.

But even if I call Candy and convince her that staying is a bad idea, I still don't have Mack. How can I leave without knowing where he is, without finding him? Even as I think this, I know that each hour that goes by lessens my chances of locating my dog. I still have no idea where he is. Any thin hope that I had squirreled away against the worst thoughts is gone. Artie isn't driving west now with my Mack alongside, riding shotgun. The unanswerable question is, Where did he abandon my dog? Ohio? Pennsylvania? New York? Massachusetts? How long would he have kept the dog with him before ditching him?

Did he at least leave Mack somewhere that a kind person might find him?

Did my impulsive ride on the back of Mitch's Harley take me *away* from Mack? Was he simply waiting for me by the exit? I feel that burn in my eyes, the hollow ache in my throat, and squeeze my eyes shut.

"I didn't realize how much you cared." Paul Rose, Jr., casts a broad shadow over me; the sudden shade makes me shiver.

"I don't. Not really." The urge to cry vanishes, replaced by the leaden taste of old anger.

"Then why did you come? You think that he'll leave you an inheritance?"

"Oh, he has. Just not the kind that's worth anything." An inheritance of bitterness.

"May I sit?"

"It's your mother's house." I don't move over until I realize he really intends to lower his bulk next to me. I squeeze against the wrought-iron railing.

He sits with a huff, as if even sitting is a form of exercise for the once-athletic Paul. "Hey, this is hard on all of us."

"Why? Why would you think that?"

Paul tugs a little at his sweatpants, loosening the obvious constriction of his crotch. "I know things got weird back then, but that's history. Old, old history."

I twist my head to get a better look at him. "Some things are always present. I don't care how many years go by."

He turns his fat face to meet mine and for an instant I see the other boy, the thin, popular boy whose best friend was Ronnie Markham.

I remember Ronnie Markham even before my father married Adele, when we went to the annual Markham Motors Christmas party with my mother. Ronnie always seemed to be crying at those parties, overtired and oversugared. By the time we were in our teens, Ronnie had stopped crying and turned into a golden boy. Girls fluttered around him. Boys like Paul simply surrounded him, an uneven admiration society. I did neither. I hung in the shadows and nearly died anytime Golden Boy cast his eye on me, as accidental as it might have been, like my being in the sight line between Ronnie and the cool girls, the popular girls he dated. I was not worthy of notice, but, like all the other girls, I daydreamed that someday he might.

"Hey, kid." Ronnie Markham acknowledges my presence there in the kitchen and I feel like a god has spoken. In high school terms, he is a divinity, a god of sports. I am two years younger and tongue-tied. I grip a glass of milk and my hand trembles with the effort not to drop it. I blush, throw a look at Paul, who is oblivious as he ransacks the cupboards for snacks for himself and his buddy. Does he notice that Ronnie has spoken to me? Somehow validated my existence?

They disappear into the basement rec room, where they will play Ping-Pong, talk about girls, and drink endless Cokes. As he pushes past me, Paul gives me a fraternal shove, making me spill the milk down the front of my shirt. I am mortified, but Ronnie doesn't seem to notice. I am already forgotten.

Ronnie Markham was the reason I plucked those damned eyebrows.

Paul turns his face away from mine. "Anyway, we're here for Dad now."

"Dad. Right." My father, not yours. I have never called Adele "Mom." The word would have burned a hole in my mouth.

It is too hard to keep going with this conversation, so I shift it aside. "How's the family?"

Paul brightens, pulls a grin, and begins to recite his kids' achievements.

I don't have to listen, just nod here and there. I am worn out with worry and travel; it is easier to let him talk and think that I'm an interested stepaunt than to keep up the volley of verbal gunfire. He can never expect me to forgive him, but at least he can relax and chat with me as if we are two strangers meeting on a bus. I'm too tired right now to care. Maybe Paul's right. Maybe it is ancient history.

"So, where are you staying? Which hotel?"

"Right here at the Hotel Meade. Nonsmoking single couch."

"That's no good. Come to my house. I can offer you a bottom bunk."

"As tempting an offer as that is, I came to be here. I've slept on worse couches."

"I don't think that Mom can keep this up. This nursing. It's why we thought you should come."

I didn't expect candor and I'm surprised that Paul is so open with the truth that I wasn't called because I was the daughter; I was called to serve. "Now it makes sense."

"But for heaven's sake, you don't have to sleep on a couch."

"Thanks. Let's just see how it goes." I guess I mean how long it takes, but that seems a weird way to put it. I also don't say that I'm not likely to stick around too long. I have a life. I know that death comes in its own time, and most likely will take longer than anyone thinks. My father is up and using a toilet, which, to me, proves that the direness of the situation was overstated. So I may not be around for the final curtain. I haven't come here to be a nurse, just to say good-bye. Not to make peace, but because Candy persuaded me to come, pushing me out the door and into Artie's rig with those rose-colored words: "So you won't live to regret it."

But while I'm here, I'll help the best I can. I won't say that I owe it to anyone; I don't owe anyone anything. I'll do it because I know how.

CHAPTER 20

Alice and the dog come in from their morning walk. She hangs the leash on one of the back door pegs they use for keys, raincoats, and grocery bags, as if it had always hung there. "He really is a good boy. He never pulls."

Ed looks up from the eight-and-a-half-by-fourteen-inch poster board that he's working on. In nearly perfect block lettering, he's written: FOUND, GRAY-AND-WHITE LONGHAIRED DOG. NO COLLAR. ONE BLUE EYE AND ONE BROWN EYE. He turns the poster so that Alice can see it. "What do you think?"

Alice thinks that she hates him. "I don't know. I guess it's all right." Her good mood of the morning is gone.

"We should try to get a picture of him to put on it."

"He's so beautiful—how will we prevent people from just claiming him?"

Ed shrugs. "I doubt that anyone would actually do that, but even so, won't we be able to tell by the way he reacts when his old owner shows up?"

"Not he if was abused."

"Alice. Really. Does he strike you as an abused dog?" Ed waves a hand toward the dog, who is daintily licking his forepaws like a cat.

"He got left by the side of the road, hungry and thirsty. That's abuse enough." Alice knows that her tone is verging on hostile. She doesn't mean to be, but it's an easy tone to take instead of just saying what she wants to say. Instead of just telling Ed that, goddamn it, they're going to keep the dog because she wants him and she takes care of the house and, like everything else, it will be her responsibility. But she doesn't. Instead, she wrenches open the refrigerator door and begins shoving GladWare containers around, trying to assemble an idea for supper hours before anyone wants it.

"I'm going to go hang these." Ed scrapes back the kitchen chair, a sound that makes Alice grind her teeth. There are permanent tracks burned into the tile. As soon as Ed pulls his keys off the pegs, the dog gets to his feet and dances to the back door as if planning on taking the ride with Ed.

"You want to go?"

The dog tap-dances, front paws doing a high step.

"Think I should?"

Alice shuts the refrigerator door, leans back against it, and studies the pair. "He looks like he wants to go. Maybe he likes car rides."

Ed pats his leg. "Let's go."

The dog yips, an easily translatable *Yippee* sort of sound.

"Leash him." Alice says that exactly as she might have reminded him to fasten a child's seat belt. A reflexive maternal remark, unnecessary but vital to say so that the protective charms of ritual are in effect.

Equally reflexive, Ed replies, "Of course."

And to their mutual amazement, the dog pulls the leash off the peg himself and brings it to Ed, sits in front of him with the black nylon leash dangling from his sharp muzzle, his plumed tail swishing back and forth on the tile.

"Wow. That's a little scary."

Alice nods. "He really is smart."

"A real one of a kind, I'd say." Ed snaps the leash on the dog's new collar. "Someone must really miss him."

"I know."

"We have to advertise him."

"I've put the ad in the *Press*." Alice has missed this week's deadline, so the ad won't appear until next Thursday's edition of the weekly town newspaper. *Found, small collielike dog. Gray and white, one blue eye, one brown. Near Old Path Road. Call . . .* Alice wishes she hadn't been so specific.

Ed retrieves his hat from one of the pegs. "Maybe no one will see it."

Alice covers her mouth with one hand. She knows, and Edward knows, that doing the right thing might mean a loss; but not to do the right thing—in this case, to properly advertise the dog—isn't an option. It's not how either of them was raised. Ed was a Boy Scout. She was a Girl Scout.

Alice Rae Thompson saw Ed Parmalee for the first time when he was standing in line at the Dairy Queen.

She's behind the counter, serving up soft-serve ice-cream cones, vanilla and chocolate laden with jimmies or a dip that hardens into a chocolate shell. This is her summer job; once she's back in class at the local community college, she'll quit. She notices that he's clean-cut among

*the young folks hanging around, his hair only a little
long against his collar, not sporting the shoulder-length
hair of his companions, and for a moment she wonders
if he's a veteran, someone who's been to Vietnam. Before
he even reaches her window, Alice decides that, no, he
can't be in the service, or recently out. His face is open
and cheerful, not like the faces of those older brothers of
her friends who have chosen the service instead of college, or had it chosen for them. They've come back, most
of them, looking thirty, not twenty. Not smiling.*

*Edward Parmalee, dark-haired and blue-eyed, top-
ping six three, slender as the basketball player he was
in high school, looks at Alice Thompson framed in the
Dairy Queen window and smiles at her. For the first
time she can ever remember, Alice full out blushes, the
warmth in her cheeks migrating straight to the roots of
her hair. She can even feel the heat prickle along the
center part that separates her hair into two long sheets
of honey blond.*

*Ed's smile opens a seam in her soul, a place that has
been untouched, unmined. She can barely stammer out
the right words to take his order.*

*"Chocolate, rainbow sprinkles, and your telephone
number." Ed has the good grace to blush himself, and
she knows that he's never done that before, that this is a
new boldness.*

*When he calls later that evening, they laugh, realiz-
ing that neither one has asked the other's name. "Is this
you?"*

"Yes. I'm Alice."

"I'm Ed Parmalee. I work at the plant."

Alice stands in the middle of her kitchen, a room she
used to imagine remodeling, with a widened doorway to

the dining room, an island counter, and a Mexican tile floor. Some time ago, she stopped thinking about changing anything in her house. Somehow it was better to leave things as they were, do nothing more than clean it and freshen up the paint now and then. A house that seemed too small for years now feels rambling, empty. The clutter and mess of a third inhabitant is relegated to a small bedroom that she dusts once a month. Nothing in that room moves out of place. The bed never needs changing.

Alice fills the teakettle, sets it on the stove, and lights the burner. She busies herself with choosing a cup, pulling a tea bag out of the box, refilling the sugar bowl. The dishwasher needs emptying. The trash is full. Homely tasks she'll take care of after a cuppa. Ed will come back with the dog, then take the bagged trash to the barrel. Ed said maybe no one will see it, the lost-and-found ad. Maybe Ed is also hoping that the dog will stay. But because he's already said no to having the dog, he will have to find an acceptable way to make it his idea. Alice pours the water into her cup, bounces the tea bag up and down a few times. She smiles a little. Edward will come around; she just knows it.

CHAPTER 21

The dog sits alert and entertained in the front seat of the Cutlass, as if he were Miss Daisy and Ed the Morgan Freeman driver, the dog's pointy snout acting like a directional aid: Go this way, now that. Suddenly, the dog gets excited, standing in the front seat and staring out the passenger window as Ed drives by the cemetery gates where Alice found him. The dog's tail wags in a broad sweep, brushing Ed's arm. Ed doesn't slow down, doesn't look in the same direction as the dog, ignoring the dog's evident desire to stop. Ed won't stop. Not there.

First to Potter's to hang a poster. Tim Potter, fourth generation of the general store–owning Potters, is busy stocking shelves. Back when Tim's dad ran the place, it was filled with useful things like sewing notions and fishhooks. Ed doesn't fish anymore, so it doesn't matter so much that young Tim has gentrified the place and no longer carries six varieties of fishing line or bait. Now Potter's offers specialty foods like mangoes and guava paste, herbed vinegars and extra-extra-virgin olive oils, kalamata olives in fancy jars, costing what he used to spend on a tank of gas in the old days. Bushel baskets are filled with cute replicas of nineteenth-century objects like handmade candles and tin cookie cutters, and old-fashioned and essentially inedible candies like horehound drops. Frankly, Ed thinks, Tim would be better served, in this fairly touristless town, if he provided cell phone chargers and poster board so that people like him wouldn't have to trek to Wal-Mart. If the leaf peepers ever ventured off the Mohawk Trail this far, then maybe ciabatta bread would sell.

"Can I hang this somewhere?" Ed holds up his home-made poster for Tim to see.

With his hands busy restocking a display of Tom's of Maine toothpaste, Tim gestures with his chin toward a small bulletin board matted with colored sheets of paper advertising a myriad of activities, yard sales, horses for lease, fund-raising events for the local elementary school and the library. "You'll have to take something down."

Ed studies the array before he removes a vintage sheet advertising a concert that took place last year. Commandeering the pushpin, Ed pokes it through the card stock of his sign. His poster is bigger than any of the others and shoves its shoulders across the one for the library bake sale and the one announcing a lecture on recycling coming up at the town hall. Maybe his poster is too big for the few words on it. He never did get a photo to add to the poster. Seemed like too much effort.

Ed takes down his sign and folds it so it's smaller, then presses the pushpin, which has a broken top and is painful against his thumb. He sucks at the offended digit. Now no one will see his sign, obscured as it is by the clutter of other, more colorful messages. Ed takes his sign down again, scans the board for a better spot, and finally pins his found poster to the very edge, where it sticks out like a dull afterthought. He should have used colored markers.

Ed picks up a package of beef jerky. He doesn't really want it, and will have to hide the evidence from Alice, but he thinks he really should buy something at Potter's, given that he's using the message board. Not that Tim looks like he's concerned, but it's the right thing to do and it's right there, close at hand, and, face it, it's a guilty pleasure.

As Ed gets back in the Cutlass, the dog is instantly alert and curious about the dried meat. "Oh, you want some, eh?" Ed shoves a piece in his mouth, relishing the salty taste. "It can't be good for you. It's not good for me."

The dog sits in the passenger seat, ears forward, eyes fixed on Ed's hand as it holds the greasy plastic sleeve, his little pink tongue licking at his lips in anticipation.

"How bad you want this?"

The dog is eloquent in his request. He gracefully sits up, dainty forepaws dangling in the air, his back neat against the seat, as if to say, *How much more do I have to do to get you to give me a piece of that?*

"Okay. Guess you earned this." Ed breaks a piece off and holds it out to the dog. The dog takes the offering with a delicate gesture, no snapping up a treat for him.

"Now say thank you."

And to Ed's complete surprise, the dog does. A quick sharp bark and one paw held out to be shaken.

"You're not making this any easier. But if you've got so many tricks, there must be somebody out there who really misses you. It wouldn't be right not to try." Driving away from Potter's, Ed tries to remember where else he wants to hang a poster. There are two left in the backseat. But it's getting late, and he still wants to get the grass cut, hopefully the last mow of the season. Plus, there's all that hedge trimming he's been putting off. How bad would it be to put off hanging another poster until tomorrow?

The dog is back to sitting like Miss Daisy, eyes fixed on their direction, except that every few minutes, he tilts his head to look at Ed, eyes full of hope that another piece of jerky will appear. When none is forthcoming, he settles down.

"You want to head home?" When Ed says the word *home,* the dog cocks his head. "Guess that means yes."

Ed drives past the cemetery gates where they had first seen the dog. As he does every time they go by, the dog begins to whine. And every time he drives past it, Ed does not stop. He won't.

Alice and Ed sit at the little kitchen table, their plates pushed aside, waiting for the tea water to boil. Alice keeps her finger in the book she's reading while she waits. Ed stares off into space.

Squeak! The dog comes bounding into the kitchen, the soft orange hydrant clutched between his jaws, and he's making it sound like it's talking. *Squeak, squeakee, squawk.*

Ed makes a grab for the toy and the dog dashes madly around the room, his tail in the air, his eyes glinting with enjoyment. He drops the toy in front of Ed and stands with front legs spread wide in anticipation of the chase. Ed pitches the toy through the archway and into the living room. In a bound, the dog retrieves the toy and pushes it into Alice's hand. She joins in the game, and in a moment, all three are playing a game of the dog's invention.

CHAPTER 22

Ed is running the mower around the backyard when Alice goes into the garage to get another box of garbage bags from their Costco closet. She has to squeeze past the Cutlass, always a little too close to the wall—she wishes Ed would get his eyes checked—and sees the white poster board still in the backseat, along with the empty beef jerky package. It feels like he's brought her flowers.

For Ed to give up on an errand is unusual. Ed is more the forge ahead, fight the blizzard to get to the store, damn the torpedoes kind of guy. Always has been. It puzzles Alice that Ed came home with the task unfinished, not even saying a casual word about why. Did he run out of tape? Was he turned away from hanging one at Potter's?

The only answer she likes is one she interprets from the way the dog and man came bounding into the house, pals returning from an adventure. The dog greeted her with enthusiasm, prancing on his back legs as if he'd never expected to see her again. Ed hung the leash on a peg, then his hat, his back to her until she straightened up from petting the exuberant dog. He was smiling an old, familiar smile, the one he used to give her when they were young and every meeting was a gift. A smile that engaged his eyes, his dark blue smiling eyes now crease-framed by years of not wearing sunglasses. Ed had been smiling, but he hadn't said anything about not hanging the posters. What he did say was, "He's one smart dog. You should see what he can do."

The forgotten posters make her smile, and in the reflection of the car's back window, she sees a vestige of her old self, a ghost of the girl who smiled like that when her man came calling.

When they had given up on ever becoming parents, it was understandable to have found some other outlet for their unfulfilled nurturing urges. They adopted two mature cats, but neither one was affectionate and did nothing to fill the void. They sent money to Save the Children and got a letter every few months from the child in Peru who was supported by their donations. But they never heard her voice, or developed any real sense of her existence. Ed took the promotion to floor supervisor, putting in lots of hours, promising the extra money would ensure a comfortable retirement. And he nurtured her, encouraging Alice to sign up for classes at the community college, to seek out activities that would give her fulfillment. The years of frustrated trying had been irrevocably lost; now they would relax and accept their circumstances and enjoy the rest of their lives. The absence of child no longer felt like a hole; how could you miss something you'd never had?

And then they did.

On the eve of her thirty-ninth birthday, against all odds, Alice found herself pregnant.

And the second time they found themselves childless, there was simply no outlet. Alice pushed away Ed's devotion. She was too angry. For a long time, there was nothing she could do but wait for each day to pass and hope to sleep for a few hours at night. A few hours, at most two or three, when the circling thoughts simmered down enough to let her rest, when the *why* and the *what if* and the self-doubt and the desperate search for a reason might give way to the exhaustion and let her sleep unmolested until she'd wake before dawn and meet the incomprehensible truth wide-eyed.

CHAPTER 23

The posters on the backseat mock Ed every time he gets into the Cutlass, nagging him with a task shirked. But he seems to forget about their existence the moment he pulls out of the garage. Especially if the dog is with him. Just goes out of his mind. Pfft. Gone. Oops, should remember to do that. Today, Ed remembers, and he takes the signs out, tears them into neat quarters, and stuffs them in the bag of trash he's jamming into the barrel for today's pickup.

Alice catches him in the act and he gets defensive. "Don't you think that it's odd that we haven't seen any lost posters? Wherever this little guy came from, it isn't from around here. He's either run away or been dumped, and there's no telling how far afield he's gone. We could be hanging posters and putting ads in all the wrong places. Let's give it a rest."

Ed doesn't miss the expression on her face, a look of relief with a suggestion of puzzled gratitude, and Ed walks out the door rather than look at her, because it has been too long since he's seen an expression like that on his wife's face.

It's not the same thing, but Ed remembers that smile the day that he offhandedly suggested that they stop birth control. It wasn't like she'd been pestering, or hinting, or sighing at the sight of babies, but somehow he knew that her thoughts, after a couple of years of marriage, were turning broody. "Let's let nature take its course." That was how he had inelegantly phrased it. But you would have thought that he'd given her diamonds, not so much that he had made the suggestion, but that he, Edward the oblivious, had recognized a need in his wife without having to be told outright. It was a big moment in their marriage. Of course, they had never expected that it would take so long to accomplish, that nature certainly took her course, but that pleased smile still lingers in his memory and whenever he thinks of the early days, the years before life got hard, he pictures Alice smiling like that.

Life is divided into uneven thirds: Before Stacy, Being Parents, and After It Happened. They are halfway to having lost her longer than having had her. And, after it happened, Ed stopped being able to read Alice. The clues and nuances became too hard to interpret, or maybe he just lost the knack for it. Maybe it just got too hard, or the telepathy they once had between them was like wires in an old electrical cord, frayed and dangerous. The connection cut in one disastrous moment.

Ed bends over his mower, a self-drive, electric start, mega sixteen-inch blade Toro. There's always a little regret in putting the Toro to bed in the fall. End to another summer. Not that anything particularly special happens in the summer. Now that he's enjoyed his first full unemployed summer, with no vacation to look forward to because, as his pals at Lil's say, every day's a vacation, Ed has had a hard time recognizing the season except for the sweltering heat of the dog days of August, when the heat lay thick in the air. That, and the endless tasks of watering and mowing. Mowing and watering, growing the grass to cut the grass. Ed wraps the tarp over the Toro, binds it with a length of clothesline, and tucks it into its corner of the garage. He'll have to get the snow blower serviced pretty soon. Don't want to wait until everyone else thinks of it and there's a rush at Stan's Tractor and Mower Repair.

A rush of despair rocks Ed with its suddenness. His whole life is calibrated by seasonal machinery. He thinks of that song: *Is that all there is*? Some singer with a sexy, husky voice. He can only recall that single line in the chorus, and it orbits through his mind: *Is that all there is? Is that all there is?*

Ed pulls himself upright. It's only from bending over that he's gotten these weird feelings. There's nothing wrong. It's fine. Mostly, day-to-day life is fine.

Suddenly, the dog is beside him, the silly squeaky toy gripped in his teeth, and he's shaking it furiously, as if it's a rodent. The thing squeaks like a mouse, so the pretense is pretty understandable.

"Hey, you wanna play? Gimma that thing!" Ed pries the toy out of the dog's mouth and plays a little hand-to-hand keep away. The dog actually looks like he's laughing and he rears up like a pony, catching the hydrant in midair as Ed tosses it.

The dog drops the toy at Ed's feet, looks up with expectation, and then sits. "You're such a good boy. Are you my good boy?" Ed swoops down and gives the dog a hug, burying his nose in the white fur of his ruff. "Who's a good boy?"

* * *

At the top of the stairs, Alice watches Ed play with the
dog. She hears the baby talk and thinks that his friends
would think that Ed had lost his mind. He doesn't look
the baby talk type. But he is. When she couldn't soothe
the baby, Ed always could. Stacy held close in big arms,
against a wide chest, a whispered lullaby. "If that mock-
ing bird don't sing, Daddy's gonna buy you a diamond
ring."

Who's my little baby girl?

Even though the man has taken him on several go-for-
a-rides, they haven't taken him to Justine. Mack loves
go-for-a-ride. At least he did until go-for-a-ride ended up
in the cab of that truck. But this man doesn't go far, or for
long, and has only left him waiting for a little while, measured in whether Mack chooses to lie down and snooze
or remain upright in the front seat, tail curled around
his forepaws, eyes on the place where the man has gone.
When the man comes back, he proffers a whole strip of
bacon. Mack, being a well-trained dog, accepts this treat
with gentleness, a tail wag, and a quick head bob. Bacon
is Justine's training tool of choice. Little crumbles just
big enough to hide in a hand, doled out at the correct
completion of his movements: circle, reverse circle, side
step. The man isn't making any of those hand signals that
mean bacon; he's just handing it over, in a strip. Mack
would be more than willing to do a few movements if
asked, but this is okay, too. So go-for-a-ride is good. But
it isn't getting him where he wants to be.

When Alice puts on her yoga pants and sneakers,
Mack believes that it means they will dance. He accom-
panies her to the back door, prancing on his little white

front feet, his pointy muzzle split into a grin. Maybe, just maybe, Justine will be where this woman takes him to dance. He will find Justine there.

When Justine first taught Mack to dance, he thought it was just more of the same sort of training that they had been doing for a long time. He enjoyed showing off to the others that he could sit-stay longer and more attentively than any of them. He loved the leaps over rails and the scurry through the fabric tunnel. He understood on some organic level that doing all these things, touching the right spots on the platform, leaping accurately and quickly over bars, weaving through the poles as fast as an otter, was the point of the exercise. When he did his best, there was always loud applause, and sometimes he got to stand by himself in the ring while the Important Person presented Justine with objects that Justine smiled to receive and always let him nose. No other dogs, just him.

Then Justine began to ask him to weave not through poles, but between her legs. Leap, not over a pole, but over a short cane. Rise up on his legs and wriggle his tail. Walk backward, forward, and place his paws against her back. Some hand signals were so subtle that he had to keep his eye on her at all times, sometimes having to decide what it was she wanted, because the movement was only a degree different from another one. A bow instead of a cocked head. Walk or army crawl.

So when Alice pulled on her yoga pants and tied her soft white shoes to her feet, Mack got excited. Those were practice clothes. When Justine wore those clothes, they'd head to the high school gym and meet up with Saundra and her pack. Juicy was always there, and Sambucca, the blue-eyed husky Mack has always had a crush

on. And sometimes Griff, who was a slow learner but
tried hard.

If Alice hadn't put on her go-to-dance clothes, Mack
would have settled for another day of waiting. But she
had and now he was excited. He even barked. One short
piercing bark, just to let her know that he was pleased to
be going back to work. Maybe Justine would be there.

But then Alice hadn't taken him where she was going.
And when she came back, she smelled of sweat but not
of other dogs. Not of Justine.

Go-for-a-ride is good. And walks are good. The kibble
is different but good. The couch is okay, a little firmer
than the soft cushions on the couch Mack uses at home
with Justine. When Alice leaves the house or goes upstairs, he settles down on the right-hand cushion, balling
himself up tight, nose tucked beneath tail. It's his default
position, the one from which he takes the most comfort.
Once asleep, he will unfurl like a flower, stretching to
take up half the couch. But to start, he likes making himself small and compact, pretending he's a wolf on the
tundra. At first, Alice made him get off the couch, but
now she understands that snuggling on the couch is a
good thing. Mack has taught her that it is nice to let him
rest his head on her legs and stroke him. She's learned
already about the nice soothing spot in his ear. They still
haven't learned his name and he's not sure how to teach
that to them.

Ed has learned about the ball. That's a good thing, especially since he throws it a lot farther than Justine does,
so the game is much more challenging. Mack likes the
long slope of the backyard and the way he has to dig in
his feet to prevent himself from crashing into the bushes.
Snapping up the ball, he runs pell-mell to the top of the

hill, where Ed waits, slapping his knees to encourage
speed. He's good with the squeaky toy, too. Knows the
same game of keep away that Justine plays.

Mack doesn't know how long he's been here with
Alice and Ed. He doesn't know how long it's been since
Justine disappeared. Time is nothing to him, measured
out in meals and walks but never adding up. Mack has
adapted to the rhythms of this household, knowing that
she rises first, that he goes to bed last. Breakfast is eaten
in silence. The routine is more obvious to him now than
it was at first. Like Justine, Alice has a set pattern that
includes food, exercise, and baby talk. Ed has a less pre-
dictable pattern, but he seems to be the one with the car
keys.

Alice takes him for walks. Although sometimes when
they go, she talks to him in a serious, sad way. When
she does that, Mack has learned that a joke is a good
way to change that tone. So he'll grab her sleeve gently
in his teeth, or fake nip at her heels as if to say, *This is
about fun. Keep moving.* Sometimes he just barks until
she breaks out of her mood with a laugh and halfhearted
warning to stop it.

There has been a change in the air. Not only are the
days a bit cooler, but the people in the house are treating
him in a new way. At first, being shy, they treated him
with courtesy and a little distance, which was appropriate. He was a stranger in their home. But now, now they
are more casual with him, easy. Ed keeps bringing him
new toys. Today it was a stuffie. Mack loves stuffies, and,
unlike his terrier brethren, he doesn't gut them to extract
the squeaker, but gently bites the fuzzy bone-shaped toy
to get it to emit the irresistible noise, then uses it as a
pillow.

There's lots to like about being a guest here, but he still wants Justine to come and get him.

Every time they offer Mack go-for-a-ride, he thinks that Justine will be there. Every time they pass the cemetery gates, he asks them to let him out to see if there's a hint of her scent on the ground, to see if Justine has come to get him. But they never do.

CHAPTER 24

"He should have a name." Alice says this around a mouthful of spaghetti, as if slipping the concept of naming the dog around food disguises the larger concept of keeping him. The dog, for his part, sits at a distance, but his eagle eyes are alert to her right hand with the upraised fork. He isn't begging per se, but he is certainly interested in their mealtime.

Ed tears a hunk of Italian bread off the loaf on the table, butters it liberally with the fake spread that Alice buys because it's supposed to be healthier for them than the margarine she used to use. He doesn't respond, but she knows he's thinking. She waits patiently, familiar with the signs of Ed's thought process. He never voices his internal debates. Finally, just as she's taken another forkful of spaghetti, he sets his fork down. "What do you want to call him?"

"I don't know. Something different. I wish we knew what he was called."

"Then we'd know where he came from."

"How about Silver? Because of his color."

"Nah. What about Butch?"

"Never. Carlton?"

"Carlton? Why Carlton?"

"I like the name."

"Oh no. Not Carlton. I just can't see me owning a dog named Carlton."

"Then come up with something."

Ed just shovels another bite of spaghetti into his mouth. "Buddy. It's a good name. Watch." Ed swallows the spaghetti, scrapes his plate with the chunk of bread. "Here, Buddy."

The dog is by his side in an instant.

"See? Maybe that's really his name. He comes to it quick." Ed puts the plate on the kitchen floor. The dog happily licks the plate with a dainty tongue, scouring it for any hint of sauce.

"Ed. I'm shocked at you." Alice leaves a tiny bit more sauce and a scrap of sausage on her plate. "Okay. Buddy it is." She takes up Ed's sparkling plate and gives the dog hers.

"Well, I'm shocked at you. Letting a dog lick your plate. How uncharacteristic." Ed grabs both now virtually clean plates and sets them into the dishwasher. "I guess if we're going to keep him, we need to get a license. I'll do it tomorrow."

Alice is glad that her back is to him. She was expecting an argument. She was prepared for it, loaded, as they say, for bear. Ed has left her with her figurative powder dry and it is all she can do to stop from laughing out loud. "Sounds good." Alice bends over the dog to stroke his muzzle, to keep her surprised smile from belonging to Ed.

* * *

Nothing is ever cut-and-dried. That's what Ed thinks as
he leaves the town clerk's office without a dog license.
Buddy needs proof of a rabies shot before he can get a tag.
Now he's got to find a vet, make an appointment, spend
who knows how much, and then, only then, can he get
the ten-dollar tag. No wonder people become scofflaws.
"What do you say, pal, want to live outside the law?" The
dog is more interested in the scents surrounding the trash
can outside the town hall.

They used to take those two ornery cats to the
Moodyville Vet Clinic over on Route 101. It's been a long
time since the last one moved on to mouse hunt on a
higher plane, and Ed wonders if the place is still there.
This time, he thinks to call Alice and tell her he's going
to be late for lunch.

"Well, we probably should get him checked out anyway. See if you can get squeezed in today. If not, I can
take him, as long as you can make an appointment that
isn't on my day at the library."

"Do you want me to pick you up?" Ed holds the cell
phone tight against his cheek. He still doesn't believe
that you don't have to shout into them. "There's no way
I'm going to remember your schedule."

There is no hesitation in Alice's reply, "Yes."

By the time Ed pulls into the driveway, Alice has
called ahead to the clinic and gotten an appointment,
which she knows will please Ed, who hates to wait for
anything. Fortunately for them, there was a cancellation.
Buddy is relegated to the backseat as Alice takes her
place in front. He rests his chin on the seat back, suggest-
ing that there is room for him between them. When neither of the people invite him to move up front, he settles
into the left-hand seat to watch the scenery go by.

The Moodyville Veterinary Clinic is a much different

place from the one where they used to take the cats. The boxy cedar-shingled building with the two chain-link runs outside has evolved into an architecturally designed animal hospital with tended gardens, and if there are runs, they are well hidden behind a flourishing boxwood hedge. The practice has clearly grown, and now there are four vets on staff instead of just old Doc Creighton, whose family has been so long in this town that there's a road named for them. Creighton's name is still on the masthead, along with those of his daughter and two others.

A staffer hands them a clipboard with a form on it. "Do you have insurance?"

Ed wonders if he's accidentally brought the dog to a people clinic. "Insurance?" His question is lost as the staffer grabs a ringing phone. Since when is there health insurance for animals? Is this in Obama's health-care package? Is that why people are so bent out of shape? Alice takes the clipboard and checks off "No" to that question.

They really don't know anything about him, and it shows. The form is mostly empty except for their names and contact info. Name: Buddy. Breed: Shetland sheepdog? Age: unknown. Last vaccination: unknown. Any health problems? unknown. Microchipped? Alice looks up from the form and points to that question. "What if he is?"

"Then we find out who he belongs to." Ed takes the clipboard from Alice.

There is no animal smell in the waiting room and barely any in the exam room where young Dr. Creighton meets them after a tech does all the routine things like weight (thirty-two pounds) and temperature (normal). Buddy takes it all like a champ. Like a dog quite used to being vetted. The clipboard with the microchip question is now in Dr. Creighton's hands and she is asking questions that Ed lets Alice answer because it isn't unlike being in the pediatrician's office with a child. A mother should answer those questions. Fathers should stay in the background.

Good appetite. Healthy bowels. No coughing. Playful. He sleeps on the couch; is that a bad idea? The whole time the vet is asking her general health questions, Alice is stroking Buddy, her fingers raking through the thick fur of his ruff. Little drifts of loosened hair float into the air.

Ed waits for the vet to ask where they got him. And if she does, will she insist on seeing if he is chipped? She opens Buddy's mouth and looks at his teeth, runs her hands down his sides and under his belly, where she spends a little longer palpating. She takes a look inside his ears and into his eyes. Ed watches as the vet's hands glide down the length of his back. She gives him an attaboy thump. "Good boy."

Buddy seems to agree. He nuzzles the vet's face.

"He has a little scar on his belly, which I think must have come from surgery. If he's been anaesthetized, he might have a chip. Do you want me to see?"

Alice doesn't answer. She wraps the leash around her hand, holding it tighter.

"He's not chipped." Ed puts a hand on Alice's shoulder. "The people we got him from didn't chip him."

Under his hand, Ed feels Alice's relief.

Ed gets the feeling the vet's not buying his story, but she isn't going to press the issue. She administers the rabies and distemper vaccines, draws blood for a heartworm test, and shoots a little medicine up Buddy's nose for kennel cough. "He's a lovely dog. You're very lucky. His former owners certainly took care of him."

"Yeah, they did. Till they couldn't do it anymore."

Two hundred and twenty-five dollars later, Ed, Alice, and Buddy head home. This time, Buddy sits in front.

Mack has never lived with two people at once. There have been visitors, even overnight guests, but never two people under the same roof, sharing a bed and bumping into each other in the hallway. He watches Ed and Alice as they go through their days. Her tongue language includes recognizable words like *dinner;* his, the word *no.* Ed says no to Alice a lot. Mostly when she asks him a question. "I don't know." "No thanks." "How should I know?" When they talk to each other, the sentences are short, and even a dog can tell that it isn't conversation as much as routine fact finding. The interesting thing is that when he is alone with either of them, their tongue language is smooth and flowing, filled with nuances and that chirpy sound that humans make when they are amused. Suddenly, they are using a word with him that he recognizes is what they want to call him. Buddy. That's okay. It's a familiar term and he'll respond to it if that's what they want.

What's hard is that they spend very little time in the same room. Buddy/Mack, still new to the double responsibility of two humans, goes between the television room and the kitchen, staring first at Ed, then at Alice. They should be in the same place; that's what his herd-dog requirements ask. Then Alice moves to the television room and Ed disappears into the bathroom. Buddy/Mack waits patiently, sitting just inside the archway so that he can monitor the television room and the bathroom. Ed comes out, and he wags his tail in relief. Okay, now he can move Ed into the same room as Alice. But Ed slips past him, giving him a pat on the head, going into the bedroom to watch the other television.

This is the first day that Alice hasn't been at home with him. Buddy/Mack recognized the word *work,* so he thinks that she may come back tonight smelling like food. That's what Justine always smelled like when she told him she was going to work. Food. Buddy/Mack licks his chops in anticipation that maybe tonight these new people will present him with a treat from work. After their daily ride, Ed has also left him alone in the house while he is outside. Buddy/Mack would like to tell Ed that he's perfectly dependable about staying in the yard, but he has no way of letting Ed know that. So he jumps onto the couch, circles, and buries his nose beneath his tail. He'll doze a little, one ear positioned to catch the sound of returning humans.

Since choosing to remain here to wait for Justine, Buddy/Mack has not slept. He has only dozed, and the lack of deep sleep is beginning to wear on him. Afraid that he'll miss hearing Justine's arrival, and a little nervous about being in the care of strangers, he hasn't allowed himself the healing sleep of the content. He has not dreamed running dreams. He hasn't dreamed chasing dreams. He sleeps the primordial sleep of his ancestors when hunting alone, always on the alert.

Today is the first day that he feels himself go into a deep sleep. Buddy/Mack isn't conscious that he's entered into REM sleep; he just knows that he is in a safe place and that he can finally slide into the relaxed sleep of a sheltered dog.

Buddy/Mack sighs, letting go of all the tension of the past few days. He tucks his nose deeper beneath his tail and falls asleep, his new stuffie tucked under him.

He is certain now that if Justine comes, she'll wake him up.

CHAPTER 25

Alice walks through the kitchen door and Buddy greets her with a little dance of happiness. She barely has time to put down the green sack of groceries as he dashes around her in circles, making a little yipping noise of welcome, demanding her attention. "How's my boy? Did you miss me? I was gone a whole five hours. Did you think I wouldn't come back?" Alice says all this in a baby voice, the same voice she used to soothe her baby; the same voice she also used to mock her bad moods when Stacy was half-grown. "Who's a good boy?"

"Buddy's a good boy." Ed appears in the archway between the kitchen and the dining room. He's got a streak of something on his cheek, something automotive. Every now and again he decides to do his own servicing. "We visited Stan's today. I left the snow blower."

Alice shrugs off the light jacket she's wearing. "Looks like you might have thought about doing it yourself." She points to a spot on her cheek that corresponds to the streak on Ed's face.

"Huh? Oh." Ed wipes the streak with a finger, then wipes his finger against the leg of his old green work pants, which have been softened by years of abuse. "Did I get it?"

Alice wets a paper towel, beckons Ed close, and rubs hard against the smudge. Buddy watches with herd-dog intensity as the two of them face each other. "That's it. Don't you dare sit down with those pants on."

"I won't."

"I thought I'd take Buddy for a walk to my mother's before I start dinner." After her shift in the library, it took Alice longer in the grocery store than she'd planned and all the time she was waiting in line behind some dimwit who didn't believe in the grammatically suspect 12 ITEMS OR LESS sign, she worried that Ed would have already taken Buddy out for his late-afternoon walk. She's never said how much she looks forward to it, as much for the casual saunter down the winding road to the conservation land, the scent of the forest and the quiet solitude after a busy day as for the obvious enjoyment the dog gets from the walk. She wants to be the one to give the dog this pleasure.

"He'd like that. We've mostly just done errands. He pooped in the backyard." Ed unbuckles his belt and lets his filthy pants drop to the kitchen floor. "Not much excitement for him today." He steps out of the pants, his heel catching the cuff, so that one leg is pulled inside out. He stands there with the tail of his denim shirt keeping him decent, long legs pale against the dark of the shirt. "Unless you count the pooping."

Alice takes the dirty pants from Ed's hands, rights the inverted leg. Despite the many years pounding the factory floors, his legs still look pretty good. Ed hasn't run to fat the way most men of his age have, but then

she's a good cook, not a fancy one. Never got into lavish sauces or fancy desserts. Good nutrition, just like she
was taught in home ec. Basic food groups, plus a treat
now and then. Alice sniffs when she hears about the public outcry about obesity. Not in her family.

"I thought about taking him for a walk, but I knew
that you'd want to do it when you got home."

Alice is surprised by that, by Ed's getting it.

Buddy flops down on the floor, his thumping tail the
only thing to suggest he's not resting, but hopeful of
some activity. Ed nudges him with his toe. "Hey Buddy,
don't lose heart. Alice will give you what you want."

The dog jumps to his feet, yips a little.

"Guess I'll just go take a shower."

It's his using the word *just* that pricks Alice's conscience, making him sound something like a boy who's
been left out of the game. Ed's had the dog all day, so
why should he feel deprived? Alice wants her solitude,
and this walk has become the only way she gets it now
that Ed's been laid off. She wishes he wasn't so stubborn
about finding another job, one that would at least get him
out of the house with more purpose than coffee at Lil's.
He is too present.

Ed bends over the dog, ruffling his fur all the way to
the base of his tail. The dog swivels his head to look at
Ed with those mismatched eyes, tongue lolling in doggy
pleasure.

Alice woke up on the dawn of her wedding day and
wondered if she'd been flattered into marrying a man she
knew was kind, charming, and supremely confident of
his decision-making abilities. A trait that, even then, in
the full blush of romantic love, Alice knew would evolve
into always thinking that he was right.

"Will you leash him for me?"

Buddy knows enough English to react to Alice's words, and he jumps up and dashes to the back door, ready to perform one of his tricks.

Alice did wake up on her wedding morning excited, nervous, maybe even a little nauseous, but she didn't wake up doubting her choice. That's a recent spin; that's three and a half decades of experience coloring in the outline of that young bride's expectations.

And in the last decade, Ed has learned the hard way that he isn't always right.

Ed takes the leash out of the dog's mouth and clips it to the collar. The fire hydrant–shaped license tinkles against the metal clip, a reassuring doggy sound. Alice wants to get a name tag as well, with their number and address printed on it. It's a good idea. No sense taking chances.

"Have fun."

Alice leaves the house quickly, just a little ashamed of herself.

Buddy/Mack stretches out on the sun-warmed deck, a long sigh of released energy shuddering through him. Alice has been grooming him, and his skin feels tingly in a pleasant way. Drifts of loosened hair float on the light breeze, up and away, too late for songbirds to use as nesting material.

Alice has on those clothes again, the ones just like those that Justine wears to dance with him. Buddy/Mack gets up from his idle sunbathing and prances, demonstrating to Alice that he can go with her to the dance place. In his dog's mind, it isn't unreasonable that Alice will take him to a place he knows and that Justine will be there waiting for him. He doesn't know why she's being so stubborn.

"Oh no, Buddy. You can't go to yoga. I'm sure that Ed will take you somewhere." Buddy/Mack understands only that she isn't taking him with her, not the tongue language. He doesn't understand the problem. Alice has on dance clothes. He always goes to dance when he sees those tight black pants and white shoes, the car keys, the water bottle almost like the one Justine shares with him. He can overlook one time when she might not take him, but not again. He stands on the alert, his blue eye and his brown eye fixed on Alice's face, waiting.

Then Alice makes a gesture. Even a dog knows that she doesn't mean to get him to react to it, but he does, happy to show off his talent. Alice flips her right hand, palm up, and Buddy/Mack rises to his back legs and spins. He can tell by her expression that she is surprised. Humans reveal so much with their mouths. Buddy/Mack watches to see if she'll try any other familiar gesture, and he isn't disappointed. A quick hand to her brow, and Buddy/Mack, still on his back legs, maneuvers himself behind her, the back of his skull fitting neatly against her backside. She moves forward and he moves with her. She moves to the side and he keeps with her. He waits for another signal, then decides on his own that back-to-back is over and, still balanced on his hind legs, chooses to hip-hop back in front of Alice. She reaches for his front paws and he extends them to her. His muzzle is split in a wide grin. She's dancing with him.

Now can we go?

CHAPTER 26

I've worked in a nursing home. I once thought about getting my certification as a nurse's aide, but I never got around to it. I did learn how to change a bed with a patient in it. I learned about bedsores. I watched the CNAs as they fed, bathed, changed, and spoke in humiliating baby talk to the old people, treating them like unthinking imbeciles simply because age or disease had taken away their speech or their mobility. I'm not squeamish. A woman who has had to support herself and a child alone can't afford the vapors when a good job pays up to seventeen dollars an hour.

I stand over my father and wait until he signals that he'll take another spoonful of soup. He can feed himself, but he prefers being helped to having tomato stains on his pajamas.

"Ready for another spoonful?"

"No. I'm done. Take it away."

I look down on his blanket-covered knees and try not to think how emaciated this disease has left him. Adele can stuff him with all the soup and protein drinks he can tolerate, but there is no reversing this decline. I take back my earlier assessment; this wait will not be long.

"Just one more." I sound like I did when I was coaxing Tony to eat peas.

"I said no. I'm not hungry." My father sounds like Tony when he wouldn't eat those peas. Petulant. When did this grown man become petulant? I remember him as silent, accepting, probably cowed by the woman he replaced my mother with, but never petulant.

"Okay." I pull the tea towel out from under his chin.

"Give me the remote."

Fighting the temptation to make him say *please,* I hand him the clicker and leave the room.

Adele has gone to lie down, so I am alone in the kitchen to clean up the minimal debris left from heating a can of Campbell's soup. It may only be a saucepan and a ladle, but cleaning up without making a sound that might disturb the resting and the dying is hard work, and at the end of it, I am exhausted. I sink onto a kitchen chair, which I instinctively choose, the one that was mine for all those years, my back against the wall. There is a notepad tucked into the napkin holder on the table and I take it and find a pencil. I need to figure out what to do next. I hunt down the New Bedford phone book, right where it has always been, in the top drawer, and try to think of whom to call. Maybe the local rescue can get me started with a search. What I really need is a computer and Internet access. I need to get online and map out a nationwide strategy. I open the phone book, searching for "Animal Rescue" in the Yellow Pages, and there it is under "Automotive": Markham Motors.

For forty years, my father worked for Markham Motors. He sold Chevrolets until Markham Motors expanded into the foreign car market, and then he sold Toyotas, although he always drove Chevys. Every year, Markham awarded sales prizes and almost every year my father came away with another bronze plaque to hang on his wall at work. The name Markham was sacrosanct in this house. It wasn't like it is now, people changing jobs and moving from one career "path" to another. In those days, and especially with a man like my father, loyalty to an employer was admirable. As long as he identified himself as a Markham man, my father was happy. He never anticipated anything other than retiring from Markham Motors.

I pull my finger away from the listing and flip the Yellow Pages back to the animal listings. Before I can find what I'm looking for, my phone rings. I don't recognize the phone number on the display. Then I do. "Mitch?"

"Hi. Just thought I'd check in and see how you're doing. Where are you?"

"I made it to New Bedford."

"And the dog?"

"Nothing yet."

"I'm sorry."

"Thanks." I am touched by the fact that this stranger whose body I clung to for a hundred miles is thinking of me. "I have a couple of leads. The truckers are using their CBs to try to locate Artie." It's a bit of an exaggeration, but I comfort myself by just saying it.

"I've posted your lost dog story on my Facebook page. I've gotten lots of comments."

"That's sweet of you."

"So many people out there can relate to losing a pet. Makes you want to cry."

The image of this tough-looking, one-legged, Harley-riding violinist crying makes me smile.

"And how are things in New Bedford?"

"All right." And that makes me feel a little better, too. "How did your concert go?"

"Same old, same old. A little Vivaldi paired with a modern piece that has no discernible melody."

I laugh. "Maybe someday I'll go to one of your concerts. I'd like to hear the Vivaldi." This is true; I'm not just making conversation. Over the years, I've developed a taste for good music. Candy doesn't object too much when I pop a classical CD into the player as we close up the bar for the night, although she won't let me do that until the last customer is gone.

"Look, Justine. I have a little break coming up. We've just finished the last of the summer season and rehearsals for the winter series don't start for a couple of weeks."

It's the "Look" that alerts me, a verbal hint that something more than a change of topic is coming. "A little vacation, then. What will you do?"

"Thought I might jump on the bike and go see the Whaling Museum in New Bedford."

"It's a nice museum."

"I can be there tomorrow, day after if I take my time."

"That would be nice. But I don't think you should."

"Because it would be inconvenient?"

"Sort of. I'm staying at my father's house. I don't know for how long."

"Not because you are being too polite to tell me to back off?"

"No. No. It would be nice to have a friendly face here." I can conjure up the feel of Mitch's leather coat on my cheek, the scent of him, but not the eyes that were behind sunglasses the whole time we rode together. "It would be nice to have a friend, but I don't think that this is the time."

"I understand."

"It's just . . ." Just what? Another guy hitting on me? Something that has happened to me all my life and I'm no longer flattered? It doesn't feel like that. It feels like something I would encourage. But not now. I have too many emotional irons in the fire to think about encouraging a man to drive from Cleveland to New Bedford on a whim. "After this. When I leave, maybe I can . . ."

"No problem. Really. It was just an idea. Stupid. Of course you're all tied up. I was being impulsive."

"Mitch. It's fine. A really sweet idea. Maybe on my way back to Washington I can stop."

There is a quiet moment while we both adjust our thinking. He wants to come; I won't let him. He was a ride when I needed it; now he thinks of me.

I hear Adele talking to my father. I need to get off the phone and see what else she has in mind for me.

"If I had a picture of your dog, it would help. On the Facebook thing."

For the first time, I wish that I'd invested in one of those fancy camera, e-mail, text, do-your-laundry phones. But all I have is an ancient Nokia that simply acts like a phone. "I don't have one with me. But my friend Saundra does. I can have her send you something." Saundra is the unofficial photographer at our freestyle competitions. She has dozens of photos of dogs performing, and surely one of Mack can be e-mailed to Mitch.

I get his e-mail address. "Thanks for helping, Mitch. And thanks for calling me. I really appreciate it." I just can't appreciate his showing up. That's the thought dangling out there. For once, I have to keep my eye on the ball.

"Don't hesitate to call me if you need to." He sounds sincere, but I doubt that Mitch will repeat this act of kindness. In the old days, I would have told him to come. But I'm older and wiser now; I know how tempting a distraction is, and how destructive.

After I left Anthony, I headed south, attracted by the warmth and the purported lower cost of living. I waitressed in Orlando, worked in a nursing home in New Orleans, got a receptionist's job in Dallas. By the time Tony was five, I was hollowed out. I was exhausted from the responsibility of being the sole source of emotional strength, of decision making, of punishment and reward. The girls I met at my various jobs were still playing. They made plans to meet at nine at night; I was in bed, my son safe in his own bed, the night-light illuminating the dinosaurs on his sleeper. They invited me out of politeness; I declined because I couldn't do it, leave Tony with a babysitter I couldn't afford to drink margaritas I also couldn't afford. To be reckless when I was the only support for a little child. I had taken on single motherhood by my own choice, and I was dedicated to it. But even a dedicated mother gets tired and resentful and frustrated.

The first time Dan asked me out and said he'd pay for the baby-sitter, I told myself that it would be fine. And it was. Then it was Carl, then Bruce, then a host of other men willing to see me as more than just a mommy. Their attention, however brief, reminded me that I was still young, still in my twenties, and maybe I didn't have to be alone. Didn't I deserve a little adult time? A few hours more with a sitter at the end of the workday wasn't going to warp my kid. Even a two-parent child got left with a sitter.

I loved having a little grown-up time, and it became a habit. Dressing up and going out told me that I could have a life outside my role as a mother and provider.

Talking about something other than homework and play dates, being kissed—both reminded me that I still had a Life.

And then they each moved on. Leaving me lonelier than ever. Although they never exactly said it, I knew that having a kid was a drawback, especially as Tony grew up and was no longer easily charmed by presents and being tossed into the air; when he no longer went off and played by himself as my guest and I waited for the sitter to arrive, but wanted to be a part of the conversation.

When push came to shove, they all wanted an unencumbered woman. Each time, each disappointment, and I'd swear to myself that I'd stick with my little boy and forget men. I just didn't realize that Tony wasn't an oblivious little child; he was growing up and was all too aware of my failures.

No, I don't need a distraction now. I need to stay focused and leave comfort aside for now.

"Justine." Adele is beckoning from the sickroom.

I snap my phone shut and head in to get my next set of orders.

CHAPTER 27

The chief help I seem to be able to give is to run errands. Adele sends me to the grocery store, to the pharmacy, to the jewelry store, where she's left her watch to be repaired. She thinks of these tasks individually, so that I am out of the house more than I am in it. As if by summoning me, she surprised herself and now needs to remove me. I go, happier to be driving around on fool's errands than sitting in that house, waiting to feed my father his next bowl of soup, or sit on the surprisingly comfortable couch, waiting for my next order. This is when I miss Mack the most; the reason I wanted him with me. To give me an ally. A reason to leave the house, a reminder that I am important in the life of at least one creature.

So far, Adele has done the more intimate nursing tasks. My "help" is mostly kept outside the bedroom door. I think that she's a little afraid to leave me alone with my father. Afraid of what I might say, or of what he might admit. So I run to Stop & Shop and to CVS and linger a little while at the North Dartmouth Mall before claiming her watch from Zales Jewelers. I use the time to check in with Candy, joining the club of women wandering the mall avenues, cell phone pressed against an ear, isolated in a crowd by the voice of a distant friend. When I hear Candy's "Candy's Place," I so want to be home, home with Mack.

"Any trucker who comes in, I ask if they've seen Artie, but no one has, and most don't know him at all. It's like he disappeared off the edge of the world."

"Or he's hiding from me."

"One guy did say that he thought he knew who Artie's agent is. But he couldn't remember the name. Says he'll find out and get back to me. I didn't want to bother you with that bit of noninformation."

"Artie is like the invisible man. No one sees him. No one knows him."

"What if he was in an accident or something? Maybe that's why he's invisible."

It's a good idea, and I wonder if I can get the state police to tell me if an Arthur Schmidt was involved in any accidents, is maybe dead. As long as he didn't have my dog with him at the time, it wouldn't break my heart. But the idea doesn't take hold. "He's a gypsy driver. Accountable to no one that we know of. Rockin' Roadie. That's all anyone on the road knows him by. He could have gotten a load and headed to Canada, or gone down south, or driven anywhere but back to Washington."

"Justine, he's got to be somewhere, and so does Mack." I can tell by the tone of her voice that Candy is distracted, customers coming in for an early-morning pop. It's only nine there.

A beep beckons me away from Candy to another call. I wouldn't jump from Candy's call except that it might be the one that I'm waiting for, the next call to move me closer to finding Mack. Every time the phone rings, my heart does a little dance of useless hope.

It's Adele, wondering where I am and why am I not there. Could it be because she sent me away? There have been a couple of moments when I've wondered if she is all right mentally. She's made little slips that have puzzled me, like when she lost the word for toilet paper, or when she told me something that just didn't add up about Paul's kids, as if she was talking about much younger children. I've worked in a nursing home. I've been assigned to the Alzheimer's wing. I know the difference between forgetfulness and senility. But I have never been there at the beginning, when the mind begins to retract. I'm not sure if incipient senility is what I'm seeing, or if my opinion of Adele is so harsh, I'm wishing.

"Are you on your way back?"

"In a minute, I'm waiting for them to find your watch."

"Don't wait for it. Come now."

Normally, that demand would have been spoken in Adele's naturally imperious tone. Not this time. She sounds panicked.

"I'm fifteen minutes away. I'm on my way."

Adele ends the call, as she always does, without saying good-bye.

I bang through the back door and drop everything on the kitchen table. Adele is in my father's room and I hear her voice and the sound of the television tuned into some chat show where the audience is compelled to applaud at every line the host utters. I snap it off. In the sudden quiet, Adele's voice also shuts off. My father is lying flat on his back, his mouth gaping open, and the odor of urine is pungent. Adele is standing over him, a wet washcloth bunched in her hands.

"He won't wake up."

"How long has he been like this?" I reach for the bed-side phone.

"A few minutes."

"But he was he like this when you called me?"

"Yes."

"Why didn't you call the ambulance?"

"I don't want him to go."

I dial 911.

"Where's Paul?" I assume she tried him first.

"I didn't call him."

"Okay. I'll call him." I don't want to be alone with his mother in this.

Adele keeps wiping my father's face with the cold washcloth. "I don't want him to go to the hospital. He should be here."

"He'll need to go for a little while. We'll bring him back." I don't know why I promise this, except that I'm pretty certain the outcome isn't going to be one that gives us a choice in the matter. These are cheap words to offer. In the same moment, I realize that this means I will never get from my father what I've wanted since I was seventeen years old—an apology. No cheap words for me now.

Done with his first year at college, Paul came home that summer and fell back in with his friends from high school. They were jocks, three-season athletes. One or two had gone to good schools on athletic scholarships. More of them had stayed in New Bedford and gone into their fathers' businesses, or gone to technical school for the nine months between graduation and an apprentice license as electricians or plumbers. Those were some of the kids Paul hung out with. They met together every night to act out Bruce Springsteen's "Glory Days." They were still underage, so their preferred hangout was the outdoor basketball court at the high school, where they could sit in a car, between games of skins versus shirts, and knock back Bud Lights without too much scrutiny from slow-rolling police cars. In their minds, anyone who might see the former heroes of the basketball court, or the baseball diamond, or, best of all, the football field, playing a pickup game would think back to those golden hours and be charmed by the scene of these gods on earth still flaunting the jump shots of their high school years. The drunker they got, the more those glory days revealed the flaws in their postgraduation lives. Some were doing grunt jobs, ordered around by bosses who had once themselves been glory boys. Or, they were like Paul, an average student but a moderately talented athlete, which got him a scholarship to play on an average state basketball team that never even made it into the play-offs.

Ronnie Markham was one of the boys who made it to a big school on an athletic scholarship. They always talked about how someday there would be a trophy named after him; his athletic prowess had put the school on the map time and again. It helped that his father had the largest, most successful car dealership in the area. Markham Motors, three generations old, enjoyed a fair amount of signage on the playing fields of our high school.

It had been a while since Ronnie had hung out with Paul. A year older than Paul, he had finished his sophomore year at BU. They'd reconnected on the basketball court and now Ronnie showed up at our house three days out of four. He and Paul would go out, shoot those baskets at the high school, and then do whatever it was that they did until the early hours of the next day. Sometimes

I'd open the door and there he'd be on our front step, still the Greek god of New Bedford. "Hey, kid. Where's Paul?" That was the sum total of his interest in me.

And then it wasn't.

That summer, Markham Motors did a little trimming. Cost cutting. Belt tightening. My father's job was on the line; it had been a few years since the last bronze plaque.

I can hear them talking about it through the thin walls of my converted closet, Adele's badgering tone, imploring my father to call a meeting with Markham and point out all his years of success and experience. "Tell him that if he's smart, he'll make you the manager. Put the experience at the top of the heap." I'm a smart kid, and I know that experience isn't always the best card in the hand. Youth is. After all, youth rules, no old folks in the commercials.

My father's reply is muted, his words mostly inaudible through the wall. Just one coming through: "Can't."

"Won't is more like it."

My father must be moving around the room, because suddenly I can hear his voice clearly. "We have the rents. It'll be all right."

Adele's reaction to that is plain: "Not enough."

"We don't know that Markham will let me go. Let's not worry."

"That's all right for you to say, but I have to run this house on your salary. It's not easy. It's never been enough. Don't you think I want a little luxury now? A little improvement? Some of the things that I've been putting off for years? If he lays you off, how far do you think those rents will take us? They barely pay for the upkeep on that house. We'll have to raise them. Bottom line. We raise the rents."

*This isn't the first time I've overheard that conversa-
tion. Adele is obsessing on what she thinks is inevitable,
while my father keeps his head buried in the sand. The
discussions have moved out of their bedroom and into
the kitchen, where the staple diet of conversation is the
relentless conjecture: If Markham fires my father, how
will we survive?*

When Ronnie Markham began to show up at our house,
my father did everything to encourage the friendship.
Everything. In the end, Markham didn't fire my father.
I've never been able to decide if it was because of Paul's
friendship or my spectacularly bad date with Ronnie that
kept my father employed until retirement.

The ambulance has arrived; the flashing lights bounce
off the bedroom walls. I take Adele by the hand and drag
her out of the room so that the EMTs can transfer my father's inert body to a stretcher. Someone is trying to extract information from Adele, but, for once, she is silent.

CHAPTER 28

"If he's so smart, why don't you check out doing obedience with him?" Sally Perkins, Alice's coworker at the library, pushes the cartload of books to be reshelved. It's midafternoon, a slow time on a weekday, too early for the kids who come in to play computer games instead of doing their homework, too late for the senior citizens who come by the little bus; the nonworking mothers are about the only people drifting through the stacks, killing time before the little kids get off the bus, poking through the romance novels and the self-improvement books.

Alice has been telling Sally all about Buddy's spontaneous trick of standing on his hind legs and spinning. She is ahead of Sally in the stacks, straightening out the disorder of improperly shelved books. How come patrons can't put them back where they found them? The one marked 941.45 HE belongs left of 941.45 HI. Alice reverses the order of the nonfiction on the shelf. "He already knows the basics. Sit, stay, down." Buddy even heels, although she's never asked him to. Every time he performs a trick or obeys a command, Alice tries not to make too much of it. If he's this clever, someone spent a lot of time with him. And that line of thinking makes her nervous. It isn't hard to put herself in the place of whoever has lost this dog.

"Then you could go into an advanced class. It'd be fun." Sally has been a dog person all her life. Alice is discovering that a lot of her friends like to label themselves "dog person." Like Mary Jackson. Alice has known Mary all her life and knows that she's never been without a dog, but it wasn't until Alice began to talk about Buddy that Mary opened up about her beloved shih tzu, as if she was talking about her kids. Sally, too, was going on about Ralphie, her rescued pit bull. Suddenly, this common ground has added a dimension to their friendship. Or maybe filled a gap.

After it happened, Alice's friends stopped talking about their children. Alice knew that it was their way of being sensitive to her loss, and their way of keeping Alice's bad fortune away from themselves. It was something beyond trying not to remind her of what happened, as if silence would prevent her from thinking about it every minute of every day. It was also their being afraid of her, of what had happened to her, afraid that it proved that their children were vulnerable. That the worst thing *could* happen. It hadn't helped that Alice had withdrawn into herself, finding any conversation at all abrasive to her tender nerves. She did not care about the price of peas at Potter's. She couldn't raise the least bit of interest in the latest small-town scandal, when the church secretary was discovered embezzling funds to support her scratch-ticket habit. Alice found herself angry at everyone, thinking, Do they not know what has happened? How can they care about a television show or the outcome of some baseball game? For a long time, Alice resented everyone for having a life without a lost child.

"I don't know. Is anybody doing dog training around here?" Alice switches a couple of out-of-order books. "Besides, he's trained enough for us. What would be the reason?"

"Just to have fun. You could enter him in obedience shows. They earn letters, like college students earning a BA or a BS. Dogs get a CD—companion dog—or something. Or maybe he'd be a good therapy dog. You could take him to the nursing home."

Alice imagines her silver-and-white dog resting his head on the knee of some wheelchair-bound elder, the expressive little black eyebrows making him look interested in whatever the oldster might say. It seems like something the dog would do well. He sits with his chin on her legs all the time, those mismatched eyes studying her face, as if he expects her to do something. Alice thinks of the feel of the dog's soft fur under her hand, how easy it is to get lost in stroking him.

Sally reshelves a book from her rolling cart. "I'm thinking that I might get another dog. There are so many out there needing homes. What if I got another and we could go together?"

Alice pokes David McCullough into his correct space on the biographies shelf. "What would you get?"

"Probably another pit bull. Maybe a puppy rescued from that New Bedford raid."

"So you've been thinking about this?"

"No. Well, maybe. Hearing about those puppies just got me thinking. And when you got Buddy, my dog-parent juices started flowing again."

Alice takes the last book off the cart and studies it. *Merle's Door.* She tucks it under her arm; she'll take this one about an author's observations of life with his free-ranging dog home to read. She's already zipped through *Marley & Me* and is grateful that the dog she found isn't a giant slobbery Lab, but a well-mannered, dignified Shetland sheepdog. She's pored through the one book in the library about the breed and now she knows that Buddy is a blue merle and that blue eyes are common. She has confirmation of what she already knows: This is one smart breed of dog. One that likes to have a job.

She thinks that Sally is right: It might be fun to do something with him like obedience or therapy training. "I'll think about it. Might be fun."

When she couldn't get pregnant, Alice read every book on the topic. When she found herself a late-in-life expectant mother, she scoured every book on pregnancy. By the time Stacy was six months old, Alice didn't have the time or energy to read. After it happened, well-meaning friends foisted memoirs and essay books on her, books meant to explain the inexplicable, to make it comprehensible and maybe even acceptable. They sat piled like unused bricks on the coffee table, where she would occasionally run a dust cloth over their covers. She returned them, one by one, never saying that she hadn't read them.

CHAPTER 29

Ed drives past the cemetery gates; from their road, it's not possible to get to the main route in Moodyville without passing this way. As he does every single time they do this, Buddy arches his neck, swivels his ears, and points his nose at the place where Alice first saw him. His mouth opens and his tongue lolls out; he pants, short intakes of breath, not like he's hot or has been running, more like a vocalization. A question: *Huh? Huh?*

Usually, Ed speeds up at this point, pressing the accelerator to kick the old Cutlass awake, but today he pulls to a stop across from the cemetery driveway. Buddy jumps from front seat to back, a blur of silver and white. He climbs over Ed and presses his front feet against the driver's side window. His excitement is obvious, and Ed can't fathom what is causing it. He opens his door and the dog leaps out, the leash whipping after him and out of Ed's reach. Thank God there are no oncoming cars. If anything happened to this dog . . . Ed cannot finish that thought. This is a bad idea and he regrets whatever impulse made him stop.

The dog is in the cemetery, coursing up and down the cracked and weedy drive. Must be squirrels, Ed thinks. The dog is mad for squirrels. But the dog doesn't run toward the tree line. He stands there, sniffing the air with an upturned snout. He tracks along the drive, going farther than Ed should let him go. For an instant, Ed is afraid that the dog will desecrate a grave, but he doesn't.

Ed leans against one of the pair of painted brick columns that flank the cemetery drive. The white paint has flaked away, leaving the bricks exposed. This old cemetery is fairly neglected; the grass gets cut, but little else is done to it. Only the more recent graves look visited. Some folks still have room in family plots owned since the eighteenth century. So many of the ancient stones are wafer-thin, like graham crackers left out in the humidity, their legends obscured by time and climate. Every Halloween, there is another one toppled. Old-fashioned angels sit in faceless guard over family plots, the history of the town in brownstone and granite. Founders and scoundrels.

A few yards further and he would come to the place he hasn't been able to bring himself to visit, the place that Alice spends too much time tending. He gets mad at her sometimes, devoting all that attention to it, as if it's a flower bed; it wasn't good for her then and it still worries him when she gets into one of those moods. It can't be healthy. He doesn't have to read a headstone to remind himself of what happened. It doesn't make him more accepting, or content, or reconciled. It just pisses him off. And Alice doesn't get that. Goddamn chrysanthemums aren't going to change things.

The dog returns to Ed, leash trailing behind, no longer excited. He sits, but his nose keeps working and his ears twist like little radar dishes. Ed needs to talk himself out of thinking that the dog is waiting for someone. Still, the dog looks disappointed. That is as clear as day.

"Time to go." Ed picks up the end of the leash.

"Watch me, Daddy!" A little girl in a polka-dot bikini, her hair long hanks of dark seaweed against her shoulders. "Watch me!" For the hundredth time, Stacy launches herself off the side of the pool into the churned-up water, bobbing to the surface, laughing and grinning, proud of herself for conquering a seven-year-old's fear of submersion. She paddles to the ladder and hauls herself out, water streaming, a human naiad. She shivers and looks pale and blue-tinged in the pool lights. The vaulted ceiling of the indoor pool room at the Holiday Inn echoes with her glee. Ed knows that he should make her come out, but he doesn't.

Buddy/Mack just doesn't understand why Justine wasn't there. Ed took him there, as if he also expected that Justine would be waiting in that place to pick up the end of the leash and take him home. So why wasn't she there? Buddy/Mack doesn't have the capacity to think, Maybe next time. For him, there is no hope beyond a few minutes, a hope contrived by human action. He cannot hope that Ed will go back to the cemetery, to "there," because it's not in his power to hope. He can only expect. He has begun to expect the ride in the car to Lil's. He expects two meals a day. He expects a walk, because Alice is a creature of habit.

When Alice accidentally signals a movement—a spin or a stand, a bow or a rump wiggle—Buddy/Mack doesn't hope that she will dance with him; he expects

that she will. And when she doesn't, he has to be satisfied with her laugh. Sometimes he thinks that these new
people are hard of hearing. They don't understand his
very simple requests, suggestions, and comments.

The good news is that lately, at night, after Alice finishes banging around in the kitchen and Ed has taken the
trash out, they sit side by side on the couch so that he can
lie between them. He takes turns resting his chin on their
legs. First, Ed strokes him, and then, when Ed gets up
to get a drink or use the bathroom, Buddy/Mack shifts
over to Alice. She twiddles his ears in just the same way
that Justine does, so he stays longest on her lap. They
have begun talking over him. Talking about him. He
hears the Buddy word over and over, sometimes with
that little sound in the throat that means people are in a
good mood. Once in a while, he lets them know that he's
listening by thumping his tail. Ed plays with the thing
that Justine calls a "clicker." Buddy/Mack doesn't know
what Ed calls it, because he hasn't asked him to fetch it.
If Ed had the word, the command, then he'd get a big
surprise when Buddy/Mack dropped it in his hands. But
Ed doesn't ask, so Buddy/Mack doesn't fetch.

Buddy/Mack stretches out between Ed and Alice; the
distance between them is exactly wide enough for him
to have his head on her lap and his back legs on Ed's.
They've stopped talking now, but Alice's fingers still
tickle the inside of his ear and Ed's hand still strokes
Buddy/Mack's rump.

CHAPTER 30

It is Stacy's birthday. It's hard to fathom, but she would have turned twenty-two today. If it hadn't happened, she would have been out of college. By now, Stacy would have had a fantastic career. She talked about becoming an archaeologist or a doctor. At ten, anything seemed possible; at thirteen, the choices were unlimited. Maybe she would have been engaged, or traveling through Europe with friends. Maybe all the things that everyone else's child accomplishes by twenty-two would have been celebrated today. Maybe fifteen wouldn't have marked the end of all dreams.

Buddy sits in what has become his place of choice, a corner of the kitchen where he's out of the way and yet able to keep his eyes on her. It's only when she's done in the kitchen, heading off to make the bed or get the laundry together, that he settles on the couch to wait for the next event. Today, he follows her to the bedroom, sits in the doorway. Alice stuffs a tissue in the pocket of her jeans. Good dog. He's watching her, little tipped ears cocked and listening as she breathes in one sigh after another. She sits on her bed and fights the urge to crawl back in, to draw the covers over her head and stare at the filtered light. Ed is out doing who knows what. Anything so as to not be in their house today. Anything to avoid her.

Maybe she should have arranged to work today, so that for a few hours she would have been forced to talk with people, hear the sound of voices other than those occupying her mind, reminding her of all that is lost. That's what she should have done, but she looked at the schedule and never thought to ask for a different one. It's hard enough on Sally to arrange the cobbled-together schedule so that everyone, part-timers and volunteers, gets what they want.

Buddy woofs softly from his place in the doorway. It's an interrogatory woof, as if to ask her, *Are we going to do anything today?* He cocks his head, clearly wondering why she is sitting there. Even the dog knows that she never sits down until the last task is done. He woofs again, this time a little more insistently, a little more *I need.*

"Do you need to go out?"

The dog responds by standing up, shaking himself from the tip of his nose to the tip of his tail. Excited by her words, he does his little two-step prance.

"Okay." Alice lets go of the blanket she's balled up into her fists. "Let's go."

You can't drive around to get away from your thoughts. They just sink in deeper, unperturbed by the need to pay attention to the road or the scenery passing by. The radio does nothing to mask the insistent thoughts, only exacerbates them with evocative music like Fauré's Requiem, and talk radio fades into background noise. But having

Buddy sitting beside her in the minivan seems to help. He points the way with his nose. They pass the cemetery gates and he whimpers, but she doesn't slow down. She'll go later, deadhead the mums. It hasn't rained, so she'll give them a drink. Whisper "Happy birthday" under her breath. As usual, Ed won't go with her. He thinks she is obsessed. He's deluding himself if he thinks not seeing the grave makes one iota of difference; he can't pretend it didn't happen just because he doesn't help her plant flowers.

It's not that she even offers prayers. She just needs to have one task still connecting her to Stacy. She's not one of those parents who talk to a gravestone, pretending their child is attending their every thought, or blame minor coincidences on an angel that was once their daughter. Alice is grounded in reality. Her child is dead.

The dog trainer Sally recommended is in Amherst. It's a pretty day, and the ride up route 181 is pleasant and will take long enough that if she includes lunch at Panera, plus an hour or so poking around the JC Penney at the Hampshire Mall, this little jaunt will take up the hard part of this day. Alice has called ahead and the trainer has agreed to meet for an assessment. Kids have assessments; so, apparently, do dogs. Buddy will certainly assess at the top of the chart.

Alice finds the place after a couple of missed turns. Expecting a kennel, she is surprised to find a modest Cape-style house on a side street not far from the University of Massachusetts. No dogs bark as she and Buddy stand on the stoop, but there are the telltale flags arrayed around the tiny lot, signifying underground electric fencing to keep an animal in. She rings the doorbell twice. Finally, a woman comes to the door, a bundle of fluff cradled in the crook of her elbow.

"Come in. Don't mind the mess."

The mess seems to consist of several unoccupied dog beds and two dog crates with artistically draped scarves over the tops, as if to convert the cages into furniture. The house definitely has a thin suggestion of animal, but otherwise it is quite clean.

"Arabella. And you're Alice?" Arabella plops the ball of fluff into one of the crates. Its secret identity revealed as a tiny dog, it curls its lip at Buddy, growls once, and then curls up for a nap, exhausted by the effort.

"Yes, Alice Parmalee, and this is Buddy."

Arabella doesn't bend over to acknowledge Buddy's existence like everyone else who meets him has done. In fact, she stands quite deliberately away from him, but Alice sees that her eyes are glancing at him, assessing him.

"He's pretty. How old?"

Alice has prepared a story. "He's a rescue, an abandoned dog. We just adopted him, and the vet thinks he's no more than four. He's very smart."

"Any behavioral problems? Biting, chewing, peeing in the house?"

"No. He's very well behaved. Not one mistake."

"Then what do you want from me?"

"My friend Sally thought he should become a therapy dog."

"What do you think?"

When Buddy so clearly asked her to do something today, he was being a therapy dog, but she doesn't say that. "I think he's perfect for that. He's also got a lot of tricks."

"Maybe he could become a circus dog."

"He's certainly that. Watch." Alice flips her hand over, but the dog sits looking at her as if he's never seen that hand signal before. "Buddy, you know that that means."

Alice tries again, adjusting the plane of her hand. Buddy doesn't rise to his back legs. He just shakes his head and sneezes. "Really, he does this little spin on his back legs." Alice tries again, and again the dog just sits there.

"Maybe he's being shy."

"Maybe." If he'd been a child, she would have given him the evil eye to let him know they'd be having a little discussion in the car. But he's a dog. There's nothing to discuss.

"Well, here's what I can do for you." Arabella outlines her program for developing therapy dogs, ending her spiel with her substantial fee, the amount of which drives Alice into a noncommittal "We'll see." That's a lot of money for a hobby; Ed will blow a gasket. She gets into the minivan, snaps her seat belt into place. Forget Ed; if she wants to do this, she will. Ed has no right to an opinion.

Ed has spent the day making up errands. He stopped by Toolie's to see about a tune-up for the minivan. He never drives Alice's car and it's always last on his list of things with motors to tend to, but he thought of it this morning and pulled in to get an appointment. Afterward, he and Toolie, who has been his auto mechanic almost since the day Ed moved to Moodyville, shot the shit for a while. Then Ed lingered at Lil's long enough that she asked him if he wanted a lunch menu. He did.

After a BLT, Ed knows that he's out of stuff to do to keep him away from the house. The fact of his leaving Alice alone on this day doesn't escape him, and he takes the long way home with a guilty procrastination. It's just that this particular day, even more than the other anniversary, is the hardest on her, and his inability to make it better feels like a failing. Every time he's tried to distract her, or reason with her, or change Alice's focus on this day, his efforts have been met with anger and accusation and no relief for either of them. There have been years, especially the first two or three, when neither of them spoke to the other because there were only terrible words to say.

Ed knows he is avoiding the inevitable, but he takes the long way home.

The second bay of the two-car garage is empty. Ed pulls the Cutlass into its berth, shuts it off, and triggers the garage door to shut. The slow-rolling thunder of the automatic door closing behind him masks Ed's sudden weeping.

It's a brief jag, and Ed backhands the tears away, draws a long breath, and pushes open the car door, banging it, as he so often does, into the plastic Costco closet.

Seven years and uncounted sessions with grief counselors and well-meaning clergymen haven't erased the questions. Nor have they provided a good answer to the big one: Why?

Alice has left him a note and a sandwich, which Ed eats, even though he's just had a BLT at Lil's. Their bed is unmade and strangely welcoming. Ed lies down, stretching out full length on his back, staring at the ceiling with its faded water mark from the roof leak that no one can seem to fix. Alice doesn't know when she'll be back. She's got the dog and she's going to see a trainer. Ed would scoff at the idea of turning Buddy into some kind of performing bear, but the idea has gotten Alice out of the house today, and for that he's grateful. This dog has been good for her. After it happened, Alice became this shadow woman. Most days, he can only see her outline as she goes through the motions of day-to-day living. Somehow, having this dog in the house, with his needs and his antics, has begun to put color in the old Alice.

Now he's the one alone in the house. Even the sad presence of his wife is preferable to the loneliness of being in the house with only his thoughts to keep him company. As pleased as he is that the dog is with Alice on this critical day, Ed wishes the dog were here, keeping him company instead.

Ed rolls off the bed and goes into Stacy's room, which is opposite theirs. The room is filled with Stacy's things and completely devoid of life—a stage waiting for the play to begin. No, a stage after the play has ended. They have left everything as it was, just as if Stacy has walked out of the room. It is a room clearly once the domain of an adolescent girl. The Barbies have long since been packed away in the closet, instead of scattered all over the room, to be expected when a girl enters high school. Novels and poetry line the bookshelf instead of The Baby-sitter's Club. Plath, Woolf, and Shakespeare— typical reading for a girl in honors English. On the wall, a famous print depicting Ophelia floating down the stream, looking peaceful and untouched, her arms open and her gaze upward, singing. Stacy had brought that back from some school field trip to a museum.

Ed touches the trophy Stacy earned in the eighth grade for soccer. He turns it a little, just enough to dispel the museum-quality stasis of Alice's rule over this room.

As he leaves the room, his foot hits something. Ed bends down to retrieve the dog's latest stuffed toy, a faceless teddy bear. Ed can't imagine how the dog's toy got here.

Today's go-for-a-ride took him too far from where Buddy/Mack thinks that Justine will find him. At first, he thought Alice was going to take him all the way home. They were in the car for far longer, even by a dog's reckoning, than ever before. Which might have meant it was time to go home. When they ended up at that house with the dog smells, Buddy/Mack expected that something was going to happen. Nothing did, except Alice's clumsy attempt to get him to perform. All he could think was that Alice had come to the wrong place to find Justine. It was a little like Saundra's house with her pack, but the silence was unnerving. Who had dogs that didn't welcome visitors? Finally, Alice put him back in the car and they drove home, Alice talking the whole way home, as if she was trying to convince him of something.

When they came in through the back door, Ed was there and greeted him with a long back scratch and lots of soft words spoken into his ruff. Then Ed straightened up and went to where Alice remained in the doorway. They stared at each other for a moment, long enough that Buddy/Mack got worried. They were like two stranger dogs meeting for the first time, studying each other for signs of fear or friendliness, aggression or attraction. Finally, they did something that Buddy/Mack hadn't seen them do before: They touched.

Buddy/Mack watched with careful shepherd eyes as Alice and Ed touched and stayed close for such a long time that he felt he had to interrupt. A dog needs dinner, after all.

CHAPTER 31

"If you had music, that would look a lot like dancing."
Jen puts her hand out and takes the beer from her boyfriend, Derek. Jen Coulter has lived next door to the Parmalees since she was in sixth grade, and when they had
Stacy, she had been their baby-sitter, practically living
with them. When her parents moved to Florida, Jen, a
nurse practitioner, bought their house, and she now lives
there with Derek, who is beginning to look like a keeper.
Stacy had outgrown needing a baby-sitter, but Jen had
remained a good friend, the teenage baby-sitter growing up into a good neighbor, and she is the only friend
who always remembers this difficult day. It has become
a tradition, this spontaneous gathering on this particular
September day. No one plans it, at least not officially.
And maybe someday Jen won't come; she may forget
the significance of this date and go on with her life.
But it is nice when Jen calls and says, "You up for company?" And then Ed brings home a six-pack, even before
he knows they will come. And Alice just happened to

thaw out the roast beef she's had in the freezer for a few weeks. All the seemingly accidental decisions converge for a midweek dinner at which no one speaks of the real reason they are together. Alice is glad that she spent the day away, and just as glad she got home in time to throw the roast in.

"That's not all; watch this." Alice turns to face the dog, who is still up on his back legs. She twiddles her fingers in a rough circle and the dog spins. Then he drops to all fours, his eyes fixed on Alice, waiting for the next thing. "Now why he wouldn't do this for that dog trainer is beyond me. He was like a kid refusing to perform in front of company."

"Ed, do you have a CD player or a radio?" Jen hands the beer back to Derek.

Ed does, and he brings out the little player that he keeps in his workshop. He's pulled out a few CDs from his collection, which tends toward classic rock.

Jen flips through the selection, choosing the Beatles' "White Album." "Pop this in and find 'Ob-La-Di, Ob-La-Da.'"

Ed does, then stands back to give Alice and the dog more room on the deck. Derek holds his new iPhone in position and Ed fires up the tune.

With the catchy tune playing, the dog's motions suddenly take on a meaning. Jen is right: This dog is dancing. Alice takes him through certain moves that she has inadvertently discovered, then tries a couple more purely invented signals to see if something else will happen. At first, nothing does; the dog stops. She tries again, and suddenly he's backing up, then pivoting on his rear legs in a perfect circle. He stops, waits for more from Alice. She waves at him. He comes forward, but on his fore-arms, his rear end up in the air, his tail waving like a pennant in the breeze. When everyone applauds, the dog tucks one forepaw under his chest, dipping his head in a perfect courtly bow.

"Do it again, Alice. See if you can get it smoother. Derek, are you getting the video?" Jen starts shoving the deck furniture out of the shot. Someone flips on the floodlights against the growing dark.

Alice waits for the music to start. "Ready, Buddy?" She flips her hand over and Buddy repeats his first moves. For half a minute, they perform a dance routine, the dog contributing several movements ad lib. At the end, the people all laugh and clap and the dog barks and barks, clearly pleased with himself. Derek has caught it on his new iPhone with its multitude of apps.

Jen and Derek leave around nine, the good-bye hugs maybe just a little tighter, a little longer than a casual dinner among friends might suggest. Ed and Alice stand on the front steps, waving them off. Ed drapes an arm around Alice, squeezes her shoulder gently. She doesn't pull away but releases a soft sigh. Buddy/Mack pushes his way between them, fitting himself against their legs. They stand that way, the three of them, long after the porch light next door shuts off.

The three of them sit at the kitchen table, a small cake laden with sixteen candles glowing in the dimmed dining room light. Stacy stares at those candles as if hypnotized. "Make a wish, honey." Ed has the video camera pointed at her and they wait for the moment when Stacy will make a wish and blow out the fifteen candles, plus one for good luck.

Stacy looks up from her trance and points at Ed, who's holding the camera. "Don't."

Ed reluctantly lowers the video camera.

Stacy sweeps her hair into her fist and leans toward the candles. When she is done blowing, one candle remains lighted. She reaches over and snuffs it out between pinched fingers.

Buddy/Mack lies on the deck, his position sphinxlike, his attention on the distant sound of a woodpecker hammering a tree. He'd like to see a squirrel to chase. He'd be off the deck in a split second, in full voice, and catch it. He always expects to catch the squirrels he chases. That's his dream.

Alice is in the house, pushing the vacuum. Ed is in the garage, doing something with the car. Buddy/Mack is enjoying a few minutes by himself. Unlike Justine, who left Buddy/Mack alone for good chunks of time, these people seem intent on keeping him company. It's not that companionship isn't nice; it's just that he can't get a full nap in. There is always someone there to stroke him, or speak to him, or make him move over; some adventure being cooked up, like go-for-a-ride or go-for-a-walk. The day-to-day activity of these humans, who continually wander around their house, needing to have an eye kept on their movements, keeps him busy. Following them as they go from bedroom to cellar to kitchen to living room is an exhausting business. He's glad Alice suggested that he wait on the deck while she uses that infernal machine, has let him go out on the deck to watch the wildlife, catch a few minutes of a nap, and expect that there might be a squirrel to chase.

Then, miraculously, there is a squirrel. It's brazenly creeping across the expanse of backyard, stopping here and there to root around for whatever it is squirrels like to find. It sits up, something in its little useful hands, then drops to the ground and continues to hunt. Buddy/

Mack is on his feet, the growl rumbling in his throat, the pulse of defender of the territory pounding through the length of him; he beats a quickstep before launching himself after his nemesis. His toenails scramble against the decking, unable to gain a purchase. He flings himself toward the steps and comes to a complete choking halt. He is tied.

This has never happened to him before. No one has ever tied him up. A simple "Stay" is enough to keep even Buddy/Mack from hurtling after squirrels, even though the command is frustrating. But this, this restraint, is shameful. Buddy/Mack shakes, whines a little as the squirrel continues on its unthreatened path, then resumes his sphinx pose. But the fun has gone out of it. How do these people expect him to defend their property if he's tied, like some cur, to their deck rail? Why have they figured out the dance part of his repertory but not the simple obedience words he lives by? It's the same as when Alice takes him on a walk. He wants to tell her that he can be trusted to return to her at a call, but she won't ever let him off the leash. Off-leash work is puppy work. He's been doing it for years.

Buddy/Mack remembers that he's waiting for Justine. This is just what's happening today, this being tied business. He is waiting for Justine, but these people don't seem to understand that. Justine will tell them in their tongue language that he is not the kind of dog that is tied. He needs to get back to the cemetery gates, where he thinks that Justine will come to get him.

He is still nursing his frustration when Ed comes to the sliding door and offers to take him on go-for-a-ride. And, as he thinks every time Ed suggests a ride, Buddy/Mack hopes that the cemetery will be the destination and that Justine will be waiting for him.

CHAPTER 32

Ed sits in the Cutlass but doesn't start the car. Buddy is sitting beside him, waiting patiently for the ride to begin. Alice is doing her usual morning routine of vacuuming, something she's doing more often now that they have this furry dog living with them. He's on his way to Lil's. Again. Ed sighs. What would be the harm in changing routine today? He's already had two cups of coffee. He doesn't need a third or fourth. But what would he do? He's run out of household tasks. In the year of his un-employment, aka retirement, he's painted the trim and edged the walk, taken care of all those little jobs that had been waiting for him to have the time to attend to. Turns out, there weren't so many after all. Now he's left with puttering—cleaning out the workshop, sorting through nails and screws. He's not the kind of guy to sit around watching daytime television; he's a doer, not a sitter.

It is a crisp, clear September weekday morning and the best he has to do is sit in a coffee shop with guys he has little more in common with than their early retirement, or their living in this little town. Their allegiance to the Sox. Okay, so a few things in common, but is it enough? Ed gets out of the car. Buddy looks at him anxiously, as if to say, *What? No ride?*

"Be right back."

The dog seems to nod, but Ed knows that's just his imagination.

Ed lets himself into his workshop. The garage of the raised ranch leads directly into his work space and Alice's laundry room. The washer is beating out a rhythm as he opens the cabinet filled with his paint supplies. Ed grabs his wire brush, a whisk broom, and a dustpan and dumps them in the trunk. He has a purpose.

Buddy is furiously excited to stop at the cemetery. He's behaving like a little kid being taken to the circus, jumping from front seat to back, making this little yipping noise that almost sounds like hiccups. This time, Ed parks the car just inside the flaking pillars and lets the dog out. As he has done before, Buddy courses up and down the driveway until he collapses in the shade of the car. Overprotective Alice would be royally pissed that the dog isn't on a leash, but that's their little secret. Buddy isn't going anywhere.

Ed gets to work scraping the flaking paint from the left-hand column. He'll give Buck Franklin a call tonight and let him know that if the cemetery commissioner won't take care of this part of the cemetery, he'll be losing Ed's vote in November. The paint drifts down like lead-based snow, covering Ed's shoes and his face. His bare forearms begin to speckle. He probably should have brought a mask.

The wire brush sings its own song against the rough brick. Stacystacystacy, it whispers.

When Stacy was born, a seven-pound-four-ounce beautiful baby girl, he dreamed of those iconic father-of-a-daughter moments, teaching her to drive and walking her down the aisle. But as she grew up, he found that he got to do those things he might have expected with a son. He taught her to throw a knuckle ball, dribble a basketball, understand football strategies; how to kick a soccer ball.

"Did you have tryouts today?" Ed has seen the high school athletic department's announcement on the marquee, donated by the class of 1975, for fall sports tryouts. Stacy had been the high-point earner on her middle school soccer team, playing forward, and everyone assumes she'll be a shoo-in for the JV team now that she's in high school.

Stacy is dressed in jeans and a T-shirt, no sign of the soccer clothes that she lived in for most of middle school.

"I forgot." Stacy ladles a spoonful of chili out of the simmering pot on the stove. Alice is in the laundry room, and Ed can hear the bang, bang, bang of a sneaker in the dryer.

"How could you forget?"

"I just did. No big deal."

"Can you try out later?"

"I don't know. Maybe."

"You don't sound like this is important to you? Don't you care?"

Stacy licks the back of the spoon, focusing on anything but looking him in the eye. "I guess so."

"You guess you care? If you don't want to play, that's fine; just don't 'forget' to try out."

"I just did. People forget things. It's, like, not the end of the world."

Ed knows that he needs to back off. In a moment of

sharp parental self-awareness, he wonders if it is he who wants her to be on the soccer field. He'd been a decent basketball player, and he understands the benefits of being part of a team, of being active, of being a little bit celebrated while in high school.

Ed thinks that maybe Stacy is just coming into her antijock phase, and he is mindful to let her make her own decisions. But he can't help asking the question: "Are you afraid you won't make the team?"

Stacy takes another mouthful of chili. "More like I'm afraid I will."

Ed rasps the wire brush across three courses of brick, over and over, until his right arm aches and a thin line of sweat darkens the back of his shirt. This is going to be more than a one-morning job, but Ed has plenty of time.

Finally! Finally, Ed has realized that they should wait here for Justine. Such a relief. Ed has found something to do, which seems like what this human requires for happiness—activity. But there is something about the manic way he's going about this task that keeps Buddy/ Mack alert and concerned. Ed is going at the task like he's in a battle.

They are there from when the shadows cover him entirely until the shadows disappear and, even in the cool air, Buddy/Mack gets warm. He stands and shakes. Sits, watches Ed. Walks around, sniffs. He hears a squirrel and ponders the chase.

Ed finally tires of his activity and sinks down to sit with his back against the pillar he's been scrubbing so vigorously. Buddy/Mack comes over to him and sits down, happy that they both will sit here waiting for Justine.

After a few minutes, Ed gets up, complaining in tongue language as he climbs to his feet. He opens the car door. "Let's go."

Buddy/Mack's ears droop in disappointment.

Justine has still not come.

CHAPTER 33

He's doing the same damn thing with the dog that he did with Stacy—being the fun parent, being the entertainment, monopolizing him. Arms crossed, Alice stares out the living room window, waiting for Ed to return with the dog so that she can get to his first training class on time. Ed knows she's doing this today, so why ever did he take Buddy with him?

When Stacy was born, it was a no-brainer, as they say, for Alice to quit her job as a medical secretary outright and become, at age forty, a true stay-at-home mom. Eight hours or more a day were spend being in charge, caring for their daughter, planning meals, and watching out the back window as Stacy and her pals played in the backyard; being the taxi driver and the negotiator; being disappointed when Stacy refused to go back to dancing school, and signing up for booster club when she took up soccer. And yet, when he was around, it was Ed who dazzled their daughter's eyes.

And now it's Buddy who dances and prances when Ed comes in the door.

Even before Ed shuts the car off, Alice is out the door. "I'm going to be late."

"For what?"

"His first class."

"I forgot."

Alice gets a good look at Ed as he climbs out of his car. Head to toe, he's covered in white flakes. "Is the dog as much of a mess as you are?"

Buddy jumps out of the Cutlass and stands beside Alice. His pink tongue lolls out of his mouth; it's not because he's panting, but from that happy look that he gets when both of them are there.

"Where is his leash?"

Ed doesn't answer.

Alice checks the dog over, clearly annoyed. She brushes a hand over the dog's back, clips on the requisite six-foot training leash, and points him into the open door of the minivan.

Buddy looks inordinately pleased to be asked to go for another ride.

"He might need some water before you go."

"Take him in, but hurry up. I have to get to Amherst."

Once, Ed had taken Stacy to the shoe store three-quarters of an hour before she was supposed to be at a game. Neither one of them remembered the game, and Alice was left on the sidelines, furious, apologetic when the coach came looking for his player, and, finally, worried. Eventually, they showed up, sheepish but not nearly contrite enough. That might have been when Alice insisted they invest in cell phones.

Buddy takes no time at all to lap up some water and races back to the garage to take up his place in the minivan.

"Have fun." Ed presses the button to raise the garage door for Alice.

It is suddenly too much like being a mother. Alice gets to the end of their street and has to pull off the road. It is too familiar, this going to a lesson, not quite déjà vu, but something so close to old habit that she tastes the past on her tongue. The smell of a September Saturday afternoon, something in the way the light hits the road, and Alice is transported back to the years when she spent more time in her van, this minivan, than she did in her kitchen. The dog sneezes, and the ghost of another passenger sits behind her.

Alice reaches back and strokes the dog's head. It's a dog, a silent companion, not a child back there. They are going to a dog class, to learn how to make sick people feel better and old people happy. "Come on up." Alice pats the passenger seat. Buddy hops into it. Maybe they should invest in a dog seat belt. She puts the car in gear and pulls away from the stop sign.

Alice tries not to blame Ed anymore. She's been advised by grief counselors that blame is destructive and no one can be blamed for what happened. Still, once in a while, when memory and the scent of September air remind her of the abrupt cessation of being a mom, the mother of a living child, Alice blames Ed.

Alice emanates unhappiness and Buddy/Mack whines softly in response. In the minivan, they are divided by the center console, so he is unable to rest his head in her lap, which was a technique that always proved successful with Justine when the low scent of unhappiness radiated from her. Sometimes this would happen after she tossed her cell down hard; sometimes it would happen in the middle of the night, when he would work his way up

from the end of the bed to press himself against her until
her arm would go over his body and she would draw him
close to her.

Alice, because she still forbids him to climb on the
bed she shares with Ed, has not yet snuggled him close,
but Buddy/Mack knows that if she would, she'd feel better. He's watched them as they sleep, two people with
the space of a foot between them. Whenever one of them
touches the other, there is a grunt or a snort and they
move apart. Buddy/Mack thinks that that space between
them in the bed would be just about perfect, exactly the
right dimension for him to slip his body in and become
the final link in the chain.

Squirrel!

Buddy/Mack sees the little rodent dash across the
road in front of them. Alice slows, avoids contact. *Let me
get him for you!* But Alice keeps driving, oblivious to the
skilled hunter in the seat beside her. He vocalizes, not a
bark, but a complaint that Alice is a lousy partner.

Alice comes to the cemetery and, lo and behold, she,
too, pulls between the gates, going all the way up the
drive before stopping. But she doesn't let him out of the
car, even as she gets out and stands in front of one of
the stones.

Buddy/Mack does bark, his place short and demanding. *Please let me out; please let me wait with you.*

Alice pauses only a moment, brushes something from
the top of the stone, plucks a dead bloom from the chrysanthemums, shudders, and then gets back into the car.
"What's all your noise about?" She strokes his head, nose
to ears, over and over, until Buddy/Mack senses that the
unhappiness has ebbed and Alice is ready to move on.

PART III

CHAPTER 34

I never would have pegged Adele as the stay-by-the-bedside type. They've assigned my father a bed on a quiet floor, where the only other inhabitants are several doors away from him and one another, as if making it easy on nurses isn't the plan. At this point, the doctors all seem to agree that he isn't dead, but comatose, and that he most likely won't wake up from that, but sink deeper. My stepmother can't seem to wrap her mind around the ultimate eventuality and acts like this is some sort of television drama where keeping up a constant patter of chat saves the patient. Then again, Adele, as long as I have known her, has kept up a constant patter of chat. I guess it doesn't matter if the person she's talking to is unconscious or not. I am uncharitable enough to imagine that my father is sinking faster and deeper just to get away from the persistent sound of her voice.

Any idea that this vigil is based on true affection is ludicrous. Adele is auditioning for the role of martyr. I can hear the ladies at bingo singing her praises: *She stayed by his side, la da la da, by his side, by his side, la da, la da.* I image it sung as a Strauss waltz.

Adele is so relentless in her vigil that I am stunned when she finally goes out of the room, leaving me alone with my father. We're both a little squeamish about using the lavatory in the room, so I realize that she's gone to the public ladies' room down the end of the hall.

My father is tilted up at a slight incline, as if he might want to relax in bed and watch the news on the suspended television. I reach out and touch the undisturbed thermal blanket, which is just a little off center, gently teasing it into plumb. As I do, I feel the warmth that still radiates from his yet-living body. There is a tiny flutter of breath. I stare at him, trying hard to find something to anchor me to the moment, to the right emotion, to the *feelings* I should have. What good memory should I cast back for? What bad memory should I cast off?

I remember wandering into Adele's kitchen, to find my father staring out the window, looking across the fence to our house. It was before they got married, it must have been, because I was wearing a pair of sneakers that were too short for me; I got new ones just before the wedding day. Why this image sticks with me is because I had never seen such an expression on his face before. It was not grief, not even lingering sadness, but almost that of panicked regret.

"What's the matter, Daddy?"
    "Nothing."
    "What are you doing?"
    "Thinking."
    "About Mom?"
    "I guess. Yes."

"I miss Mommy." I am still talking to his back. He rubs his face with both hands but says nothing.
"Is Adele going to be my mother?"
"Yes." His voice is raspy, as if he has a sore throat.
"Daddy, I want to go home."
"This is home now."

Another man might have reached out and hugged his daughter, but the great withdrawal had already begun. Adele walked into the room and he quickly turned around and reached for her.

I give the thermal blanket another adjustment, just to feel that he's still warm.

Adele is back, and I move away from him.

I am not staying by his bedside. I am at Paul's office, checking my e-mails. There are the usual junk e-mails, a couple of notifications that my online bill pay is about to take money out of my account, a thought that chills me to the bone until I check my bank account and see that my dear friend and boss, Candy Kane, has direct-deposited an unearned paycheck into my account. I don't normally get weepy, but that brings tears to my eyes. I fire off a thank-you e-mail with a promise to work it off. There are e-mails from Candy and Saundra with messages of hope and "Hang in there."

But there is no e-mail to say "Found your dog." I scroll down, check the junk-mail folder. I don't know why I think an e-mail will save my life, but I do, and the lack of an e-mail with that subject line is monstrously disappointing. Alerts have been posted across the country on a million Web sites devoted to lost pets, Shetland sheepdog rescues, animal rights and the like. I follow the list of links Saundra has given me, but not one has a clue as to Mack's whereabouts, only gentle, supportive comments.

Back at the hospital, Adele is still talking to my comatose father. The relentless beep of the monitor is the only thing telling me that he still lives. I watch it as if it's live television, rapt with the spikes and valleys of the constantly streaming green line. I really don't know what it means, just that as long as it maintains its steady beat, we remain here.

I've brought back lunch. Adele slides the bedside tray table away from my father, who for some reason has been given lunch, although he is clearly nonfunctioning. She looks at the ham and Swiss on rye with a little twist to her mouth. "No mayonnaise?"

"In the packets, in the bag."

"These are always so hard to open."

I take the mayonnaise and the mustard and bite into the tough plastic, ripping both open with my teeth. "Here. Squeeze."

Adele takes the packets from me like they might be contaminated, but she squeezes both condiments liberally on the bread.

We are on death watch and we eat every bite of our sandwiches.

"I've been telling your father that once he's out of here, we should be thinking about selling the house. We could move into one of those residences they built in that warehouse complex. You actually have a view of the water. The house is too much for him to keep up."

I look away from staring at the monitor. Adele is fiddling with the arrangement of covers over my father. She is telling my dying father that she has plans; that they'll take up housekeeping in an expensive retirement community when he dodges death. And then I get it. Adele knows perfectly well that she will be making that move by herself, but she doesn't want my father, if by some miracle he's still cogent beneath the surface, to think she's leaving him behind.

"If you sell your house, you'll be able to live pretty well. Or maybe sell both houses. That should keep you going for a long time." I'm just making conversation here, nothing more.

Adele purses her lips in that familiar way I remember so well from my childhood, a sour "I do this for your own good" look she'd get when she was about to impart her peculiar justice. Controlled anger. "What do you know about it?"

"What do you mean?"

"You have no idea how hard it was."

"I think I do. I fed my son oatmeal for dinner often enough."

"That was your own fault. You left home; you got pregnant and left your husband. Now you think you can swan back here and take over."

This leap from simple conversation to attack makes me think my earlier impression—that Adele was showing signs of dementia—was more accurate than mean-spirited.

"I'm not taking anything over."

"We needed those rents, Justine. We still do."

The tiny hospital room is filled with the mechanics of keeping my father alive. Adele sits at his side in the only comfortable chair. I am perched on a closed commode. The air is tainted with the scent of disinfectant and bodily functions. The single window, a solid pane of immovable glass fretted with wire, throws a glare into the room, so that the white of the thermal blanket and the white of Adele's hair appear haloed. I throw back the rolling commode and leave the room. I'm done here.

Once again, I wish that I smoked. I could join the small band of hospital employees huddled across the street, puffing on cigarettes, flicking ash into the gutter. A couple of them sip from paper cups. There's a small coffee shop halfway down the block from the hospital entrance, and I find myself jerking the door open to the sound of clanging bells. I order a large coffee to go and then wonder where I'm going. As I pay, my cell phone rings. I wonder if my heart is going to keep leaping like this every time it does. It's Troy.

"I found him."

"Mack?" I have to lean against the faux-marble counter in order to keep on my feet. My heart bangs against my chest with an audible thump. Mack!

"No. Sorry. Rockin' Roadie. His rig blew a rod and he's been cooling his heels in Worcester for the past few days. One of my regulars was on the horn with him just this morning. Got a location, if you want it."

I will not let my optimistic mistake show. I shove too much money into the hand of the barista. I grab a small table and a napkin. "Shoot."

Troy gives me an address and simple directions to the A-1 Truck Service Center.

"Troy, did your guy mention if Artie still has my dog?"

"I would have said that first. No. Course, he didn't ask him, either, so maybe he does."

I hold back the disappointment. "I owe you, my friend."

"No biggie. Just go find him. Let me know what happens, okay?"

I know where Artie is. I'm a couple of hours away from tagging him. My only problem is, how am I going to get there?

When we took up canine freestyle, no one knew what I was talking about. Dog dancing? What, like waltzing? Like circus dogs? Then the British version of that television talent show featured a young woman with her dog, a Border collie, dancing to a James Bond theme. Even the professionally dour Simon Cowell was impressed. The video went viral and dog dancing entered the world of YouTube. Even Mack and I have made it onto the Internet. Saundra records all our competitions and demonstrations and posts the best of them. What Mack and I like to do best are the demonstrations. These usually take place during lulls in big dog shows, sort of like half-time performances. The crowd can really get into the act, clapping in time with the music, laughing, cheering us on. Mack is a real ham and loves it—the louder the crowd, the better. I'm always mindful of his dignity and will never subject him to some of the weirder costumes my peers often inflict on their dogs, especially the small dogs. Not for Mack some gold lamé outfit. With his natural silver-and-black coat, he needs only a "formal" collar that looks like a black tie. The black tie looks so snappy against his white ruff. Oh how happy he is when he sees me pull out his "tie." He wriggles and makes this little chuffing noise in his throat, telling me in no uncertain terms that he's ready to party.

Everything that has been going on around me fades into the background. I have my first real chance at recovering my dog. My dancing dog.

My mind is racing. How am I going to get to where Artie, miraculously, is held up? I have to get there now;

if his truck is fixed even by this afternoon, it will be too
late. I have to go now. I can make it from New Bedford
to Worcester in two hours, two and a half at the worst if
the Pike is backed up. It's already 1:30. He could be on
the road by four o'clock. I need a car. I need to get the car
keys from Adele. My heart races and my forgotten con-
tainer of coffee sloshes in my hand as I race back to the
hospital, where I dump it in the nearest trash can.

The visitor elevator tortures me with its slowness
in arriving and with its painful floor-by-floor ascent. I
should have taken the stairs. When I get to the room,
Paul is there, occupying most of the rest of the available
space in the room. "Paul, can you take Adele home? I
need to borrow the car."

Paul turns to look at me with a crumpled face. "Justine, he's gone."

I wonder for a split second how Paul knows that Artie
is gone. And then I understand what he means.

My father is dead.

I am not prepared for this. Ridiculous, I know, since it's
why I'm here. But still, the fact, the hard, cold fact of his
death, has stunned me. It's like being on a roller coaster.
You know it's going down, and you're going to have that
swooping feeling of lost gravity and maybe your breakfast rising, but you're surprised anyway. You scream. I
don't scream, but I do reach for the wall to support myself as the room spins just a little. Adele and Paul step
apart and I see him there: pale, waxy. The hands that
once wrote sales contracts by the dozens are now stilled.
Even when he was comatose, they had not seemed inert,
devoid of life.

I wish, vainly, that I could be properly grief-stricken.
And then I find myself weeping, and the grief is real.

Adele sits on the bed, her back to me, one hand on my father's left hand, which is free now of the web of plastic tubes. The monitor with its incessant beeping is quiet, shoved off to one side. I should have realized the minute I walked into the room that it was quiet and in that silence heard the news that Paul, with his large weeping face, has given me. But I was so noisy with my own news that I couldn't hear the silence.

Someone, a nurse maybe, or an aide, has tidied him up. Someone else, a doctor maybe, has granted "the family" permission to sit as long as we want to with the deceased. So we sit, as expected, with the fragments. Who will be the first to blink? What next? We don't speak, pretending to be contemplating the meaning of life. Praying. I should be praying for my father's soul, but I am praying that Artie stays put.

"They'll steal his clothes. Make sure that you get everything of his out of the cupboard." Adele's first concern is equally practical and offensive. Who is going to want the old man's underwear? He arrived without shoes. I want to scream at Adele, tell her to leave it all here. It's useless. Better for to it disappear than have someone take it to Goodwill. But I don't. I get up and squeeze around Paul to open the cupboard, where a blue bag hangs, containing the pitiful pajama bottoms and socks in which my father left his house for the last time. It smells.

"Can you take Adele home?" An hour has slipped by, a precious hour. If I can get on the road now, I can be back by early evening. There is nothing to be done now. The undertaker will be in soon to take the remains once we vacate the room. Adele is Paul's mother; let him deal with her. Tomorrow, we will make the arrangements. Today, I can find Mack. They won't miss me.

"Where are you going?" He is incredulous that I'd bolt now. I'm a little incredulous myself, but there's nothing I can do here, and I'm mere hours away from reclaiming my dog. If I miss this chance, I may never have another one. It's colossally bad timing, I know, but I can't help it. There's no way I'm not going to try to catch Artie.

I don't answer Paul's understandable question; it would be too hard to explain. "Please, it's important."

Finally, he nods, and I run out the door. As soon as I get to the car, I feel like the weight of darkness in my life is beginning to lighten. I am suddenly free, and if this wasn't Adele's car, I am not certain that I would turn around and come back once I find Artie and, God willing, Mack.

CHAPTER 35

"Is Andy going to be my father?" Tony is leaning into the doorway of my bedroom. He's ten years old but has the world-weary look of a thirty-year-old whose plans haven't panned out. Andy has left, dragging himself out of bed to get to work on time. He's a framer, and his day on the job starts early. We've been together for a few months, maybe half a year, and Tony likes him. He likes it when Andy pays attention to him. Maybe because Andy is still a boy himself. He's younger than I am, by a couple of years, and his sense of play hasn't been squashed entirely. Andy hooked up a PlayStation to my TV and he and Tony play for at least an hour every time Andy comes, which is getting to be more and more often. The sleeping-over part has commenced and the next step will be to move some of his stuff into my house.

I don't know how to answer Tony. This isn't the first time that he's asked that question. He asked it about Mark, and about Teddy, two guys I dated fairly seriously when Tony was much younger. Since then, he hasn't *paid much attention to my boyfriends, so asking about Andy is a big deal to me. I like Andy and have a good feeling about this one. Still, Andy hasn't been making any sounds of commitment.*

"I don't know, honey."

You are never truly separate from an ex; despite distance and years, you are still connected if you have a child. Even though Anthony willingly let us go, over the past few years he's taken to calling us and adding more money to the child support, even though I've never asked. He's even visited Tony twice, taking him out to dinner and letting him pick out some desirable new toy. I'm ambivalent about this contact; he's not exactly a presence in the boy's life, just an interruption. Tony doesn't call him "Dad." He doesn't call Anthony anything anymore. Long ago, he stopped asking when Daddy was going to come. Now he takes Anthony's phone calls and mumbles replies. I can't tell if there's some resentment Tony has toward his father, which would be understandable, or if it's simply that the man is more of a stranger to him than, say, Andy is at the moment. Which makes me smile. "Would you like him to be?"

Tony pushes himself away from the door frame. "No. I'm just wondering when he's going to leave."

"Why would you wonder that?"

"Because they all do."

I get a call from the school. Tony has been in a fight. I leave work to get my bruised son, mother bear furious at the other kid.

"Ms. Meade, Tony admits to starting it." *The teacher, Miss Fletcher, folds her arms across her chest and turns a teacherly scowl at me and my son.* "Tony can be very provoking. It's not the first time he's done this."

"Is this true?" I squat to face Tony. "That you started the fight?"

"Maybe."

"Why?"

"Dunno."

He is awfully young to be so sullen. "Tony, why did you fight with him?"

"'Cause I didn't like the way he looked at me."

The big-haired Dallas debutante teacher pipes in, as if she knows my son better than I do. "That's not a reason, and you know that, young man. Actions have consequences."

"I'll handle my own son, if you don't mind. I'm sure there was a reason he got mad. People get mad."

"People get angry, but even a child knows better than to throw punches. We use our words. We discuss our issues."

I take Tony by the hand and walk out of that classroom and out of that school.

We left Dallas and headed for Los Angeles. I had a friend we could stay with till I found a new job. Tony would start at a new school and get a fresh start, make some new friends, have another chance. Andy was gone anyway, the romance evaporating in direct contrast to my desire to move on to the next phase of the relationship. Apparently, Andy got cold feet at the thought of living with me and a ten-year-old.

I shoot up Route 24. After a clot of traffic breaks up around the Silver City Galleria, it's clear sailing to the 495 West exit. Four ninety-five opens like a smooth pathway for me; even the inevitable road construction doesn't slow me down appreciably. I feel like I'm flying. A look at the speedometer and I realize that, actually, I am. I slow it down from eighty to a more reasonable seventy-five and hope that no cop in the area will believe that a dull brown Chevy is doing ten over the speed limit. I am prepared to cry if stopped. I'm prepared to convince any trooper who might stop me that he should give me an escort all the way to Worcester—sirens blaring and lights flashing, letting everyone know they need to make way for an outraged woman.

I fluctuate between believing that Artie has kept Mack with him all this time and dread that he has no idea where the dog might be.

In what feels like a lifetime, I haven't allowed myself to think about not recovering Mack. I won't think about life without him. I will go to the ends of the earth to find him. Too many others in my life have chosen to live without me; I will not choose to live without Mack. Not when there's the slightest hope.

Mack and I are performing during the lull before best in show is judged at a benched show in Portland, Oregon. It is by far the biggest event we've been to. Saundra and some of the other members of our freestyle club are here and have already performed. Mack and I are going to premier our newest dance, choreographed to the Beatles' "Help." It is a change from "Puttin' on the Ritz" and has lots of new moves.

I come out by myself, pretending to be a lonely woman. Once the lyrics reach the words "but now I'm not so self-assured," Mack comes dashing out of the wings, prancing around me, pulling playfully at my pant legs, and leaping into the air to bounce over my bent back, portraying someone trying to cheer a friend out of a funk. It is a showy piece, featuring his high-jumping abilities and comedic skill.

The crowd loves it. Suddenly, Mack comes down a little hard on one leap. For one brief, horrible moment, I think he's injured. But within a second, Mack shakes off the pain and is watching my every signal. For first time, I wonder how long we'll be able to continue these performances. There will come a day when he'll be too old to do it. We'll have to retire. At my subtle command, my dog—my partner—rises on his hind legs and pirouettes around me in perfect clockwise rotation, a little furry ballerina. I relax. It will be a long time before we stop dancing, and only when Mack tells me he wants to.

I touch my mouth with the memory of Mack's happy jumps. I miss him so much. In my life, he is the only one who hasn't let me down.

Los Angeles was pretty good for a while. I had a nice job at a health-care center, where I did patient intake. I liked it, a first for me. Tony entered junior high there. He seemed to like school, had a few friends he hung around with, boys from around the neighborhood where I had found us a small place to rent, a neighborhood that edged up close to South L.A.

"Mrs. Meade, we found your son with three other boys and a bottle of vodka." The principal is a burly guy, Hispanic, and fighting hard to keep an unruly school population in check. He uses the words *"zero tolerance"* like a cudgel. My pubescent boy is being suspended.

"It's Ms., not Mrs. What am I supposed to do?"

"He'll have to keep up with his schoolwork. His teachers will give you what you need."

"I mean, what do I do to prevent this from happening again?"

Mr. Chavez just looks at me, a flicker of something that might be sympathy in his eyes. "Keep him away from those boys, first. Second, keep him busy. Third, you might want to see about counseling. I wish I could say that this is a boyish experiment, but there have been other incidents, as you know."

I do know. The fights, the inappropriate language, getting caught smoking in the boys' lav; the bad grades, which weren't a result of not understanding the material, but of failing to do the homework. It's overwhelming. I have to work; I can't be on him every second. Besides, that never worked for me, so why would it work for Tony? He's my baby, my only family, and lately he's become a stranger to me. Secretive, rude. I feel the tears working their way into my eyes, but I won't let them come. "I'll take care of it."

I've reached the MassPike and I am impatient as the tollbooth attendant languidly passes out tickets to the five cars ahead of me. I wish that the car had a Fast-Lane transponder so that I wouldn't have to stop again, just glide through the exit at Worcester and catch up to Artie. Immediately after getting on the Pike, I pull off at the Westboro service center to pee and to call the truck-repair place. I'll ask them to keep Artie there. Bladder empty, phone in hand, I am ready to confront Artie Schmidt.

As soon as I punch in the telephone number that Troy has given me, I suddenly wonder if this is a good idea. I'd like to know if Artie's still there, but what if they

tip him off that I'm coming and he bolts? In the end, I
snap my phone shut. A quick study of the napkin with
the scrawled directions and I'm fairly confident that I can
find A-1 Truck Service. It's just off Exit 11. Bang a right,
a left, and then take the next right. It's bound to be easy,
so that all these big rigs can locate it without any trouble;
there's probably one of those huge signs visible from the
highway. On the road, I dig out the money needed for the
toll and drive with it gripped in one hand. I can't waste
any more time.

We left California when Tony was thirteen, ending up
in Kanab, Utah, on the promise of a hotel manager's job
in what turned out to be a seedy, run-down motel on the
main drag. The first thing I did was to move us out of
the manager's pitiful accommodations and into an apartment. In all our moving around, this was by far the nic-
est place we'd ever lived. Instead of renting a furnished
place, I found an empty two-bedroom apartment on the
third floor of a Victorian house complete with ginger-
bread and a circular turret. The bulge of that turret was
our living room and we looked out toward the mountains
that rose like protection around us. I slowly filled the
place with secondhand but decent furniture, some of it
donated by our landlords.

Marta and Henry Sanchez were the grandparents
Tony had never had. He spent more time in their kitchen
than in ours, sampling Marta's cooking—tamales, chi-
michangas, homemade red and green sauces. We spent
Thanksgiving with them, and popped in for Christmas
Eve eggnog. Henry taught Tony how to drive a nail and
change the oil in a car. Marta simply loved him.

It wasn't the job of my dreams, but moving to Kanab

put the brakes on Tony's bad behavior. Maybe time would have done that, but Kanab and the Sanchez couple were good for him.

Things went much better in Kanab, until I had an offer I couldn't turn down.

CHAPTER 36

"You should have seen him. Arabella thinks that he can get his therapy dog certification in four weeks. He's a natural." Alice is gushing and she knows it, but this half hour of dog training has pumped her up. She drapes the leash over the peg beside the back door.

"Well, we know he's a smart boy." Ed is scrambling Buddy's fur with both hands, all the way up and down the dog's body. Loose hair floats into the air, but Alice doesn't mind.

"Once he has that, we can take him to the nursing home a couple of times a week. The residents love having animals come because it makes them feel at home and not so alone."

"You can practice on your mother." Ed has finished mussing up the dog's coat. Buddy has flopped onto the floor beside Ed's chair. "She'll love that." He suddenly realizes that Alice has said "we."

"Not a bad idea." Alice drops into a kitchen chair,

runs a hand along a spray of loose hair, and tucks it into her twist. "How about a cup of tea?"

"Sounds good." He's still pondering her use of the plural pronoun. Alice hasn't included him in anything more than obligatory family gatherings in years. Slip or significant?

Alice leans across the table. "I think that this is going to be a good thing. Having Buddy is a good thing."

Ed reaches across the table and extracts one of Alice's hands. "I'm glad we decided to keep him."

Alice keeps her hand in Ed's, squeezing his fingers a little. Significant.

Buddy slowly rolls over onto his back, stretching his forelegs and hind legs in opposite directions, so that he looks elongated. He doesn't wriggle, but lies still, flat on his back. He lifts his head, looks at them, as if to make sure they notice, and then flops back, all crocodile sunbathing in the Nile.

"I think he wants a belly rub." Alice takes her hand away from Ed.

Ed slides off his worn slipper and starts rubbing the dog's exposed belly with his toes. The dog wriggles with pleasure. "So, do you want to walk him over to your mother's in a bit, let him practice his therapy?" He is warm from the experience of holding Alice's hand, an action so out of character that he is nearly embarrassed. His wanting to take it, and the equally surprising fact that she let him, has infused Ed like a tea bag in hot water. Not a sexual response, but a thawing. Ed keeps rubbing Buddy's belly, keeps his eyes on the dog, but he is acutely aware of Alice in the room, the soft squeak of her sneakers on the kitchen floor, the opening of the refrigerator door. It's almost like someone from his past is visiting. Ed shakes off the notion. It's just Alice.

Alice leans over Ed to place a mug of tea in front of him. As she does, Ed recognizes the visitor. It is cheer. Alice is relaxed and cheerful. Her dark shadow is, for a little while, gone. Buddy stands up and shakes, tap-dances a little. Ed contemplates the tea bag in his mug. Alice sits down, pushes a plate of Pepperidge Farm cookies toward him. She's still talking about the dog class. She's repeating herself, going on about Buddy's cleverness, aptitude.

Ed looks up from his mug and smiles at his wife. She is beautiful.

The dog sits; then, having realized that the people are going to stay put in the same room for a little while, he gets up and goes into the living room to jump up on the couch. Ed dunks his tea bag and then drops it back into the mug. "Buddy, come here."

The dog bounds into the kitchen, fully ready to take on whatever challenge or treat Ed is thinking of.

"Sit."

Buddy does.

"What's the command?"

"Arabella asks for 'greet.'"

Ed taps Alice's knee. "Buddy, greet."

Buddy rests his head on Alice's knee, raises his eyes to her face. Ed watches—not the dog, but the woman. There it is. The look that has eluded him for seven years. The look on Alice's face that means she's moving ahead. Not happiness—neither one of them is allowed that again—but some measure of contentment.

"Good boy." Ed lifts the dog into his arms and buries his face in his ruff. "Good boy."

This new work is fun, but certainly not demanding. The woman Alice calls Arabella clearly understands about command and patience. But all of the commands are puppy commands: sit, stay, down. Buddy/Mack executes them in an offhand manner and then looks at Alice for a more challenging set of commands. Then there is something new—well, not new, but a variation on a puppy task. Sit quietly with chin on knee. No sniffing, no licking, no wriggling. The old person they are asking him to do this with gently strokes him on the head. So, big deal. When are they going to let him leap or spin, even climb up the ramp he sees in the corner of the small yard? Buddy/Mack feels like a professional being asked to begin over at the elementary level. He sighs, adds a little variation of his own. One little white paw extends and joins his chin on the old person's knee. The people around him seemed pleased with that. He lifts his eyes to the face of the old person, sets his ears back in passive greeting. Everyone pets him. "Good boy!" they say.

Alice is clearly pleased with him and praises him for ordinary behavior all the way home. The unhappiness that she had emanated earlier is gone and she is singing along with the radio. In the dog's eyes, Alice is lighter.

It's nice to be in partnership again with someone. But if this primary training is the limit of what Alice wants to do with him, he's disappointed. He's already shown her how to dance; why doesn't she want to do that? For such a simple act, which he would do without command, Buddy/Mack is given the kind of praise that only Justine has ever given him. Not the praise of food, or "Attaboy," but the praise of connection.

Ed has signaled that he is ready to partner up. Hanging out with him isn't the same thing as partnering. Ed has been a good host, but now it feels like he's ready to connect. Alice has long since done that, so it is nice to think that if Ed is equally on board, Buddy/Mack may find it easier to get the two of them into the same room. Already they're in the kitchen together for a longer period of time than to eat, and together they took him to an older person's home to work on his "greet" skills. Sweet. They are doing more tongue language that isn't directed at him, although he hears this word *Buddy* frequently enough that he knows they are talking about him. He likes the sound of Ed's soft, rumbly voice, which he has been using at night when they climb into the bed. Alice doesn't always talk then, but sometimes she sighs or laughs in response to something Ed has said. Last night, they invited him into the bed. He burrowed into the space between them, feeling the double weight of their arms over him. It was nice to be invited, but he only stayed till they slept. He heads back into the living room to stretch out on the couch—the better to keep an ear out for trespassers.

Buddy/Mack knows that he is no longer a guest. He is now responsible for the safety of this place.

He is their Buddy.

CHAPTER 37

Jen Coulter is at the door, a basket of late-season vegetables over one arm, a bottle of wine in the other. "I can't stand any more squash. You have to eat these or throw them out when I'm not looking." She puts the basket on the counter beside the sink and hands Alice the bottle of wine. "Somebody at work gave Derek a ticket to the Sox, so he's in Boston and won't be home till midnight. Thought we could both use a little company."

Jen knows that Ed's out tonight at the semimonthly zoning board meeting, vainly attempting to preserve the rules without giving into the variances that are beginning to change the face of their town. Jen is young enough to think that Alice would prefer company over a solitary evening at home watching her favorite shows without argument. The new television season is about to begin and she was really looking forward to it. Alice smiles at Jen and takes the bottle of wine, wishing that she had one of those DVR things that would allow her to stop time.

"Have you looked at the YouTube clip yet?"

Alice is hunting down the corkscrew. "What YouTube clip?"

"Of you and the dog dancing. Derek posted it on the Internet. All of our friends are raving about it and it's gone viral."

Alice finds the corkscrew and brings down two wineglasses. "So you're saying that the whole world can watch me being foolish."

Jen takes the opener, digs the tip of the screw into the soft cork of the bottle, drawing it out with a soft pop. "It's not foolish; it's great. Pour us some wine and then we can go look at it on your computer."

"I'm not sure I like the idea of being on the Web."

Jen just laughs, as if Alice is hopelessly naïve. Sometimes Jen feels like a peer, and at other times, like right now, Alice feels the generation gap and remembers that she's old enough to be Jen's mother. More than old enough. Jen's mom and she are exactly the same age. If she'd had Stacy earlier, Stacy would have been Jen's friend, not her charge. One of the maybes that tortured Alice was the fact that she was forty when Stacy was born. Just as Stacy entered a very difficult adolescence, she'd reached menopause. Ed called it "menopause meets puberty—clash of the hormones," but the strength, patience, and flexibility Stacy had needed was subsumed by hot flashes and irritation. Maybe if she hadn't felt so edgy and overwhelmed by her own physical changes, she would have been more aware of Stacy's own difficulties. Difficulties that weren't obvious to the naked eye, beyond her physical changes. Taller, but not tall; built like a soccer player, then suddenly thin as a reed. Silent, not quiet. A new tendency to insomnia.

* * *

"Jen's a nurse, Alice. She knows what she's talking about." Ed paces in front of her. It is a beautiful Saturday afternoon and Stacy is in her bedroom, the door shut, not even the sound of music leaking out from under the locked door. Sleeping, or crying—they can't tell which. *"She thinks that we should take her to someone who can help figure out why she's so unhappy."*

"She's a kid, Ed. An adolescent. They invented angst." Another hot flash is beginning to rise up out of her core, flushing her cheeks and making her want to throw off her clothes and run out into the chill March air.

"This is different and you know it." This is classic Ed, the authority, the knower of all things. The insister.

"See, here it is." Jen has booted up their PC and signed into her YouTube account.

Alice watches herself and Buddy dance right there on the little screen. He looks so happy, and his soft grey-and-white coat with its wash of black sparkles in the floodlights of their deck. Derek had even gotten a good shot of Buddy's odd blue and brown eyes. The dog pirouettes, dips, and bows. Alice is charmed, and pleased that she doesn't look entirely foolish. She actually looks fairly good. The clip lasts little more than a minute, so they play it again.

"Let's get you set up with your own account and then you can look at this anytime. We posted it so anyone can see it. Just search for 'dancing dog.' There are a lot of them—you wouldn't believe it—but his is popping up almost at the top. You can save it to your account."

"Ed will love this." Alice sips at her glass of wine and replays the video one more time. The Beatles music is going to be stuck in her head for hours, but it's such fun watching the dog's antics. Jen is right; there is a whole strip of thumbnails offering dog-dancing videos. The still photo in one of them even looks like Buddy, except that he's wearing a little black bow tie.

Alice lets Jen set up the account. Maybe tonight, if Ed doesn't get home too late, she'll play it for him.

CHAPTER 38

It's almost like a noir movie. There's been an accident, and two miles from the Westboro plaza the cars are stopped dead in the water. Or maybe it's road construction. Whatever it is, I crawl along the center lane like a wounded ant. My heart is pumping as if I'm running a half marathon, but the speedometer reads fifteen miles per hour/ten miles/five miles/fifteen miles per hour. I begin to worry that Adele's car might overheat. God only knows the last time it was serviced.

I feel the panic rise in my throat in the same way a nightmare about being late or not finding a door or running away from something bad will choke you until you wake up and realize it's only a dream. Except that this isn't only a dream. Every inch I crawl along the MassPike is one inch closer to Artie. But it's only an inch and time is going by. I'm already at least a half hour later than I hoped to be. I had hoped to be standing in front of Artie this very minute. How long before his truck is fixed and he's back on the road? How late is A-1 Truck Service open?

It's already past four. I should be there. I could be mere miles away from getting Mack back and still miss him because of this mess.

This is torture. I am running in molasses; every step of the way is barricaded or delayed, thwarted. I feel like God is laughing at me. Or maybe mad at me. Is this some kind of divine retribution for loving a dog more than almost any human? For running out on Adele and Paul; for leaving an hour after my father has died?

I'm going slowly enough that I consider hitting that call button. The number for A-1 is still on the screen. One push and I can reach them and ask if Artie is still there, beg them not to tell him I'm coming. Appeal to the stranger on the other end of the line, saying that they need to keep Artie where he is. Strangers have been helping me all along—Mitch, Tyler the car-rental kid, Troy. I just need one more savior. Then, for no apparent reason, the traffic picks up and I'm back up to seventy-five.

The one blessing is that the A-1 Truck Service center is easy to find. Detached rigs fill the parking lot, and the noise coming from the three monumental bays is deafening with the roar of diesel engines being gunned. I squeeze Adele's car between two trucks like a slice of ham between bulky rolls. I leave everything in the car except the keys, which I pocket. I want my hands free. I take a quick look around the parking lot of waiting behemoths and don't spot Artie's truck. I don't know whether this is good or bad, but it leaves me with one last hope that one of the rigs currently occupying the garage has to be his.

I walk slowly past the open doors. A sleek black truck is in the first bay. A dented red dump truck is in the second. The third bay contains a green rig with its hood

yawning open. I have only to walk in to be able to read
the lettering on the door. I can see the Washington State
tag on the front. I walk in, ignoring the sign forbidding
anyone but personnel to enter. Arthur B. Schmidt Trucking. I quickly jump up on the running board and haul the
door open, squeezing my eyes shut in a frantic prayer.

The cab is empty. No Mack. I even call his name,
but I know even before opening the door that he's not
in there. If he was anywhere around, I'd hear his joyful
bark. He'd know instantly that I was here. That I'd finally
found him.

I am suddenly very thirsty, parched. My tongue sticks
to the roof of my mouth. Confrontation does this to me. I
am going to kill Artie Schmidt.

"Can I help you?" The voice is clearly annoyed at
finding an interloper in his secure manly space. I turn to
face a barrel-chested guy in a smoke-gray uniform with
the name Al stitched over the A-1 emblem. There is a line
of grease on his face that makes me think of war paint.

"I'm looking for the owner of this truck." I shut the
door and place a hand on the fender, as if I think this guy
won't understand which truck I'm talking about.

"He's in the lounge. Over there." The mechanic jabs a
finger toward a glass wall. I can see the backs of heads as
the room's three occupants sit in a line of chairs facing a
big-screen TV that's tuned to ESPN. There's a baseball
game on. I think it's clever that A-1 faces its customers
away from watching what's happening with their trucks,
mesmerizing them with the lure of big heads on bigger
screens. Each one of the lounge sitters wears a cap. They
sit apart, like strangers in an airport, one or two chairs
between them. From behind, I can't tell which one is
Artie.

"Thank you." I start toward the glass wall.

"You get in through the office." Al nods at a metal door at the far end of the garage.

I feel his eyes on me as I walk to the door. I throw a little sashay into my walk. I might need this guy if Artie gets nasty.

I have imagined this moment for a week. I have pictured myself grabbing Artie by his filthy shirt and shaking him like Mack shakes a rag doll. I've pictured myself screaming at him, calling him foul names, even slugging him. I've imagined him defiant, aggressive. What I haven't pictured is the sheer surprise on his pug face when I suddenly reappear in his life. The entrance to the lounge puts me exactly in his sight line. At first, he looks at me as men often do, with that "Well, well, what have we here?" look of a man who has no idea how unattractive he is. Then he recognizes me. Then his expression drains from recognition to realization. Here in the flesh is the woman he abandoned on an Ohio highway, the woman whose dog he stole. Artie looks right and left at the two guys in the room with him, as if looking for back up in a shoot-out at the O.K. Corral. They are also looking at me, but their interest fades as something important happens on the muted television. They cheer, throwing themselves out of the plastic chairs. Artie and I face each other.

"Hello, Artie."

"Justine. Hi. How are you?" Artie sweeps off his gimme cap and squeezes it between his hands. I feel like I'm looking at an actor portraying an embarrassed man. But Artie's color deepens, going from his normal gray pallor to the color of meat that's gone bad.

"Where is my dog?" I have gone from sweating with anxiety to feeling ice-cold. The room, even on this September day, is air-conditioned. But it's more than that; I am solid with the ice of fear, fear that he's about to say something that will wreck me.

Behind me, the silent television no longer holds the interest of the other two men. Suddenly, Artie and I are of interest.

"How'd you find me?"

"Where is Mack? Just tell me."

"Tell her, man. What'd you do?" These two strangers get off their chairs and flank Artie. I manage a grateful smile at both of them, a nod to their chivalry.

"I don't know. I don't know where he is. He, uh, ran away." Artie keeps looking behind me, as if I might have a Hell's Angel tagging along.

These two strangers, one a little older than a boy, the other a man old enough to be my father, step closer to Artie.

"That's crap, Artie, and you know it. What have you done with my dog?"

"You're the guy, the guy who ditched a woman and stole her dog." The younger guy points a finger at Artie. He looks back at me, looking for confirmation. "Is he?"

I'm surprised beyond words to hear my story come out of the mouth of a stranger. Then I get it. "Yes, this is Rockin' Roadie." My story has been traveling from CB to CB all around the state.

"What'd you do with her dog?" The older trucker drops a meaty hand on Artie's shoulder, clenches his fist, and Artie winces like the victim of a Vulcan pinch.

"Get off me; I'll have you arrested for assault." Artie squirms, but the big guy doesn't let go.

"Where's the dog?"

It seems like such a simple question. But Artie is clearly unwilling or incapable of answering it. If I wasn't so angry, I could almost feel sorry for him as the guy continues to trap him between his fingers. When tears actually come to Artie's eyes, I call him off. "Enough, please. It's okay. Let him go."

The older man drops his hand reluctantly, clearly not pleased to be stopped. He has the look of a dad whose daughter's boyfriend has broken her heart. A man bent on exacting payment.

Artie grabs his shoulder and rubs it. "Look, I don't know where he ended up, but I left him near Exit Eight—eastbound."

"Oh my God, you left him on the side of the MassPike?" The ice unblocks from my veins and the heat of despair causes me to break out in a sweat. How would my dog survive that? A loose animal on that major highway is doomed. Driving here today, I have seen the carcasses littering the shoulder—raccoons, a fox, lost pets. I can't breathe.

"You shit for brains. Why'd you do something like that?" The younger guy raises his fists but doesn't step any closer to Artie.

Artie fixes his eyes on me, all indignant. "Your goon threatened me. If the dog wasn't with me, they couldn't prove anything."

"They who?"

"You know." Artie drops his voice to a whisper. "The Hell's Angels."

"If you'd answered your phone even once when I was trying to reach you, he wouldn't have had to threaten you." Clearly Mitch's voice-mail message had an effect.

"I didn't know I had the dog. Honest. When I finally saw him, we were already into Massachusetts. What was I going to do? Turn around? I had a delivery." Artie slaps his cap back on his head. He looks at the other two truckers for understanding, for sympathy, or empathy, or whichever one it is that will make him feel like he didn't do a stupid, cruel thing. He gets nothing.

"You fuckin' left a woman alone at a rest stop and then think it's okay to toss a dog out onto a highway?" Young Trucker is up in Artie's face now and Old Trucker does nothing to back him off. I am so weak at the knees, I sink onto one of the orange plastic chairs. I put my head between my legs. I am either going to pass out or throw up.

"What are you going to say to this lady? Huh? What have you got to say, mister?" Young Trucker takes on the school bully persona that is at odds with a rather baby face. He's probably had to kick ass more than once to prove his masculinity. He jabs Artie in the chest with a slim, clean finger. Old Trucker stands behind Artie so that he can't back away.

I need to stop this. "Thanks, both of you. He's told me enough. There's nothing else he can say." I really don't care if this kid beats the crap out of Artie; I just need to think for a few minutes. Neither one of them backs down. I can nearly smell the testosterone emanating from two guys who see a chance to blow off some steam.

"What kind of asshole are you to ditch this woman and dump her dog?" Clearly, Artie hasn't answered this question to the satisfaction of Young Trucker.

"She was making me late. You know what that's like, keeping to schedule. And I didn't know her goddamned dog was in the backseat—where he didn't belong." Artie raises his own finger now, waving it in the kid's face.

"Arthur Schmidt? Your truck's ready." Al's sudden appearance at the doorway to the lounge snaps all of us out of the drama.

Both of my knights step away from Artie, letting him take the invoice out of Al's hand. Al looks at all of us, shrugs, and leaves the lounge. As long as Artie pays his bill, it's nothing to Al if three strangers gang up on him.

Old Trucker is still behind Artie and now he leans in so that his mouth is next to Artie's right ear. "What are you going to do to make this right?"

"What can I do? I don't know where her frickin' dog is. What am I supposed to do?"

Old Trucker smacks Artie against the back of his head, tipping his dirty cap forward. "Apologize, you shitwad."

I could almost laugh. Almost. The look on Artie's face is priceless, but it isn't the price I want him to pay. For what he's done to me, there is no price. Apologizing can't bring Mack back to me. And I highly doubt that Artie has the capability of apologizing with any sincerity, or any true sense of being in the wrong.

Nonetheless, Artie pulls his cap off his head and nods. "Justine, I am truly sorry for leaving you behind. But you—" Another smack from Old Trucker stops his feeble attempt to pin the blame on me. "I'm sorry."

"I don't care that you left me behind. I do care that you were so cruel to my dog. An innocent animal. Why didn't you—" This time I'm cut off.

"There weren't a lot of choices out there. If I'd missed my deadline again, that would be the last time my agent was gonna get me work. It was my last chance."

"Then why not just hang on to him? Take him to Boston with you. Make your deadline. Then call me to come get him." I am suddenly gasping for breath, as if I have asthma. "Why didn't you just answer the phone and we could have straightened this all out?"

Artie squeezes the bill of his cap and then replaces it on his head. "Didn't think of it. I have to go. See you around."

He almost gets away, but one look from me and my two new friends block his way. "Is there something you'd like us to do, ma'am?" The older guy meets my eye; then the pair of them take Artie by either arm. We all look through the glass to the garage to make sure we're unobserved.

"I can do it myself." I punch Artie in the gut with all the force of my anger and grief for my dog. The two let go and he drops to his knees.

"One thing's for certain, Artie Schmidt. Don't you ever show your face in Candy's Place ever again."

Artie leans on one of the plastic chairs to get to his feet. This time, Old Trucker and Young Trucker let Artie leave the room. They drift back to watching the ball game and I stand at the glass wall, watching as Artie makes it back to his truck. Then I remember something. I race back to the bay.

"Wait." I run to the right side of the truck and swing open the door, climbing up on the running board to get inside. I find what I'm looking for easily. Mack's collar is caught in my sleeping bag. I retrieve my last connection to Mack. The feel of his leather collar in my hand pushes a new surge of anger and despair through me. My dog was abandoned on the highway.

Artie has climbed into his seat and is staring at me, as if he half-expects I'm going to stay in the cab.

"You never fulfilled your promise. You took my money and dropped me. The way I see it, you got me only halfway to where I was going, so you should give me back half the money."

"You know I don't have it, or didn't you just see me pay Al?"

I don't have my knights with me, so I end negotiations. "You are a piece of work. Get out of my sight."

I stand aside as Artie guns the big engine and laboriously emerges from the open bay. Cranking through the gears, he makes his way to the exit and pulls away.

I need to get back on the road. Paul and Adele will be gnashing their teeth at my absence. I'm sure they'll want her car back sooner rather than later. But there is something else I need to do. Before I pull out from between the rigs, I call Tony. He's never met this grandfather, but he needs to know that he's lost one.

Typically, his phone goes to voice mail. Is this the kind of message you leave on voice mail? In this case, it is. "Tony, your grandfather died today. Peacefully, I think. I don't know the plans yet, but I guess I'll be heading home soon."

I should point this car west. But I don't have my duffel, and I don't relish being accused of being a car thief. I find the eastbound Pike entrance and collect my ticket. Even before I reach sixty-five miles per hour, I have to pull over onto the shoulder. Cars whiz by me and Adele's car is shaken by the backwash of a semi like a mini earthquake. How in God's name could Mack have survived this?

I am awash in tears, snot runs down my nose, and I bury my head in my arms, hoping that no well-meaning Samaritan knocks on my window. What would I say? As a human being, I should say that I'm crying for my father, for his merciful death. But I'm not weeping for that. I am weeping for Mack, for his loss, for imaging the worst death right here on this road.

The car rocks violently with the rush of traffic. I have no tissue and I'm reduced to using my sleeve to wipe up the mess. I fumble in Adele's glove compartment and find some Kleenex. I am choking on the fear that my dancing dog is dancing in heaven.

CHAPTER 39

Alice paces past the breakfront cupboard with the old videotapes, waiting for Ed to get home, impatient. She can't wait to show Ed the YouTube video of Buddy and her dancing. His meeting seems to be taking a long time, or maybe it's always this late and she's never been awake to notice. She knows that sometimes he goes out with one of the other board members for a quick beer. He never used to do that, back when he was working, but now, without an early get-up, he can. He creeps in as if he won't disturb her if he's tiptoeing, which, of course, only disturbs her more. He tries so hard not disturb her, awake or asleep.

In the little video, Derek has caught Ed watching her dance with the dog. His expression is so unguarded, so full of the laughter that they never seem to enjoy with each other anymore. This dog has made them both laugh.

Jen has gone home, leaving the squash on Alice's counter. Buddy, after having escorted Jen to the door like a polite host, curled up on the couch, looking at her with one eye, as if to say, *Come sit with me*. Alice did and flipped on the television just in time to catch the end of her program. Now the news is on and she watches the murder and mayhem channel with scant attention.

Suddenly, Buddy's head goes up, moments before Alice hears the garage door rumble open. He jumps down and stretches, bowing deeply, his tail swishing over his back. He goes to the stairs leading to the basement level and sits, waiting for Ed to appear. Alice stands behind him, one hand tucking loose strands of hair up into her knot.

Ed comes up the stairs quietly, head down, shoes off. He looks tired, Alice thinks. It must have been a tough meeting. Buddy runs down the stairs to meet him, and Ed, not seeing her there, bends to accept the dog's greeting, muttering soft words into Buddy's ears. The weariness lifts. Is there no greeting more perfect than that of man and dog?

Then he looks up and sees her standing there. "Oh, I didn't expect you to still be up." Maybe there is a more perfect greeting—that of man to wife after a hard meeting. Ed swoops the dog into his arms and comes up the short flight of steps, then second-guesses his pleasure in seeing her waiting up for him. "Is there something wrong?"

"No. No. I have something to show you." Alice feels like a kid, wanting to show a parent a new trick. *Look what I can do.* Like Stacy learning to ride her bike, or maybe more like when she learned to whistle.

They sit side by side in front of the computer. Alice logs on to her brand-new account and asks for "dancing dog" in the search bar. "Watch this." They wait while the array of dog-dancing clips load. There's Buddy, a little triangle placed over his body for her to click on. "Jen's so smart with these things. But, really, it isn't hard. Now watch."

The tiny square opens up to reveal their dog bowing and crawling, leaping and pirouetting. Dancing for all he's worth, his open mouth so much like he's smiling, keeping uncanny time to the Beatles' music.

Ed and Alice sit still. He's dancing to "Help"; he's dancing with someone else.

"That's not Buddy." Ed pushes away from the computer. "Obviously similar, but not our dog. Where's the clip with our dog?"

"I'm sorry, I thought it would be the first one." Alice slides the cursor down the array and finds the one she knows is theirs. "I guess he's not the only Sheltie who likes to dance."

"Some coincidence." Ed has his hand on Buddy's head, cupping the narrow skull with his whole hand. "Just find the right one. I'm beat."

This time Alice has the right clip. She plays it twice for them and they both laugh where they should at the sight of Alice and Buddy performing their impromptu pas de deux, but underneath the enjoyment is the thought of another dog, so similar, doing the same thing.

"That's wonderful. Really neat." He logs out of the program and shuts down the computer. "Well, time for this one to go out."

Alone in the third bedroom, still in front of the computer, Alice hears the slider open as they go outside. She worries that Ed won't have leashed Buddy. She worries that he'll dash off after some night creature and disappear. In a moment, she hears the slider open, listens to Ed talking to Buddy and the distinct sound of the clip end of the leash banging against the wall as Ed hangs it up. She lets out the breath she's been holding.

CHAPTER 40

Alice is at the library and Ed is left at home. It's rain-
ing, which is a good thing, as it's been a very dry month
so far. Still, it keeps him inside, bumbling around the
house, looking for a task that will occupy him. He wants
to get back to wire-brushing the cemetery gates, but that
will have to wait. Buddy patiently follows Ed around the
house: down into the basement to get a screwdriver, back
upstairs to fiddle with the loose doorknob, back down
into the garage to pull a fresh box of crackers out of the
Costco closet, upstairs to make lunch, then into the third
bedroom, where the computer lives.

Ed boots it up and finds YouTube on the Web. He
doesn't even log on to Alice's new account, just types
in "dog dancing," and public videos crop up, a long line
of "dancing" titles, including theirs: "Dog Dancing with
Buddy." Ed is annoyed at Jen for not safeguarding their
privacy and keeping this one-and-a-half-minute clip in-
accessible. The nerve. These kids nowadays think that
everything should be out there, available to all. The fact

that it pops up almost at the top just means that more people will see it. But Ed isn't looking for Buddy's clip. He scrolls down slowly until he comes to the image of the other Sheltie.

The light from the monitor glows like a lamp in the rain-gloomy room. This is a neutral space. A bed is set up for the rare overnight visitor, but otherwise it serves, as it always has done, as a sewing room, a computer room, a room where they keep off-season clothing in the good-size closet. North-facing, it is never as bright as the other bedrooms. Because they have this room, they never had to change a thing in Stacy's room. All the bits and pieces that belonged to her that had drifted into other parts of the house have long since been moved back to her room. The torn athletic shorts, now mended, are in the bureau drawer. All the tiny patterns Alice used to make toddler clothes and the remnants of homemade Halloween costumes are all packed away. There is nothing of their daughter in any room except her own.

They called it "depression." A common-enough word. A meteorological word, a financial word. An emotional word. Apparently, a treatable word with the right drugs. Drugs for a child.

Drugs that came with a booklet of contraindications.

Ed clicks on the image of the dog that looks like Buddy. A showy announcer's voice booms, "Introducing Justine Meade and her wonder dog, Maksim." At first, there's only the woman, a tall, lithe-looking woman dressed in a stretchy white suit with sequins sparkling in the lights. The Beatles' familiar song "Help" begins and she mimics loneliness. Suddenly, the dog, her dog, races into the spotlight and teases her into action. He leaps and spins and literally sails up and over her back. At the end, the announcer repeats their names: "Justine Meade of Seattle, Washington, and her Sheltie, Maksim. Good job, Justine and Mack!"

Buddy is sitting behind Ed, looking every bit like he wants to watch this video, too. His ears are on the alert and he keeps his eye on Ed, waiting for some signal, waiting for some action. Ed looks at the still image of the dancing Sheltie. Both of the dog's eyes are visible. Unmistakable.

"Mack?"

Mack hears his name and cocks his head. He knows this word. This is so exciting. Finally, this guy remembers what to call him. Mack jumps to his feet and barks a short, sharp yap, just to say, *Yessss!* Spontaneously, he spins around, pivoting on his back legs. He barks again. *Woohoo!*

Then Ed says something else, using the *Buddy* word this time. Mack doesn't understand what he says, but he hears the grief in the saying of it, which stops his barking and spinning. He flops onto the carpet, down but keeping his eyes on Ed. He's not sure what Ed wants. A good dog, he focuses on the man's face and waits for clarity. For a long moment, nothing happens except that Ed's head is down and his hands are clasped together between his knees.

Suddenly, Ed rolls the desk chair away from the computer table and calls the dog over. Buddy jumps up from his self-imposed down-stay and snuggles up between Ed's knees, happy to have the back scratch, hoping that maybe they'll go someplace. But Ed's touch feels unhappy. Buddy presses himself closer.

When Ed gets up, Buddy follows him out of the spare

room and down the stairs to the garage. Excited, anticipating a ride in the car, Buddy makes a little chortling sound, encouraging Ed to get a move on. Maybe just a quick run to Potter's for jerky, or another ride to Lil's. It doesn't really matter; a ride is just fun. Ed lets Buddy into the Cutlass and the dog assumes his shotgun position, ready to navigate. Ready to do this job that Ed has given him, to be a good passenger and point out squirrels. He swings a look in Ed's direction. *Ready? Let's go!* Finally the rumble of the garage door signals departure. Ed starts the car and backs out of the garage. He hasn't said a word, not the *Buddy* word or the *Mack* one since leaving the spare room, but now Ed begins to talk. Ed uses another word; his monologue is laced with it until Buddy gives up trying to figure out if it's meant as a command or a praise word; a random vocalization or a human word not meant for canine comprehension. *Stacy.* Buddy doesn't know what Ed is saying, but he grasps what he needs to do.

Buddy moves from his shotgun position to the middle of the front seat, scooting his rump over so that it touches Ed's hip. Ed wraps his right arm around the dog. He keeps talking, his voice streaming out a story that even a dog can understand, because he's felt the same way.

Lost.

CHAPTER 41

The rain is slackening off, and Ed kicks the wipers back to intermittent. He has no idea where he's going, a fact that bothers him. He wasn't brought up to do meaning-less things. Every car trip must have a purpose; every man feeds his family. The weight of his unemployment, call it that, a more accurate name for early retirement, feels like shame. Even in the darkest days after Stacy's death, he had his job, his work to retreat into. Retreating from Alice, from her unassailable grief. He grieved, too, but Alice's grief was like a mushroom cloud, obscuring and consuming. He might have believed that she loved her grief. So he worked. He kept his distance. He allowed his own sorrow to form a thick scar of manliness. No one ever asked him how he was doing, patted his hand or his back. The workers in his plant did treat him with a softer deference for a few months, but then they allowed him to master his tragedy.

"So, where're we going, Buddy?" Ed pulls gently on the dog's ear.

The dog sighs, a rattling exhalation. He seems to sense Ed's distress and leans against him as if to help shoulder the burden of his thoughts.

"I know where."

The rain has stopped completely as Ed reaches the old pistol factory ruins. A rude parking lot has developed alongside the road, where fishermen and hikers leave their cars. Shattered glass, cigarette butts, and soggy beech leaves litter the stony turnout. The place is empty right now, midday, a school day, a workday. He and Buddy are the only souls there. Ed realizes that he has no leash; he's left the house in such a hurry, he's forgotten it. Rather than chance the dog's getting hit by an oncoming car, Ed takes him into his arms and carries him across the road to the ruins. The dog doesn't even squirm, but he does lick Ed's nose, as if to say, *This is cool.*

The brick facade of the pistol factory is intact, although all the windows are gone and the interior has been gutted over the past hundred years. Rumors at the zoning meeting last night suggest that some developer has a plan to buy the place and turn it into something. Someone said condominiums; someone else had heard shops. Locals chuckled at the notion that anyone would buy a condo in Moodyville, much less draw the traffic that would support a bunch of chichi shops. Ed would love to see it purchased by a small manufacturer and have it restored back to its original purpose. Maybe not pistols, but certainly something could be produced here. The place still has good bones.

Ed sets Buddy down and he and the dog climb down the steep stairs to the apron that runs around the building to the millpond and the steps that lead to the old path. Immediately, the dog sets about squirrel hunting. "You already scared them off." He pats his thigh and the dog comes bounding back. "Stick close. It can be dangerous here."

The millpond is low, a good foot beneath the lip of the dam, as the dry summer has depleted the dammed river of its volume. It halfheartedly escapes through one open sluice gate. Today's rain has given the usually placid surface a little motion, and leaves float like little empty boats, ganging up where the unseen force of the thwarted river pushes them against the stones.

Ed hasn't been here for seven years.

Ed stares down into the bronze-colored water of the millpond. The power of the moving water to make the shaft work is in the flowing of it into the waterwheel, long since gone. Only the real old-timers remember when it was there, and even then just a broken vestige of industry.

Five feet deep. A mere five feet of accumulated river water, and all the power of strategically released water moves the wheel. Five feet. Deep enough to swim in. Deep enough to keep the trout alive. Deep enough if your pockets are full of rocks.

Moodyville doesn't have a police force. When emergencies happen, car crashes and the like, the resident state trooper does what is necessary. A 911 call will get the volunteer fire department out, and the EMTs. Neighbors. Colleagues. When a fisherman who was hoping only to catch a fish on opening day snagged his line and discovered the drowned body of a young girl, it was left to the resident trooper, arriving after the fire department and the EMTs, to make the unhappy connection between the girl in the pond and the parents who had made the missing-person call two days earlier. The fire department lieutenant and the driver of the town ambulance looked each other in the eye and were glad that they, who know the Parmalees well, wouldn't have to make that visit. No one wants to bring that kind of news into a neighbor's house.

They think that she's run away. Unlike many parents who would default to a belief that their daughter has been abducted, Ed and Alice both know that this is Stacy's doing. Although there is no note, no missing items—not even her stuffed rabbit, which, even at her age, she still clings to—they know that there is no outside force. When she was a little girl, maybe five, she decided to run away and got as far as the end of the road before turning back, informing her parents that she had decided not to run away that day after all. Alice, who had watched her march down the road, her stuffed rabbit tucked under one arm and her Barbie backpack bouncing against her little bum, thought that the few minutes it took for Stacy to "run away" felt as long as the time it had taken for her to take her first breath; it felt similar, the wait for the breath of life, or for the childish threat to resolve. Would she take that first gasp of air? How long to wait before running after her?

Stacy has seemed so much brighter in the past month. She has smiled more, listened to more cheerful music, spent more time with them at the dinner table. She even went to a sleepover. Ed has begun to relax, thinking that if things continue to improve, it will just prove that he was right to insist on her taking this course of medication. He has been collecting the evidence of Stacy's being more like herself, like the self they understand, to show for his bold defiance of his wife. This running away is a mistake, a misunderstanding. They know that the antidepressants can cause odd behavior as a side

*effect. They call her cell phone and it rings in her empty
bedroom. They call all her friends, but no one has seen
her. Her bike is in the garage. Her purse is on the counter.*

*And then the resident trooper, Trooper Rossman, is at
their front door. He is the same trooper who took their
missing-person report, asking questions about Stacy's
friends and whether they thought she took drugs.*

*"Antidepressants." Alice spit the word out, and Ed
knew that however this ended, he might never be forgiven.*

*Ed had insisted that they follow doctor's recommen-
dations and put Stacy on the antidepressants. The side
effects were simple legal jargon to cover the pharma-
ceutical company's liability. "We have to try. She needs
a little help so that the counseling can help."*

*"No." Being her mother, Alice had known that this
was a bad idea. Stacy didn't want to take them, and Alice stood by her right to defend her daughter's decision.
She wasn't a little child; she was a young woman who
knew her own mind.*

Overruled.

*Trooper Rossman holds his hat is in his hands now.
Uncovered, he looks younger, more human. Regretful.*

*It is an April afternoon, the sun just sliding behind
the hills to the west. The air is fresh but damp; rain is
imminent—the first of the April showers. Alice is standing behind Ed as he lets the trooper into the house. Ed
knows he is letting death in. By opening the door, death
is invited in. He should have shut the door and barricaded it with his shoulder.*

*They don't go into the living room this time; for some
reason, Ed leads them into the kitchen, where he gestures for the trooper to sit at the table. He then holds*

a chair for Alice. She doesn't look at him as she sits. She has barely spoken. The prescription bottle is on the counter, its label facing the wall.

Alice says nothing as Rossman gently breaks the news of finding Stacy in the pond.

"But I went to the pond. She wasn't there." Ed isn't calling the man a liar, just mistaken. "How could I not have seen her?"

"She was under the water."

Ed has to ask if it was an accident, and the need to ask that question reveals his deepest fear. "She fell in? How?"

"There will be an investigation."

"But you think that it was"—Ed hits upon a word he can't utter—"not an accident?"

"As I said, there will be an investigation." Rossman has set his trooper's hat on the empty chair at the table and he touches it gently on the crown. "I have to ask. Is there a note?" He asked this before, when Stacy was simply a missing person. This time, it is less of a question and more of a demand for a piece of evidence.

Ed remembers the warning on the bottle: Thoughts of suicide may increase when first taking this medication.

Alice stares at the trooper, great tears running unchecked down her cheeks, into the grooves that have appeared at the corners of her mouth; she makes no noise, makes no attempt to wipe them away. It is as if she has no idea that she is crying.

Trooper Rossman stands up and gathers his hat to his chest. "Mr. and Mrs. Parmalee, I am sorry for your loss."

Ed sees the trooper out. He turns to take Alice in his arms and is met with a flat-handed slap.

"I never want you to touch me again."

*   *   *

Buddy whizzes past Ed at a dead run, the lure of low-hanging squirrels too much for him. Suddenly, the dog finds himself perched on the lip of the dam. Daintily, he travels the edge like a gymnast on a balance beam, moving skillfully away from Ed, toward the opposite bank of the pond.

"Buddy!" Ed watches the dog disappear into the woods. "Goddamn it! Buddy!" He's going to have a heart attack right here and now. "Buddy! Come!" He tries to whistle, but his mouth is too dry. He claps and calls, shouting the dog's name. He's never not come before. Every time Ed has let him off the leash, in defiance of Alice's overprotectiveness, the dog has come like a shot at his call. Now the only sound is the brush beneath the trees rustling as the dog moves away from him. Ed braces himself against his knees and fights a surge of panic. He's been their dog for only a little while. What if he's running away from them? "Buddy!"

Then the dog is back on the dam, trotting along the six-inch-wide coaming as unconcernedly as a high-wire walker on pavement. He sees Ed and picks up the pace.

"Easy, slow down." Just as the dog reaches Ed, who is kneeling on the rain-slick cement of the abutment, his hind foot slips on a scattering of wet leaves and suddenly he is scrambling. Ed reaches out and grabs the dog by the ruff.

"Sweet Jesus, I thought I'd lost you."

CHAPTER 42

I make it back to Adele's house, only to find it empty.
She's probably at Paul's. That makes sense. Why would
she come back to this empty place, be here alone with
me? There's a newspaper on the front walk, and I pause
for a moment after retrieving it to contemplate the triple-
decker next door, the house that I once lived in. If Adele
meant what she said about going into that retirement
community, it could be sold fairly soon if she wants to
convert it into liquid assets. Or maybe the rents will off-
set the expense of senior housing and she'll hang on to it.

Lights are on in all three flats, diffused through drawn
curtains or lowered blinds. Even in the murky half-light
of dusk, the place looks in need of paint and a little TLC.
It occurs to me that I lived in that house almost exactly
as long as I lived in Adele's—nine years. I haven't been
inside since the day we moved out, so I still picture the
living room walls as mint green and cream, the shag rug
a blend of olive and russet fibers. Hideous by today's
standards, but what I remember fondly.

A welcome thought rattles through me: I am free. With my father's passing, I no longer have any connection to Adele Rose. As cut off as I have been, there has always been this lingering attachment I could never quite break free from. As long as my father was alive, there was communication, however sparse. Like being called here to attend him like some unpaid nurse. A Christmas card with a twenty-five-dollar check in it, signed by Adele. That will stop now.

The door of the first-floor flat opens and a woman comes out. She's carrying a casserole dish and she heads right for me. I don't know her, but she's dressed in a tracksuit that emphasizes her ampleness, big hair caught up in a topknot, Crocs on her feet. She is comfortingly like the women I knew growing up, big and generous, a little loud but kind. I can smell the cigarette smoke on her.

"Are you Justine?"

"Yes."

"I heard about your dad. I'm so sorry. I made you this." My new friend hands me the still-warm casserole. I can smell tuna and cheese, and suddenly I'm so hungry, I could sit down and eat all of it.

"Thank you so much. I think Adele is at Paul's. Do you mind if I take your dish there?"

"Not at all. Just leave the dish on the porch when you're through with it. Don't even wash it."

"What's your name?"

"I'm Diane Santos. We've lived in that house for ten years. Your dad was so good to us. I'm going to miss him." Unbelievably, she actually tears up, adding to my impression that she, like so many of the women I knew around here, keeps her emotions handy.

"I don't know what the arrangements are yet, but please come if you can."

She presses a hand to my hand. "I will. And if there's anything . . ."

"I'll let you know."

Diane leaves me standing on the walk with the warm casserole in my hands. She turns and waves as she goes back into her house, into the very apartment I once lived in with two parents. I'm almost tempted to ask if I can go inside, see if there is anything there that will give me one more memory of my early life.

I walk inside and put the casserole on the counter. The delicious and familiar odor of my favorite comfort food wafts up, and I yank open the silverware drawer and pull out a fork. I'll just have a little. I'm still buzzed from the long drive and from my encounter with Artie. I can't keep the image of my dog dead on the side of the road out of my mind. I need a moment to regroup before heading over to Paul's and the fresh drama that awaits me. I have no doubt that they will be royally pissed that I disappeared for half the day on the day that my father died.

I take a bite of the tuna noodle casserole. It's every bit as good as it smells and brings me back to Tony as a little boy, when I made it for him. He would never let me use egg noodles, like Diane has, always ziti. He had his little-boy rigidness about certain things—what kind of pasta constituted macaroni and cheese, and what kind was meant for tuna casserole. Wheat bread was verboten; only squishy white bread would suffice for PB&J. I wonder if he's listened to my message about my father. Does he ever listen to my messages?

Tony was almost sixteen when I announced that I was moving us to Washington State. It wasn't an arbitrary decision; it was a fantastic opportunity. I'd been seeing a guy who was opening a new high-end restaurant. When he offered me the chance to be his manager, with a salary and benefits, I thought that it sounded wonderful. Greg was offering stability, even a career. I was still young enough to believe that there were good opportunities left in the world and that taking them was the important part. Better to try and fail than never to try at all. That's what I said to Tony.

"Fail at what? Another 'relationship'?" This from my teenager, sarcasm complete with air quotes.

"It's not about a 'relationship,' it's about being in at the ground floor on a successful business." I imitate his flippant gesture and use air quotes. "Greg's a nice guy, but this isn't romantic. Greg is a good businessman and this is a good opportunity for us."

"No. I won't go. Enough is enough. This is the longest we've ever lived anywhere and I like it here."

"I understand, honey; moving isn't easy. But this is a fantastic opportunity."

"It's always a fantastic opportunity. Or a fantastic new guy. When are you ever going to be satisfied?"

I am speechless, then angry. "You don't get to decide what's best for this family. I do."

"And you think pursuing this newest crazy idea of yours is the best thing? You'll keep moving because you can't just accept that this is the best it ever gets. A place, a job, nice neighbors. That's all life is really made up of."

"I'm your sole support, and I need to have the best job I can get."

"With the newest best guy?"

"This is not about Greg."

"Then who is it about?"

"You."

"It's never been about me, Mom. Even moving here was about that great job you were going to have."

I pace the arc of the turret six times, my fists clenched so tight that I leave nail marks in my palms. "You're grounded." A mother's weakest weapon. He is way out of bounds here. Every move we've made has been to better his life.

"Can't you at least wait until I graduate? Then we can move. You can move." His voice is still unreliable and he croaks on those words.

"Discussion over."

Tony draws himself up to full height, shocking me with the fact that he is close to six feet tall. He runs a hand through his thick, dark hair in a gesture so like his father's that I have to blink hard to dispel the notion that Anthony is standing there. "I'm not going."

"Of course you are. You're my son."

"Mr. and Mrs. Sanchez will let me stay with them until I graduate."

"I don't think that Marta and Henry are willing or able to take on a teenage boy." I take another lap of the turret. "It's a ridiculous notion."

"No, it's not. Ask Mrs. S. She'll tell you."

"Why do you think they'd be willing to do this for you?"

Tony actually blushes, the roses against his olive skin making him look equally child and grown man. Petulance and desire. "They know about all our constant moving. Ten places since I was three years old. They know that's not good. That you'll just keep moving me until I . . ."

"What? Until you what?" I should remind him that the last two moves were a partially a result of his own behavior, but some things are unfair when wielded by a parent.

"Leave home."

I take a deep breath. This is nothing more than a half-grown child's fantasy of "I'll run away and show you." I know about that fantasy. Oh yes, I do.

Tony stands before me, a perfect model of anguished youth. He isn't crying, but his mouth forms a thin line of holding back—holding back tears, or holding back very angry words; I'm not sure which. It's like watching two entities struggling to form a single unit, the blur of the child he has been, the one I know so well, and the overlay of this almost adult, this man-child who is a stranger to me. We face each other, a gap of five feet between us. My maternal instincts are to go hug him, tell him everything will be all right, that he just has to trust me. Then the shadow of the child is gone and I see the future man standing in front of me. Not quite fully formed, but no longer a boy.

"Mom, I just can't keep living like this." Tears slide out from under his lashes. He makes no move to acknowledge them, just lets them drift down until they meet the scruff of beard on his adolescent cheeks and vanish.

It is a crystal moment. I have exactly two choices: move to Seattle and take a great job, or stay put for another three years and wait for another golden opportunity to break out of the shit-job rail that I am riding. I'm thirty-six, and I feel as if life is beginning to run dry on good opportunities for me. Greg offers the best yet. Besides, Seattle is a great place, filled with opportunities for a young man—good schools, new friends, the music scene.

I know that Tony has good friends here, a world of difference from his L.A. friends; he's even joined the baseball team. He hasn't been in one fight, has even

made the honor roll. But I need something, too. I need a
better job than managing a flophouse of a motel.

Tony will just have to suck it up.

"We're moving."

"How can you not understand what I'm saying?"

"I do. You don't want to move again. I understand
that. But we have to take chances."

"Three more years, Mom, that's all I'm asking."

"I don't have three more years."

"Then you don't have me."

I finish off another big bite of the casserole and cover it
up. Time to go.

Paul lives in Fairhaven, over the Acushnet River from
New Bedford and off of route 240. He's managed, on an
accountant's salary, to buy a house with a water view.
It's a tiny house, to be sure, someone's summer cottage
tarted up, but from his back deck, you catch a glimpse of
the Acushnet and the New Bedford waterfront on the opposite shore. Once inside, I can't imagine how he raised
his two huge children in this space. His wife, Melanie,
greets me with great sympathy, assuming that I am dev-
astated. She, too, has grown large since the last time I
saw her—at their wedding. But her largeness suits her,
and she wears it with pride. She keeps hold of my hand
as she pilots me through the living room and into the
dining room, where she finds space for the deflowered
casserole among the massive collection of platters and
dishes, remnants of pies, and salads.

"Adele's resting now. If you want to go look in on
her . . ." Melanie says this without irony.

"That's okay. Let her rest. Where's Paul?"

"Outside. Eat something!"

I don't, but I do grab a chilled bottle of Sam Adams
and head out to the deck, where Paul and a host of other
men have congregated, much like this is Super Bowl
Sunday and not a sad occasion. They're laughing, until
they realize who I am. I have no idea who these people
are, but they murmur appropriate sentiments: "Sorry for
your loss." I keep thinking that they mean Mack. I'm
sure that they think that the very real grief on my face is
attributable to the human loss and natural filial feelings.

If only they knew that I lost my father years ago. That
loss is hardened into my bones. I murmur my appropriate
responses. Paul plays host and starts introducing them to
me. I shake hands and smile and keep the urge to howl
at bay. I take a quick sip of the beer, tell myself I need to
behave like a grown-up, thank them for their kindness in
being on Paul's deck on a weeknight.

"You remember Ron Markham?"

Nearly thirty years changes a man. Changes a boy
into a man. Changes sleek and Greek into a schlub. This
Ronnie Markham is soft-faced; a ring of untidy brown
hair frames a bald head, and his eyebrows are trying to
make up for the loss. He sports a bristly mustache and
looks the part of a used-car salesman to a T. His hands
are feminine, small and soft as he takes my unoffered
hand in his. He freaking pats it. "Justine, I'm so sorry
about your dad. He was always one of our best people."

"Right." I extract my hand from his. Markham's best.

*I am so excited, as only a girl can be whose dream guy
has suddenly woken up from his obliviousness and seen
her for a desirable woman. Golden boy, king of the football field, legendary Ronnie Markham is taking me out.
It is one of the few times I can remember Adele smiling
at me with genuine pleasure, as if I have turned from*

straw into gold. My dating Ronnie Markham is clearly a feather in her social cap.

I dress with such excited panic. Is the floral dress with the outsize shoulder pads the best thing? I decide that I shouldn't be too dressy. I pull on my black leggings and fashionably droopy boat-neck top. Using electric rollers, I curl my hair, and tease my bangs into a lofty height. Ron, a little early, is in the kitchen, drinking Coke with Paul. I walk into the room and, oh Lord, he stands up, like a gentleman caller, and helps me into my fake-leather bomber jacket. I hope that my deodorant does its job and I'm not going to embarrass myself with wet circles under my perspiring armpits. I am so nervous.

When Ronnie asked me out, it was an afterthought. "Hey, Justine, want to go out sometime?"

I looked at Paul, standing beside Ronnie, absolutely sure this was a joke. When Paul didn't burst into laughter, I nodded. "Yeah. Sure."

"You look beautiful." Ronnie sounds sincere, although I catch a half smile on Paul's face, just like he's in on a joke. I wait half a beat, fully expecting that Ronnie and Paul will pull the plug on this charade.

"You two kids have a nice time." Paul slaps Ron on the back and waves as we walk to Ron's car, which is parked at the curb. Predictably, his car is a brand-new Chevy Camaro with all the bells and whistles, a throaty muscle car. Ronnie pulls away from the curb like he's launching a rocket.

"I thought we'd go to the Pizza Palace and then maybe take a drive."

My hands are clasped between my knees so that Ron can't see how nervous I am. "That's sounds nice." Anything sounds nice. I've never been out with a college boy before, and I suppose that Ron won't be interested in the usual stuff of high school dates, McDonald's and the Game Room. The very fact that this isn't a double date seems so sophisticated to me, but on the other hand, I wish that I had a friend with me, someone who would be a witness to my success, or failure. Someone I could go home with at the end of the date and analyze every word and gesture for deeper meaning.

Ron has a lot of his father's car salesman charm and keeps the conversation in the restaurant going single-handedly against my tongue-tied hero worship. He talks about his athletic achievements at college. That topic moves easily into his academic stardom. In the end, he isn't a whole lot different from the other boys I date. As long as I keep nodding and smiling, he keeps talking.

I begin to relax a little, the glow of his aura dimming enough that I can actually look across the table at him. I sit up a little straighter, hoping that someone, anyone, will come in and see me, Justine Meade, sitting here alone with Ronnie Markham. For once in my life, I'm glad to be popular Paul Rose's stepsister.

Later, we drive around a bit aimlessly until we get to the beach, stopping at a point that is a popular make-out spot, especially in the warm weather, when a blanket and the sand behind the dunes make a perfect nest. The engine pings softly as we sit there looking out over the water through the broad windshield of the car.

"Your brother's a great guy."

This seems like a strange statement to make, sitting, as we are, in the most popular make-out spot in New Bedford.

"He's all right." I'm hardly going to complain about Paul tonight.

"He convinced me to take you out."

I felt like I'd been kicked. "Figures. What did he promise you?"

"Doesn't matter. The point is, I like you. I'm glad I did."

"I don't need Paul to get me dates."

"No, you don't. I was blind. Paul opened my eyes."

It is just warm enough to be outside, so Ron pops the trunk, extracting a blanket and a six-pack. We lie back on our elbows, drinking the beer, pretending to be fascinated with the stars. The beer isn't cold and tastes like metallic water, but I sip from the can as if I enjoy it. A shooting star streaks across the sky.

"Oh! Look at that. Make a wish!" I point skyward, wishing my own wish.

Ronnie pats my knee, then rubs my back.

My star wish was that he'd kiss me. When he doesn't, I kiss him.

I will always admit that I made the first move. But Ronnie Markham took things too far.

Ron Markham, not Ronnie, leans close to my ear now. The impression of softness disappears. "Did you know that your father came to me? Privately."

"No."

"Your father was a pretty big guy back then. I was taller, but he got me by the shirt and slammed me into a wall and told me in no uncertain terms that I'd better stay away from you. I told him the truth, that nothing had happened."

"What do you mean, nothing happened? Something did happen. You wouldn't stop when I asked you to."

"I did stop before anything happened. But I was turned on and didn't behave like a gentleman. I took advantage of your age, but your brother said . . ."

"What?"

"That you would. You know. Once I realized you wouldn't, I stopped. Don't you remember?"

I remember the feel of his mouth all over me, the weight of his hands on my skin after he'd managed to pull my shirt off. I remember tugging at my clothes, desperate to cover myself, the damp night air chilling me, and then walking to his car with his arm around my shoulder as if I needed help. I have zeroed out the rest.

I sat that night in the kitchen. I was sobbing. "Paul set me up." Paul had slunk off as soon as I walked in the door, my artfully arranged hair tangled and my *Flashdance* top stretched askew, my mascara streaked. He'd taken one look at what he'd done and fled.

"He told Ronnie he could have me."

"Shut up." Adele stalks over to me. "He did nothing of the sort. You dress like a tramp, you get treated like a tramp."

"I'll have a talk with the boy." My father stands in the archway of the dining room. "With Ronnie."

"You will not." Adele grabs the back of my head, twisting my face toward my father. "Are you willing to sacrifice your job for her?"

It was his silence that I took for betrayal. He wouldn't stand up to her, not then, not ever.

In all this, I have never thought about Ron Markham. It's always been my father's sin of failure to stand up for me that I've remembered with such pain. Now here is the man, the grown-up version of the boy who almost got my virginity. Never did I imagine that he, of all people, would be the one to tell me my father had stood up for me after all.

At this point, Paul has literally shouldered us off the deck and into the empty yard. I know that the people on the deck, and by now there are several wives out there, can hear every word. I'm not raising my voice, but the evening has become foggy and the fog acts like a band shell.

Out of the fog I hear her voice.

Marriage, motherhood, divorce; reinventing myself every few years, living through 9/11 and two Iraq wars, even at that, the sight of Adele Rose Meade standing on that deck, looking down on me, scares the shit out of me. In a curious way, the deck floodlights illumine her and her only; the rest of the audience, Greek chorus now, have faded into the shadows. I feel myself shrinking.

"Justine. You need to come in." The transformation is complete. I am ten.

"Mrs. Meade, give us a minute." Ron doesn't touch me, but I follow him a few steps away from the deck, deeper into the wet grass and the fog, mostly out of earshot. I wonder if this is a good idea. Not that I imagine he'll touch me. It just looks compromising, and I have an idea that his wife—surely there is one—is not going to understand this.

"Whatever happened that night, I want you to know that I am truly sorry. A boy looks at these things differently. Not that I'm saying it was right, or acceptable, but I'm sorry."

This is so unexpected. An apology. From Ron. But it's not the one I wanted.

Suddenly, it hits me: The reason my father never apologized is because he had nothing to apologize for. Tears build in the corner of my eyes.

"Thank you."

I have this strange sense of being like a creature that

molts its skin; what has held me together cracks open and I feel my life slide out, fresh. Ron Markham, in clumsy fashion, has offered me closure.

"Justine?" Adele's voice fades into the mist. A ghostly sound, meaningless.

"Puttin' on the Ritz" jangles on my cell phone, startling us both. It gives Ron an exit and he disappears into the fog, leaving me alone at the edge of the yard. Crickets are all wound up, droning their September song as I look at the display. It's Mitch, my one-legged violinist. I take three rings to collect myself, to find the voice that won't sound cloudy with emotion.

"Hey, Mitch."

"How's it going?"

We sound like two adolescents with nothing much to say.

"My father passed today, so we're at my stepbrother's, eating."

"My condolences."

"It's fine."

If only my father had said something to me, just let me know that he had taken take my side, even if I was the only one to know it. It's too late. It's like trying to turn the *Titanic* to give up my hardened sense of injustice. "The funeral's on Saturday. Then I guess I'll head home."

Just saying that pains me. I tell Mitch about finding Artie, about how Artie's scared to death that the Hell's Angels are on his trail. For a split second, I wonder if Mitch will think I blame him for what Artie's done. I don't, not really. I don't mention socking Artie in the gut, but I do tell him about the truckers. And then the threatened tears win the battle and I sob into the phone that my dog is most likely dead on the MassPike.

"Justine, maybe not. This may sound weird, but I think I saw your dog on Facebook."

"It's probably one that Saundra put up. We're in a lot of her YouTube clips." I don't want an image of Mack; I want Mack.

"Except that the woman with the dog isn't you."

This stops me. I knuckle away the tears. "What?"

"I've sent you the link. You just look at it and see for yourself."

"Mack isn't the only dancing Sheltie." I can't allow myself false hope.

"I'm not asking you to get your hopes up, but don't you want to see this?"

There is a moment of silence between Cleveland and here and I hear the Vineyard ferry horn blasting. Mitch doesn't want me to get my hopes up, but he offers me hope by telling me that someone is dancing with my dog?

If Mitch is right, that this online Sheltie is Mack, somehow safe, it means that I can't leave until I exhaust every avenue in finding him. I don't know how long Candy will keep my job open, but I've quit plenty of jobs for far less compelling reasons.

"A silver-and-black Sheltie, big white ruff, one blue eye, one brown?"

"Justine, go look at the video."

The consoling crowd has thinned out. Two of the men who were on the deck with Paul turn out to be my nephews. They call me "Aunt Justine," as if we have blood in common. They call my father "Grandpa."

"Do you guys have a computer I can use? I need to check my e-mail."

Ryan, the elder one, shows me to his bedroom, where he has a laptop. He opens it up for me and kindly leaves me to it. The room looks tidied for company, but the odor is pure man-boy, and I inhale it with a certain nostalgia. A sock pokes out from under the bed, a grayish white tongue licking the floor. I picture Melanie racing around, trying to get the place in order, never having planned on entertaining on a weeknight. Even an expected death comes unexpectedly.

I open the e-mail from firstchairharleyplayer. "I hope this is your dog."

I click on the link, hoping, too, that it is my dog.

I watch the short clip, my hand over my mouth, trying not to cry out. The sound quality is poor, the image a little jiggly, but "Ob-La-Di, Ob-La-Da" distinct as Mack does his routine. I can tell he's improvising; the woman with him isn't giving him any good hand signals, but he has figured out enough of them to know what she wants. He is that smart. Then I hear a name, Alice. "Keep going, Alice." Is that enough to be able to find my dog? A woman named Alice is dancing with him? Then I hear a second name, Buddy. That's what she's calling him. It is Mack. Even though there are plenty of blue merle Shelties in the world, only this one is mine. Unmistakable.

The relief acts like a drug, and I start shaking, my hands trembling so much that I have a hard time texting Mitch to let him know he's right. I can't talk now; I have to process this flicker of hope.

"You okay, Aunt Justine?" Ryan is standing in the doorway.

"I am." Or very nearly.

CHAPTER 43

Officer Rossman sits in their kitchen like some malevolent spirit, a tight frown on his face, as if he's practiced giving bad news and knows the right facial expression. There is something wrong with her hearing; Alice can only hear phrases coming out of his mouth, not full sentences, not complete thoughts. "There will be an investigation." "The medical examiner. . . ."

She is aware of a sound like the susurration of the ocean. It's been a long time since they went to the shore; maybe this summer they'll rent a place on Cape Cod. The susurration begins to hiss and build, until what's in her ears is a roar. Her own heartbeat, her own blood pounding up and through her brain, clouding the words coming out of Rossman's mouth, obscuring the meaning until it breaks free of his mouth and penetrates her soul.

Stacy is dead.

This is Ed's fault.

* * *

"Hey, Alice."

Alice is furiously vacuuming again.

"Alice, put that thing away and come with me." Ed was on his way to Lil's when he changed his mind. Buddy is in the Cutlass, waiting for his daily ride.

Alice can't hear him. Ed steps on the off button of the canister vac. "I said, forget this and come with me."

"I've got to finish this." She steps on the button.

Ed pushes it off. "Let's do something, go somewhere. You'll never finish vacuuming."

"Where?" She doesn't move to restart the vac. She shoves a strand of hair behind her ear in a girlish motion.

"I don't know, but it's too fine a Saturday to be wasted on vacuuming. Grab your jacket; let's go do something."

Alice stands there with the vacuum nozzle in her hands. Her hair isn't yet in its twist, just pulled back in a workaday ponytail. The morning sun filters through the window, backlighting her, so that the uncaught strands look like a halo around her head. "Like what?"

"Time for a little adventure. Want to go look at cars?"

"That's an adventure?"

"Have you looked at cars lately? They're all about the adventure."

Ed can see her debating his offer. In the old days, the really old days, there would have been no hesitation. Now everything is a debate.

"What about Buddy?"

"He's waiting in the car. We need to find something that he likes, too."

"When did we decide to get a new car?"

"We haven't. I just thought it might be nice to see what's out there."

"I'll get my jacket."

Why does it feel like he's won a major victory?

Alice pulls off the thin T-shirt she's wearing and puts on a blue oxford shirt, puts her feet into her Dansko clogs, and runs a brush through her hair, sweeping it up and securing it with a clip. She's done this so often that she doesn't think about the action, just checks the result in the mirror hanging over her bureau. She should put on lipstick.

Ed is standing in the doorway, his reflection behind hers, his eyes admiring what her reflection doesn't reveal to her. Alice watches as Ed's reflection bends to kiss the back of her neck. It's like watching strangers through a window—avatars of Ed and Alice Parmalee.

The softness of Ed's lips against her skin is not a reflection, but real, and sends a frisson of energy through her body, a quickening of something she's forgotten existed. For once, she doesn't say "Oh Ed." For the first time in a very long time, it feels like her idea.

"I forgot about Buddy."

"It's cool in the garage. He's fine." Alice sits on the edge of the scrambled bed and pulls on her jeans. "But let's go. He's probably wondering what happened to you."

Ed reaches for Alice's shoulder and pulls her down against his bare chest. "Let's not tell him."

Alice swings her feet back onto the bed and sighs. "I think he may figure it out." She doesn't struggle to break free of his embrace, but settles herself into it. "He's such a smart dog. It's like he understands everything."

"He's really great, isn't he?" Ed shifts a little, begins to stroke a lock of her hair as if he's stroking the soft ears of the dog. "I went there yesterday. To the millpond."

Alice lies very still. Her heart is beating. She is breathing. She feels the weight of each individual rock pressing against her own ribs. The water rises but does not crest the dam of her grief. "Was it all right?"

"After a while. Buddy was there and he went a little nuts on a squirrel that literally dashed right under his nose. He nearly fell in, but didn't. He did look a little embarrassed, though. Alice, he made me laugh. There. That place. I laughed."

And then Ed holds her so close that the weight of the rocks is nothing compared to the pressure of his arms and his need. The grief does not subside, but the waters do, and Alice pats Ed's arm. "It's okay, Ed. It was good for you to go. It's the same for me when I go to the cemetery. There's some comfort in the tangible."

"I thought maybe I'd figure it out, if I finally looked at it. But all I figured out is that people still fish there and it's still a pretty spot. The leaves are already changing and the big trees are reflected in the millpond, like you're seeing everything double. Peaceful. Except for that squirrel, completely still. Nothing about it explained anything. She wasn't there, Alice."

"She wouldn't be there, Ed. Any more than I find her in the cemetery. She's here. And not. We lost her. We had her for a little while and we lost her. End of story." Alice pulls herself away from Ed and they both sit on the edge of the bed. "Sometimes I think that I need to gut her room and turn it into a den or an office or something useful. Put all of it away. And then I realize that once I do, I will have accepted her death."

"I think that maybe we have accepted her death, but not the reason for it. It wasn't like a car accident, where you'd put a cross and a teddy bear at the scene; it was an illness. It was something so out of our experience, we will never be able to understand how she felt."

They are silent again. But this time, the silence isn't a wall, but a cocoon.

"What do we do, Ed?"

Buddy barks suddenly, an impatient complaint of abandonment.

Ed kisses Alice. "Let's go look at cars."

"Maybe we should turn in the van. Get a Prius. Something economical. I don't need all that space."

"The Cutlass is older. Maybe we should see what they'd give us for that."

Ed is dressed first and goes out to the garage to soothe Buddy. Alice is back in front of the mirror, repairing her hair, putting on a little lipstick. She sees herself smiling, which is a surprise. Maybe it's the diffused light through the ivory-colored shades in this bedroom, or maybe it's something else, but the reflection coming back at her isn't as pinched as it's been. She's got good color in her cheeks, probably from all the walks she's been taking with Buddy. If she turns her head in a certain way, she even looks a little pretty, a little girlish. Alice looks at herself in the mirror and sees a hint of roses in her cheeks, something besides sadness in her eyes. What they've said was hard but, in a strange way, comforting. As if they've faced a common enemy and not fled.

At first, it was nice to have the front seat all to himself. Buddy doesn't know how long Ed will be. But after a couple of minutes, he settles down, nose under tail, eyes closed, but ears alert for Ed's return. Eventually, he dozes. Then he wakes and is puzzled. He hasn't been left alone in a car for this long, and never without being someplace other than where they started. He barks. This is a little naughty for a dog who can down-stay for hours, but there was no command. He barks again: *Hey, where are you?*

Ed comes back, all treats and apologies, which is good. But still they don't move. "Backseat, boy." Ed waves

Buddy over the seat back. Now Buddy is intrigued. A passenger? This is unprecedented except when they both took him to the vet. Vet? Buddy makes a little interrogative noise in his throat. *What's up?*

Alice appears and climbs into the Cutlass. They talk and suddenly everyone climbs out and gets into the minivan. This is better. The middle seat offers a great view, which he can change by going from side to side. Buddy is excited; the routine is different. Something new is happening. Like yesterday, when he and Ed went to that pond where the squirrels were lush on the ground and plenteous in the trees. That was fun. An adventure. Except that Ed slowed down and stopped. Stood at the edge of the water without moving for a long time; stuck like humans sometimes get when their activity is invisible and is often accompanied by sighing. Not the sighing of comfort like a dog when he settles for the night, but that sighing that broadcasts human distress. This clearly wasn't meant to be a walk, just a visit. Maybe Ed thought that Buddy would rid the place of its squirrel vermin. He tried, very nearly ending up in water, something that he has no interest in doing. Water is for Labradors. That flushed Ed out of his immobility. That stopped his sighing.

This is bound to be an adventure, both humans in one place. No need to herd them; they are willingly together. Buddy sniffs the air behind the humans. He cocks his head. Notices that their hands touch now that Ed has the minivan on the road. Buddy loses interest in the scenery going by, doesn't think to look for squirrels, or cats or bikes. He keeps his herd-dog eyes on the touching hands visible in the space between the front seats.

He fails to notice the cemetery gates as they drive by, the left-hand pillar nearly scraped clean of its flaking paint; he is intent on the humans here with him now.

CHAPTER 44

I should have known that Adele would want to pull out all the stops. Rather than a simple funeral home service, she has opted for the grand send-off at the largest Episcopal church in New Bedford. My father was a Catholic when he married my mother. Somewhere along the line, Adele had converted him to what I'm sure she thinks of as her classier denomination. She doesn't actually attend the church, but she swears that we need to use the huge space for the hundreds of friends who will show up. I'm sure that the nave will look like an empty boat.

We climb into our limousine in our suitable new clothes—Adele in Lord & Taylor widow's weeds, me in Kohl's basic black pantsuit, also useful for job interviews and visiting New York—and drive in luxury to the church.

I hadn't counted on Paul's clients and Melanie's circle of friends. It's not a bad crowd, for a perfect September Saturday morning, more suitable for a round of golf than

a funeral. The four of us emerge from our limo, are met
by Ryan and Peter, the younger boy, who have come in
the family Lexus. Hugs shared all around. Paul supports
Adele, but the sight of his bulk and her bent-over figure
make me think irreverently of Shrek and a Hobbit. Then
my nephew, my stepnephew, young Ryan, offers his arm
to me, and I am touched to tears.

I have spent the previous evening looking at the face
of my dead father. In death, in this waxy repose, he was
diminished, as I guess death diminishes us all. Strangers filed in, in twos and threes; some people I sort of
recognized, old friends, most of them tottering about,
pushing walkers, aged way past how I remember them;
old customers coming in to pay their respects. They all
offered such lovely platitudes: ". . . a better place." "He
will be missed." ". . . hell of a guy." Some even cried.
Who were these people to weep over my father's death?
Adele greeted each and every one of them with what I
can only describe as queenly calm. Paul knew them all.
Teammates of Peter's showed up, stringy boys dressed in
rumpled jackets and poorly tied ties. "Sorry man," they
said, giving awkward boy hugs. Grandpa, it seemed, had
attended all the games. Had a jersey with NUMBER ONE
FAN printed on it and all the kids' signatures on the back.

I was the mystery daughter, tacked onto the end of
the receiving line. "You must be Justine!" people would
say. One person with a familiar face finally showed up,
my parents' tenant, Diane Santos. She and her husband
waited at the end of the line parading past the coffin,
made their prayer with a nice big Catholic sign of the
cross, and worked the line down to me. Diane, like so
many of these other strangers, didn't feel odd about giving me a sympathetic hug. But with Diane, at least we'd

278   SUSAN WILSON

been introduced. I'd eaten her food. I thanked her for it
with the first genuine sentence I'd spoken since this tortured evening began.

During a lull, I wandered away from the family and
took a look at the flowers that had been artfully arranged
around the coffin like floral soldiers at attention on ped-
estals. One was from Markham Motors; another came
from my father's Masonic chapter. A couple were from
distant relatives. A late-arriving spray didn't get a ped-
estal, but sat on the floor, so I bent over to read the card.
"In deepest sympathy." It was from Anthony Marcone.

That spray, pink gladioli and ivory lilies, sits on the
chancel steps, its stems crushed together with those of
all the other arrangements. When we go to the cemetery,
they'll all be arrayed around the grave, left there until the
coffin is lowered, a sight Americans don't usually watch,
despite how it's portrayed on television. Soon enough,
they'll be trashed, tossed out with the rest of the debris.

At the end of the service, before the funeral home guy
collects the flowers, I pluck that telling card from the
holder and pocket it.

Despite Tony's protestations, I moved us to Seattle,
swearing that this really would be the better life. Six
months later, I was collecting unemployment again.
When Tony didn't come home from school on a Thursday afternoon, I went into his bedroom in the sublet we
were renting and found a note on his desk. "Mom, I'll be
okay, and I'll call you when I can. Love, Tony."

My son was gone.

The family files out of the church to the waiting limo
and I follow slowly, the little card from Flora.com in my
pocket. I pause on the church steps, wishing I could just

pile into the Lexus with the boys, but the rear door to the limo gapes open, waiting for me.

"Justine?"

A man in a black suit stands on the steps beside me. Moderately tall, he is clean-shaven and has the deepest blue eyes beneath a wide forehead. His hair is short, and in the sunlight it is tipped with silver. I know him but can't place him.

"It's Mitch." He's seen my confusion. "I'm out of context. Besides, you only really ever knew the back of me."

"My Harley rider?"

Mitch, on two feet, comes closer. "I'm here. At your service again."

Going down the steps, I figure out that he's wearing a prosthesis. He's pretty facile, but there is a little hop in his gait that isn't quite normal. "You don't look like you came here on a bike."

"Left it home. That's my ride." He points to a Camry parked across the street. "Not very glamorous, but I figured that we may have a lot of driving to do.

"I don't know where I'm going next."

Mitch touches my elbow. "Wherever the search takes us."

On Saturday, Mr. Sanchez calls me to let me know that Tony had arrived at their house in Kanab. The boy had tried to swear the old man to secrecy, but Mr. Sanchez is having none of that. "I told him a man doesn't ask another man to lie. Secrecy is a lie."

"Thank you. I'm going to see if I can fly down and get him. I just have to . . ."

"No hurry. He's safe here. But, Justine, this is serious. A kid shouldn't run away."

"He's still mad that I moved him."

"How's that worked out for you?"

"I'm sure he's told you; the restaurant never even opened. I'm temping for now."

"I'm sorry to hear it." ·

For one second, I wonder if he's going to offer me our apartment back. Would I take that awful motel job again? No. That ship has sailed. "I thought that he was okay here."

"He's a boy without a good male influence, a kid who has never had any stability in his life beyond a loving mother. Justine, sometimes you just need more than good intentions."

Mr. Sanchez is breaking my heart with something I already know. I used to tell Tony that we were on a voyage of adventure, who knew what new and exciting things lay ahead of us. In the end, our voyage has hit the shoals and I have only one choice to make.

CHAPTER 45

"You missed your pals this morning." Lil swipes the countertop with a rag. "They got worried."

"That's dumb. Now I have to call in sick if I miss a morning?" Ed goes past his usual stool and slides into a booth. Alice is across the street at the tiny town green with Buddy and a plastic bag. "I can't spend Saturday with my wife?"

"Hey, I'm just saying they were looking for you." Lil hefts the Bunn coffeepot. "Can I start you?"

"Thanks." Ed sees Alice come back across the street and pop Buddy back into the minivan. She rolls the windows down just enough. She sees Ed watching her and waves.

Ed isn't sure what's happened, only that he feels pretty good today.

Alice slips into the booth opposite him. "He'll be fine out there. We won't be long."

"He sits out there every morning waiting for me. He

likes to keep tabs on all the comings and goings, the little mayor of Moodyville."

"You won't be able to do this in the summer, though.
You can't leave a dog in a hot car."

"I know. Maybe I'll do something else in the summer."

Alice studies the plastic menu. Ed has it memorized.
They both order grilled cheese—his with tomato, hers
without.

When Lil comes with their order, she slips a little bag
of bacon onto the table. "For my pal out there."

"You give him bacon?" Alice hisses as Lil drifts to
another table.

"Just a strip."

Alice adds a little sugar to her cup, stirs it with a back-
and-forth motion. "What else would you do in the summer?"

"I don't know. Maybe it's time we took one of those
vacations we always talked about. Drive to the Cape or
up to the mountains."

"We don't have to wait till summer to do that. There's
nothing says we can't go somewhere now."

Another reminder of his unemployed status. All the
time in the world.

Ed aligns his coffee cup in its saucer. "What would
we do about Buddy?"

"There're lots of places that are calling themselves
dog-friendly. We can take him."

"Where do you want to go?"

Alice shrugs, takes a bite of her sandwich, and sits
back. The bench seat is so low, she looks like a little kid
sitting at the grown-ups table. "Canada? Someplace we
can drive to. Montreal?"

"All the more reason to look at a new car. Neither

one of our clunkers could handle an eight-hundred-mile drive."

This is fun, this optimistic conversation. It's been so long since they've talked about anything having to do with planning, or adventure, or life beyond being lost parents, that Ed feels like laughing. It might not even be necessary to go on a vacation; it's just a step in a new direction to talk about it. It's a sign to him that Alice is moving out of another stage of her grief. From never leaving her bed to never leaving the house to never leaving Moodyville, Alice is contemplating a journey out of the country. Ed is fairly certain that she will begin to worry about who will take care of things while they're gone, a train of thought that will eventually derail these happy plans when she considers being absent from the graveside for more than a couple of days. Summer, winter, whatever the season, whatever the weather, Alice Parmalee tends the grave. Chrysanthemums in the fall; impatiens in the summer; greens in the winter. The tulip bulbs poking up in the spring, flanked by daffodils. He's never seen it, but he knows what Alice plants. Sometimes it's the only thing she tells him in a day. Or it was, until Buddy came along.

So, it's quite nice to have her talking about going somewhere else.

Thursday's town newspaper is still on the stand and Ed goes to get one while Alice takes another cup of decaf from Lil. Pushing the empty plates aside, Ed stretches the paper out in front of them and they check through the car ads side by side. The end-of-season clearances are going on, so each of the dealers is touting big savings and decent monthly payments. Maybe even on Ed's fixed income they can afford to do this. They've put some away; money that was meant for college is still sitting there. It seemed wrong to use it for anything else. Taking it would have been tantamount to stealing it from Stacy in the early days following what happened. But now, with Ed out of work, it sits there like a backup plan.

In this little hometown paper the lost-and-found ads are the first classifieds after the paid ads. Lost earrings and cats, found wallets and boots. Alice doesn't want to look, but she finds herself drawn to the column. First ad under the column heading: "Found, small collielike dog. Gray and black, one blue eye, one brown. Near Old Path Road. Call . . ."

It feels like a century ago that she called in that advertisement. Now the object of those few words is a member of the family. She narrows her eyes, hoping that no one will see it. She wishes that it wasn't the first ad, but was lost among all the other ads for missing sweaters with sentimental attachments and bracelets worthy of rewards. Alice breathes out. If anyone was going to call, they would have by now.

Alice starts to fold up the paper, but Ed pushes it back to the table surface. "We need to look."

She knows what he means, and the old familiar animosity rises. "No, we don't."

Ed ignores her and runs his finger down the lost ads. Alice doesn't watch. She looks out at the car, where Buddy is waiting so patiently for them. He is out of sight, curled up, no doubt, on the middle seat.

"Nothing. No one around here is missing him. We don't have to look ever again, but we had to look now. I couldn't live with myself if I didn't."

"I could."

"But now we don't have to worry about it. Free and clear. We've done what we could."

Ed wraps his arm around her shoulder and Alice lets

herself sink in next to him, tucked safely under his arm. "He's our boy now."

The scent of bacon clings to the people as they get into the car. Buddy licks his lips, but tries hard not to look like he's begging. Alice holds out a crumb and he takes it with proper canine etiquette, then finds himself whining for more. Ed usually gives him a whole piece, but Alice wants to parcel it out in bits. After two, she puts the bag away.

Buddy settles into the backseat and begins to enjoy the ride.

The not talking is a good thing. The people in the front seat of the car are gently not talking, but the silence is that of a contented nature. Buddy watches the scenery go by, alert for squirrels, but no longer alert for discord between these people. Not that they have ever raised their voices, or used hard-sounding words, but he knows the difference between tension and relaxation. This is the first time he can recall since his arrival that he hasn't felt the barrier between the two people who take care of him. Buddy is as sensitive a dog as any, and he is familiar with barriers. Justine has no barriers between herself and Candy, or Saundra. But she has barriers between herself and the males who occasionally take up her time. This barrier always made him keep his guard-dog focus on whatever male came to take Justine out of the house, leaving him behind. Or came back into the house. One or two got enough past the barrier that Mack was left on the outside of the bedroom door—but not often. The barrier smelled like distrust; the kind of fear smell a dog that never attaches gives off. That was why he kept himself between Justine and Artie. Justine's distrust was emanating from her skin. He could taste it when he pressed his tongue against the back of her hand.

The barrier he has sensed between Ed and Alice is not distrust. The barrier, diminished today, is fear-aggression. They seem to him to be like those dogs who snap and snarl at everyone because they are confused and uncertain and the only safe thing to do is growl. Even though Ed and Alice don't snap or snarl, or even raise their voices, this underlying current of snappish-ness is there, and a sensitive dog knows it. They are a little afraid of each other. But not today.

Today, all three of them glide through the scenery, unafraid.

CHAPTER 46

The car shopping has been fun, but exhausting. Too many choices and too many hungry car salesmen. They've looked at Toyotas and Fords, Kias and Subarus. At each dealership, Buddy hopped out with them, heeling prettily and sitting like a good boy as the salesman patiently explained the merits of this car or that, this deal or that. With down payment or not. Trade-in or not.

"I'm beat. Let's take the dog for a walk and stretch his legs." Ed snaps his seat belt into place. "I don't think I like any of them any better than this old heap."

"I know. They all look like oversized athletic shoes to me. I just can't picture myself going to Potter's in any one of them. But I think we still need to do it." Alice kisses Buddy's muzzle and points him back into the middle seat. "If we want to go any distance, we need a car."

So the vacation is still on the table. Ed grins and points the minivan in the direction of a state park.

The day is fading into dusk as they get out of the car, but the air is slightly warmer, as if summer isn't quite done. Alice has the bag of bacon crumbles in one hand. Buddy is more interested in those than in stretching his legs, so Alice puts him through his paces, treating him after every command. Sit, stay, heel. "You should work with him, too, so that he knows you give commands, as well." Alice hands the leash and the bag of bacon to Ed.

"Okay, Bud, heel!" Ed trots around with the dog's nose clamped to the side of his knee. He stops. "Down. Stay." Ed lays the leash on the ground and steps backward about four feet. "I bet he can do this without the leash. He knows he's not tied."

"We haven't worked off-leash yet. We're not ready." Alice folds her arms across her middle.

"I think he's ready. Watch this." Ed calls the dog to him, unsnaps the clip, and tosses the leash to Alice. "Buddy, heel!"

Alice covers her mouth with one hand, as if she expects the dog to run off. When he doesn't, when Buddy simply tags along beside Ed, jogging around the pine needle–strewn area, her hand drops as she begins to believe. Ed knows that look, a bird watching her fledgling, a mother watching her child ride without training wheels. It's that good-bye to old concerns, hello to new ones.

Ed stops; the dog stops. Buddy's eyes are riveted on Ed's. He's loving this exercise. Ed fishes another crumble of bacon out of the bag and treats the dog. "Good boy."

Ed tosses the bag of treats to Alice. "Go to Mommy."

As soon as the words leave his mouth, Ed realizes what he has said. He waits to see Alice's reaction. *Mommy.* The *m* word. It's what he called her from the moment they knew that Stacy was coming to the day she died. He hasn't called Alice "Mommy" in seven years, and yet the word came so fluidly to his mouth just now because she has been mommying this dog. He waits, horrified that he may have broken the spell of this better day with an unconscious blunder.

The dog trots to Alice, sits in front of her, herd-dog eyes catching and holding hers. Alice bends slowly from the waist. A strand of hair slides out from under her clip, dangling. She neither praises the dog nor gives him the treat he so clearly expects.

Buddy wiggles. His tail sweeps the pine needles. A soft inquiring woof. *Please?*

Alice holds the last piece of bacon in the tips of her fingers. Buddy takes it gently, his eyes fixed on hers, promising something. Straightening up, Alice looks at her husband. "Tell Daddy it's time for a walk."

CHAPTER 47

Everyone is out of the house by five o'clock. Even Paul and his family have gone home. Those who have come back to Adele's house after the service have drifted away, final condolences distributed to Adele, who sits in her living room, taking those sentiments with a royal dignity. I think she looks like she rehearsed for this role. Queen Adele. Or maybe duchess. Maybe only duchess. At any rate, I am left with the cleaning up. I sent Mitch to his hotel. No sense in him hanging around this group of complete strangers. I am meeting him for a drink as soon as I can get away. He's brought his laptop, and I am beyond anxious to get started looking for Mack.

As I'm drying the last platter, adding it to the collection of dishes on the counter that will have to be returned to mystery owners, Adele comes into the kitchen. She stands there watching me, and I can feel her need to comment on how I'm doing the dishes, or where I'm stacking the orphans, or even that I'm making too much noise. She doesn't. She sits in her usual kitchen chair,

the one nearest the stove. She's still dressed in her Lord
& Taylor outfit, but she has on slippers instead of the
good sensible shoes she's worn all day. The slippers are
threadbare, the pink terry-cloth faded to something like a
washed-out bloodstain, the cloth separating from the foam
sole at the edge. She sits and watches and stays silent until
I am done with the dishes. I take a last swipe at the wet
sink surround, squeeze out the Handi Wipe, and hang it
over the faucet.

"Don't leave it there."

Ah. I'd forgotten that faucets weren't for drying; the
little towel rack in the pantry cupboard is for drying. Not
handy, but the rule. I open the cupboard door and do as
I'm told.

"I have to talk to you about your father's will."

I have assumed all along that he would leave everything to Adele. With probably a prize for Paul for being the son he never had. And then I think of how he
grabbed Ronnie's shirtfront, and I wonder if maybe he
left me a little something, too. A memento.

"He left you the house next door. He insisted. It was
your mother's and he wanted you to have it."

I stare at Adele; I'm certain that my mouth is open.
"What?"

"I'll tell you the truth; I didn't want him to do that.
You don't deserve it; you cut yourself off from us. But he
said that's what he wanted."

When I was a little kid, I fell off my bike and knocked
the wind out of myself. There was that supreme moment
when I felt the air go out, and I thought that I would
never inhale again. This is exactly how I feel right now.
I can't get a breath. The tips of my fingers are tingling
with flight or fight.

A memento. A house. Of my own.

"How do you think you can manage it from Seattle?"

The house. My inheritance. "I don't know. I guess I'll figure that out." *My father provided for me.*

"There's always so much to be done. You have no idea. Painting and repairing the damage done by tenants. Keeping tenants happy. Shoveling sidewalks and mowing lawns." Adele is getting worked up.

"Who takes care of it for you now? You don't mow and you sure don't shovel."

"We have a man."

"Then I'll have that man, too."

"Justine, I'm not sure I can live on your father's pension and Social Security alone. I never worked. Outside, I mean. I took care of you and Paul."

"You took care of Paul. You tolerated me. Mostly."

"I took care of you. Who do you think washed your clothes and cleaned up your messes? Who made sure you had new shoes at the start of the school year? Who fed you? I did, that's who."

"I won't argue that you clothed and fed me, but you never *cared* for me."

Adele fixes a glare on me that would ice over Medusa. "You were a sniveling little girl who refused to let me hold her. I wanted to mother you, but you kicked me. You hit me. You told me I would never be your mother. Do you remember that? Remember?" Adele's icy eyes lock onto mine.

I don't remember any of that. I only remember the disbelief and betrayal of my father in taking up with Mrs. Rose before the flowers on my mother's grave were frostbitten. *He grabbed Ronnie's shirtfront. He defied Adele for me.*

Adele clasps her hands together in an operatic pose.

"He needed me to take care of you, but I needed him to love me."

I think I'm going to be sick. "And did he?"

Adele stands up, stretching as tall as she can. "Yes, he did."

My silent father doing as Adele commands—that's what I remember of their relationship. If that's love, then I guess he did love her.

"I wanted to love you, Justine. But you wouldn't let me." This is revisionist history spilling out of her mouth. Adele's version of my life as a foundling.

"I was a bereaved child."

"You were hostile and intractable."

"I believe that I still am. I didn't need you to love me, Adele. I needed my father's love. You deprived me of that."

"How?"

"By making sure every wrong I did and every mistake I made was pointed out. And everything that Paul did got a gold star and was hung on the refrigerator."

"You sound like a child. A jealous child, which you always were."

"Of course I was. I was jealous in the same way that Cinderella was jealous of her stepsisters; they had the unconditional love of their mother's husband and his own flesh and blood served them."

"You never served—"

"Adele, you're being literal. I'm saying that I felt, and feel, like a second-class citizen in this house and you made my father treat me like one. Now he's gone, and I'm done. You'll never have to think about me again. Oh, wait, you probably don't think about me anyway. It won't be a loss."

Adele doesn't say anything to that. She backs down, steps away from me, walks around the small kitchen, pushing canisters back into alignment, testing the countertop for crumbs. "Justine. What are you going to do about the house? I can't live without the rents."

I finally get it. Now, after all these years, Adele needs me. Not for myself—she's already proved that she needs my service, if not my affection—but for the one thing my father, in the end, refused her; the income from the house next door.

Adele leaves me alone in the kitchen, snapping off the overhead light on her way out, as if I'm not standing there, as if I'm going to leave it on and cost her more in an electric bill. Old people get freaky about expenses. The fixed income that they welcome at retirement must feel like bait and switch. Inflation and recession screw up the best of plans. Surely this house is mortgage-free. I have no idea what the rents are from next door, but my guess is that they're substantial enough that Adele and my father have been living comfortably on them since his retirement. Then I think of the yellowed vinyl siding and the neglected yard.

The only window in the kitchen looks out at the big three-decker. I can picture Adele standing in the window, looking over at the house on the day my father came home from the hospital with only his little girl and not his wife. Did her scheming start then, or was she honestly generous, like Diane Santos, with casseroles and kindness? There is nothing more endearing than a man alone with a child. Who could resist? And if the man came with a good job, plus a triple-decker, what woman wouldn't set her cap for him? It made sense, this moving into Adele's house, cramming me into a closet. One more rental unit made available.

Adele is in the living room, sitting on the couch that has been my bedroom for the past week. She isn't doing anything, and I get the impression that she's waiting for me. I come in and sit in the chair opposite her. Her white hair has lost the just-coiffed look and there is a tiny pull in her stocking. In the big cushy couch, she looks like a gnome. I feel the slow cooling of my stoked temper. She looks like what she is, a fragile old lady.

"The reason he wanted that house to go to you was that he thought you needed the stability."

I would gladly give up the "stability" of owning the house next door for one moment when my father opened his arms and held me.

I'm exhausted with the day and this conversation. If I had hoped to slouch out of New Bedford with empty promises to keep in touch, I know now that's impossible. I am forever tied to this woman. "For right now, we'll split the rents."

Adele's expression is more one of victory than of relief and gratitude.

There's no way I'm staying in that house tonight. I call Paul and tell him that his mother is going to be alone unless he or one of his hulking teenagers comes to granny-sit. I rip off my funeral clothes and stuff them into my duffel. My jeans and a plain white T-shirt feel like home to me. I toss on a navy blue fleece vest and run a brush through my hair. I'm out of here. Except that I have no car. I don't think I'm up to stealing Adele's car, even if only for the night. I call a cab and sit on the steps to wait for it. While I wait, I call Mitch. We can indulge in New Bedford's haute cuisine down on the historic waterfront.

CHAPTER 48

Fried clams and french fries. That's what we end up with, and they are perfect, even if I have to convince midwest-erner Mitch that consuming whole clams, with bellies, is the only proper way to eat the bivalves. Clam strips are akin to fake maple syrup—okay but not right.

Mitch pushes the mess from dinner across the table and sets up his laptop. We sit side by side, hoping to get within range of someone's Wi-Fi. The first thing we do is look at the little video clip again. There he is, my lit-tle man, strutting his stuff on some stranger's deck, his open mouth looking like he's smiling, laughing. Enjoy-ing himself. As if he's right at home. I take a big swallow of my Sam Adams, trying to push the lump in my throat down. "What do we do now?"

"Let's check out the local papers, read their lost-and-found ads."

Mitch's fingers fly over the keyboard, scouring the Internet for clues as to Mack's whereabouts. Artie said he'd left him near Exit 8, so we search for newspapers in that geographic area. We find dailies in Springfield and Ludlow, Worcester and Hartford. None of them have a found ad to give me any hope, just sunglasses, bracelets, and a trash barrel.

Out of his black suit and dressed in chinos and an untucked denim shirt, Mitch looks a little more like the guy I hijacked, and I'm beginning to feel like he has a lot of variations: Hell's Angel, Beau Brummell, and now average guy. He taps the keyboard. "Let's put an ad in all of them. Tell me what to say."

"Blue merle Shetland sheepdog with one blue eye and one brown one, missing in area of Exit Eight off the MassPike. Very intelligent. Answers to Mack. Desperately missed by owner. Call . . ." I can't even get my number out before the magnitude of this loss clamps my throat tight.

Mitch pauses in his typing to wrap an arm around my shoulders. "We'll find him."

What I wonder is how I've managed to find him, this white knight. Life is so random. I would have to be a philosopher to even begin to understand how life isn't really lived in the big picture, but moment to moment. The big picture was trying to go east cheaply; the moment was when I decided to hop on the back of a Harley behind a total stranger, panic overruling common sense. A woman alone, and this guy might have turned out to be a mass murderer.

I have no idea if there is something happening here between a single mom with a missing dog and a one-legged violinist, but for right now, it's pretty nice to have his company. I am really not in the market for anything more. I've reached the point in life when the need or desire for a permanent fixture in my bedroom is so diminished, I no longer think it's missing from my life. Still, that arm around my shoulders and the sense of someone else taking care of things is sweet.

Mitch sips at his beer as he patiently fills in all the info for an ad in all the papers. I am suddenly so weary that I can hardly keep my head up. The weight of an entire life believing that my father had turned his back on me has shifted to the weight of knowing that he hadn't. The relief that at least I know that Mack is alive is almost as heavy a burden as worrying about him. New worries have risen. Having seen him, I may never be able to find him. It is certainly better, knowing for certain that he's not dead on the side of the road, but also cruel, in fate's own way, to have him just out of reach.

Just like Tony has been out of reach for the past seven years.

I call the restaurant. I know there's no way my ex-husband is at home on a Sunday morning. Marcone's Grill serves one of the best post–Sunday Mass breakfasts in the area. He'll be there, commanding the troops. This is good for me, because it means the call will be short and to the point and done. Above all, it means I won't have to chance getting his wife on the phone. Anthony, like me, didn't remain celibate. Unlike me, he settled down. One of the very few times Tony went east was to attend the wedding. I put him in the charge of a flight hostess and spent the next two days biting my nails until Anthony put him on the return flight.

The kitchen phone rings four times before a female voice answers with a rough, get-out-of-my-way "Marcone's."

I ask for Anthony. The rough voice on the other end asks the "Who's calling?" question and I have almost no idea what to say. Finally, I just give her my name.

It clearly means nothing to this woman, and the phone clatters as she drops it onto the counter. I hear her bellowing for Anthony. "For you!" I notice she doesn't mention who's calling, even though she's got my name. This woman needs to polish her secretarial skills. It's like ambushing Anthony. Very rarely have I ever called him, and this time it's going to be far more difficult than asking for the support check a little early.

"Marcone."

"Anthony, it's Justine"

"Justine, hi. What's wrong?"

Two little words and the floodgates open.

"I just don't know what to do." *I can't quite make my mouth say what I've called to say—"Please take him"— but Anthony has figured it out.*

"Send him here. I'll take care of him. You've had him all this time, all by yourself."

It's what I know has to happen. But I don't know if it's really the right thing to do. "I don't want to lose him."

"You won't. You're his mother, and you always will be. But a little distance may be just the thing." *I remember why I fell for him in the first place, this sensible, sensitive guy. Fleetingly, I wonder what would have happened if I'd stayed with him.*

"What will Mary say about this? Shouldn't you at least talk with her?" *I realize that I am putting my son into the same position I once suffered, that of stepchild in another woman's home. I feel my knees quake. I am about to change my mind.*

"Mary will love having him. Besides, he needs to get to know his half brothers."

The difference is in the blood. Anthony's twins are Tony's blood.

"Just for a little while."

"As long as he wants to stay, Justine, he's welcome."
The phone is muffled for a moment as Anthony responds
to someone's question. In that space, I feel the last of my
anger at Anthony dissolve.

"Anthony, I really appreciate your help."

"You should have asked for it more."

"I didn't want to. I chose to cut the ties, after all."

"Justine, I never meant to be mean to you. I was just
so conflicted." This last word sounds so Brooklyn com-
ing out of Anthony's mouth.

"What did we know; we were practically kids."

"Now I have a good business, and a good home. Mary
is a great girl. I think Tony will be okay here. I'll put him
to work in the kitchen. Who knows, maybe he'll like food
service." Anthony's voice is so excited, I have a flash of
guilt that I so deliberately kept Tony away from his father.

"He's watched me in the food-service industry long
enough; I don't think it has an appeal for him."

"Fair enough. Look, Justine, I'll send you plane fare.
He can finish the school year in Seattle and be out here
for the summer. How's that?"

It was a good plan, a workable plan. A summer back
east, then home to me in the fall. Except that Tony went
ballistic.

Mitch has noticed my slump. "You okay?"

"I think I've hit my wall. I'm exhausted."

Which leaves the question of the rest of the night sitting between us.

"I'll take you back to your mother's house."

"Stepmother."

"Step, then. Or not."

It's that little "Or not" that makes me smile. "I really don't want to go back there. I'm done with that house."

"Stay here."

We are back at Mitch's hotel, sitting in the lounge, having a last glass of wine and munching the endless popcorn provided instead of bar peanuts like those at Candy's Place. Mitch leans over. "It's been hard, hasn't it?"

"You don't know the half." I am so tired that I spill out half my life story, only partially edited. I've told him about Mack and our dancing and why I am so desperate to have my dog back. I tell Mitch about leaving home the day after high school graduation and why coming back to New Bedford was supposed to heal that breach, and maybe it has. Because my thoughts have been on the past so much, I tell him about sending my son away when he was sixteen and how that made him so hurt and angry that he estranged himself from me. Mitch hands me his clean handkerchief.

I swallow back the uncontrolled self-pity and ask him to tell me about life with a handicapped plate. He talks of being a normal teenager, then not a normal teenager. About friends who were freaked-out and friends who remained loyal. About being a badass when the mood strikes and the way some music is so divine that he plays without even thinking, just letting the music take charge.

And now we're at that junction where every date eventually arrives—the yes or no moment.

"No expectations, Justine. There are two beds, and I don't think I snore." Mitch tosses this out so casually that it almost seems conceivable that I would share a room with him and not sleep with him.

"What about my expectations?"

Mitch smiles and those blue eyes, just the color of the

sky on a bright fall day, light up and he is suddenly quite lovely.

His room is only one floor up, but we take the elevator. I can see us in the mirror that lines the walls. I fit neatly against Mitch's side. My hair is scrambled and I watch myself struggle to fix it. I watch Mitch watching me, so I keep the worry off my face as the questions rise with the elevator.

Do I know what I'm doing? Is this a good idea? Am I simply giving in to all my bad impulses that I have worked so hard to control?

All questions cease when the room door closes behind Mitch and he takes me into his arms in a decidedly not-for-comfort-alone manner. We make love and then I am out cold.

Room-darkening drapes make me think that's it's before dawn when I finally climb out of the deepest sleep I've enjoyed in two weeks—dreamless, cocooned in the comfort of a hotel mattress and surprisingly cushy pillows. The length of a good man beside me, but respectfully on his own side of the bed. I reach for him and can't find him. Sitting up, I hold the sheet to my chest like a ravished virgin and see Mitch sitting at the little table provided by the hotel, thumping away at his laptop, his head moving to something on his iPod. A pair of crutches rests against the other chair. I wake up and smell the coffee. He's been down to the complimentary breakfast and brought up food. On one leg. Amazing man.

Mitch closes his laptop, winds the earphone cords around his iPod, and pushes his chair away from the table. I take that as an invitation. He takes me onto his lap and wraps his arms around me. "Pack your bags, lady, and let's get outta Dodge."

"Do you always talk like someone from the Wild West?"

"That's the Wild Midwest to you."

"Where are we going?"

"To find your dog. Look." Mitch turns the laptop so that I can read what he's found while I've been sleeping. "Found, small collielike dog. Gray and black, one blue eye, one brown. Call . . ."

I nearly weep. "That's got to be him. Where is he?"

"This is the *Moodyville Press*. I'll Google Moodyville; you call the number."

I wonder if the hope on my face will blind Mitch. My hand is shaking as I punch the number. I misdial twice before I get all ten digits right.

"You have reached Ed and Alice Parmalee. Please leave your message . . ."

Her voice. The one on the video, the one that calls my dog "Buddy." Alice. Ed and Alice Parmalee. I know where my dog is.

"Mrs. Parmalee, my name is Justine Meade, and the dog you found"—I actually have to take a breath—"is mine."

CHAPTER 49

Deep in the laundry room, Alice hasn't heard the phone ring. Ed is just coming in from getting the Sunday paper, Buddy at his feet, his nose pointed skyward in expectation of a treat. The flashing message light goes unnoticed until it catches Ed's eye as he sits down with a fresh cup of coffee.

"Who the heck is calling on a Sunday morning?"

"Maybe it's someone with a zoning board question. Or it could be Jen, asking if we want any more squash." Alice pours kibble into Buddy's dish, the musical chime of breakfast making him do his little happy hop.

"No, Jen would just leave it on the counter. Anonymously." Ed reaches for the play button.

"My name is Justine Meade, and the dog you found is mine."

The air in the room is suddenly gone, the atmosphere around Alice a vacuum, a void. She reaches for the delete button even before the caller gets to her telephone number, but Ed holds her back. "You can't."

Alice slaps his hand away. Slaps away the good feelings of yesterday, the progress, the fresh air entering her burdened lungs suddenly sucked away by a stranger's voice, a woman claiming their dog as hers, repeating her telephone number twice. It isn't enough to slap away Ed's hands; she wants more—to hurt someone or something. Suddenly, she is pummeling Ed, as if it's his fault.

"Alice, stop it. Enough. I've had enough." Ed moves so quickly away from her that Alice slips, nearly going to the floor. He catches her but holds her away. "This isn't my fault. This is just how life plays out."

"You made me put in the ad."

"We agreed we had to do it."

"We don't have to call her. Finders keepers."

"Alice, that's not how we operate, and you know it. How could you live with yourself?"

"How can I live without Buddy?"

Ed is still holding Alice at a distance, but now he reels her in, holds her close. "She's going to have to prove ownership. We can make it tough."

Alice's tears dampen the front of his shirt and he remembers the first time he held her close. How many years ago? Too many to count. He held Alice in his arms for the first time an hour and a half after they were on their first date. It was the day that Nixon ended the Vietnam War. Everyone was celebrating. The television was on in the pizza place, where they were testing the waters of their acquaintance over pepperoni. The sight of Tricky Dick announcing the cessation of the war that had ruled their young lives was enough for an embrace between strangers. At the end of it, Ed knew that they'd never be strangers again. She fit so perfectly.

Now he holds his wife and wonders if he will ever know her again. Losing Stacy had unhinged her. For a

very long time, it seemed like he would never get Alice back from the dark place she had gone. He can't go
through that again. Buddy may only be a dog, but this
new creature in their lives, this object of their affections,
has lightened up the days and made smoother the nights.
Buddy isn't a replacement for Stacy. What he has become, in this short time, is a willing receptacle for the
flow of love that has been dammed up behind the silence
in this house. Even now, the dog stands at attention, his
ears turning like radar dishes, his unmatched eyes focused on them. His mouth is a little open, and his breaths
are shallow, audible. Like he's worried about them. Like
he wants to say something.

Ed keeps Alice tight against his chest as he reaches
out to touch the answering machine. He feels her quiver
against him, so afraid of hearing that message again.

Ed feels like Michaelangelo's God in the Sistine Cha-
pel, one finger reaching out to change the world. He hits
the delete button.

Buddy can't quite figure out how the people went from
all relaxed and happy, pouring kibble in the bowl for him
and talking to each other, to this, this wounded sound
coming from Alice, and the stiff fear-aggressive posture
from Ed. He whines a little, trying to get their attention,
trying to understand what's going on. Humans are so
changeable. You just can't trust them.

Finally, the crisis seems to be over and Alice drops
to the floor to pull him into her lap and embrace him so
hard that Buddy almost whines. He understands then that
she is sad again, and that disappoints him. Alice hasn't
been sad for a few days and he's thought his job here was
done. Buddy licks her face, tastes the salt from her eyes,
and licks again. Then Alice laughs, pushing him off and

letting Ed hand her back to her feet. They sit down at the table and he's free to go eat his delayed breakfast.

The people sit in silence, facing each other. He's not sure, but they may be touching hands. He can't see from his low elevation; he'd have to be rude and jump up to see, but he's not that curious about the state of their touching. Things seemed better and now this, this return to the gloom that permeated this house when he first arrived. He's worked hard to be a good guest, and even a good pet, if that's what they needed.

Buddy knows that he needs to break this tense silence with some action. Even a good dog can lie on occasion, and Buddy decides that there is a trespasser—or a squirrel—lurking in the backyard. The rabid barking and growling get the people up from their chairs, and suddenly Buddy is hopeful that for once they'll release him to chase whatever is out there, even if it is only in his imagination. They don't, but they do open the slider, letting him out onto the deck, which Ed has recently gated. He barks some more, then gives up the pretense. The people linger on the deck with him, although they don't sit on the chairs or water the plants. They are talking quietly, and this is better than the silence, so he feels pretty chuffed with himself for getting them to move.

"Hey, Buddy. Go for a ride?"

Buddy barks an enthusiastic yes and dashes in to get his leash.

CHAPTER 50

Mitch, the first-chair violinist, doesn't play Vivaldi;
he plays Mark Knopfler and Sting. I think he does that
for me. We're on the road by nine and, unlike the day
I went to find Artie, the drive is smooth sailing—no
delays, no traffic, a Sunday, not a busy weekday. We
chat. We are quiet with our thoughts. We hold hands
every now and then. My heart thumps with excitement every time I think that by the end of the day, I'll
have my dog back. I can almost feel the tickle of his
fur beneath my chin, the weight of his little thirty-pound
body in my arms, the wriggle of his happiness as we are
reunited.

My heart thumps when I glance at Mitch, who's tap-
ping out a rhythm on the steering wheel to the percussion-
heavy music. I try not to think that he's the first decent
guy I've hooked up with in a long time. Maybe forever.
I try not to think of it as "hooking up." I try to simply enjoy the feeling. For now. After all, all we have is
the now. I know this feeling all too well; the sense of

novelty and romance inevitably grows contentious and regretted.

I'll never follow another guy. Not even this one. I learned my lesson the hard way.

Then Mitch takes hold of my hand again and squeezes it gently. Violinist's hands, and they played me last night like a virtuoso.

Before we reach the Pike, I apologize for being on my cell phone in the car, but I have to call Saundra and Candy. I wish that I could get them both on the phone simultaneously, so that Mitch doesn't have to hear my girlie squealing as I breathlessly go over the steps leading to this drive, this moment. I wish he wasn't in the car, because I hate discussing him with my pals. "Yes, he's the guy who got me from Cleveland Heights to Erie . . . well, Conneautville. Why is he here?" I give Mitch a sideways glance. "I don't know. Just is."

Mitch gives me a smile and keeps thumping out rhythms on his steering wheel.

Saundra is far less interested in human relations, just cries and tells me that Sambucca, her husky, sends her love to Mack and can't wait to see him.

The Parmalees haven't called me yet, so I call them again, leaving the same message. I'm starting to get worried, but Mitch won't let me. He shakes his head and says that we'll sit outside their house if we have to.

I shut my phone finally and bask in the warmth of knowing that I am within miles of seeing my dog, of getting him back. I feel myself tearing up and then feel Mitch's hand on mine. I marvel at the warmth of this undeserved friendship.

There is one more call I have to make. I pull the little florist's card out of the pocket of my fleece vest; "In deepest sympathy, Anthony Marcone."

* * *

Tony fought with me about being sent to his father. "He doesn't want me. You've always told me that. Why would he want me now?" He begged and pleaded, called me names, but I was obdurate. I couldn't do this alone anymore. I was exhausted with living every day waiting for the next crisis, the next rebellion.

The air between us was charged with resentment and anger and distrust—on both sides. Anthony's offer was my best chance at being a good parent. Besides, it was only for the summer, a little time to decompress and start fresh in the fall. Mr. Sanchez was right: The boy needed a father. He'd never had anyone to show him what it meant to be a man: be kind, work hard, take pride.

As good as his word, Anthony sent us the money for airfare, and the day after school let out we flew to New York. Watching Tony walk up to his father in that airport arrivals lounge was like watching the young Anthony meet with his adult self. No one could deny that Anthony was Tony's father, and it was enough to break the ice between them. If this was going to work out better than I had hoped, it was also going to break my heart.

I dial my son, who now calls himself Marcone, and, for once, he answers.

"Thanks for the flowers, Tony. They were beautiful. Adele was pleased." The last bit is a lie; Adele never mentioned them, but it would be awful for him to think his expense went unnoticed.

"Sorry about your dad."

"Thanks. He left me the house. The triple-decker."

"Cool."

"I own it. Can you believe that?"

"Will you live there?"

"I don't know. It has tenants already." I could never be the kind of landlord that doesn't renew a lease. But the second-floor tenants are a young married couple; surely they'll be moving in a year or two. I don't ask, "Would you want me to?" I don't want to hear the answer.

"Justine, I don't know how you're going to take this, but Tony wants to stay here." Anthony sounds equally apologetic and pleased.

"I want to hear him tell me that himself." It is the day he's supposed to arrive home. He should be on a plane right now. I have cleaned the apartment like a frenzied housewife and bought every snack food the boy likes. I haven't had but one phone call from him since I left him in Brooklyn, and that one was curt and a request for a CD he left behind.

"Mom. I want to stay here. I can finish school without having to worry about moving again."

"I won't move again; I promise." I haven't told him that I have a new job, a good one at a health clinic. We can start looking for a new place when he gets home. I want to surprise him.

"Yeah, right. Just like the other times."

Tony's sardonic words pierce like a harpoon into the heart of a woman just trying to do the best she can.

Tony never came back to live with me. The next summer, he was too busy working in Marcone's Grill, learning the business, and then he was in college. For spring breaks and holidays, Anthony flew him back to Seattle, but the bond we'd had when Tony was little and still sleeping with his Donald Duck pillow was gone. Tony had finally found the stability he'd needed. A permanence that I had never been able to provide.

* * *

Moodyville is one of those forgotten Massachusetts towns, not quite mid-state, not quite the Berkshires. Pretty in a rural way, not a suburban way. Train tracks bisect the country route we find ourselves on, the Albany to Worcester line no doubt. Freight, not passengers. We go over tracks and then, oddly, go under a trestle as the road curls and winds away from the Pike. I feel like I'm on a carnival ride as the road rises and swoops, narrows and straightens. We pass a golf course, a lone foursome playing a midafternoon game. The road flattens out and there are little mill houses lining the slightly wider road, antique duplexes with asbestos shingles and spartan single-family dwellings with narrow porches, all over-looking the road.

We come to a four-way stop. A gas station, a coffee shop, a post office, and a utilitarian brick rectangle that is the town's administration building. Welcome to Moodyville. The coffee shop is open, and I suggest we stop and regroup, which is a euphemism for needing to use a bathroom.

"Maybe there's a phone book in the coffee shop." Mitch pulls into a convenient parking spot and we both climb out, a little stiff from the ride.

Two burly guys sharing a Sunday *Globe* sit at the counter, one stool in between. Mitch and I take a small booth that looks out at the parked cars. The waitress brings coffee and mugs, two menus tucked under her arm.

"Do you have a phone book?"

"Sure." She fishes one out from behind the register and brings it, along with the creamers, on her next trip by our table.

Mitch opens it and quickly finds what he's looking for. "Edward Parmalee, twenty-nine Old Path Road.

Same number, and there's only one Parmalee listed in Moodyville."

Suddenly, I'm famished, and we both order the Hungry Man Special. I feel like I'm delaying Christmas with this, but we haven't heard from the Parmalees yet, and I feel for Mitch, who has driven all this way on the strength of one cup of weak hotel coffee.

The waitress is quick with our order and is back in no time with platters of eggs and bacon, then freshens up our coffee.

"Can you give us directions to Old Path Road?"

"Sure. It's easy." She begins to outline a route that has more twists and turns than a video game.

One of the counter denizens chimes in. "Lil, they don't have to go down Creighton; they can take the right at the old mill."

"Either way, they have to end up on Cemetery Road." This is from the second guy. "You folks going to hike the old path? You can start at the mill if you want."

"No, we're looking for Ed and Alice Parmalee. They found my dog."

"Oh, that's a cute dog. Ed brings him here every morning." Lil drops the check on the table. "I make sure there's a little bacon to take out to him.

I'm quicker than Mitch in grabbing the check. *Ed takes my dog on rides.*

"Ed says Alice is real attached to him. It's helped." The guy on the right-hand stool folds up the paper and spins around to face us.

"Helped with what?" I hand Lil the check and a ten.

The room goes quiet. We are, after all, strangers. Then he shrugs, as if he realizes that what he has to say isn't a secret. "They lost their daughter a few years back. Alice took it pretty hard."

"I'm sorry to hear that. Lost how?"

He clams up again, and I recognize a good old-fashioned New England reticence.

The other guy speaks up. "Drowned. Right there in the millpond."

"That's so sad."

"They thought she'd run away."

"How old was she?"

"Fifteen. Right, Lil?"

"Yeah, sophomore."

Lil leans toward me and lowers her voice. "No one likes to say, but it was suicide."

"Jesus. A child?"

She nods and drops the change on the table, where I add another couple bucks to it for a tip. The joy that's been festering under my rib cage all morning is tempered now, diminished a little. I can't help but think that it would have been preferable for the Parmalees' daughter to have run away. They could have survived that. What a tragedy. No wonder Alice has found comfort in Mack. He excels in that.

Mitch slides out of the booth. "Okay, so right past the mill, left onto . . ." He rehearses the directions until everyone in the room is satisfied that we will find Old Path Road and my dog.

I buckle my seat belt before I can say what is on my mind. "It may be hard to get him back from them, if they've gotten that attached. What if they won't give him back?"

Mitch takes my hand. "Justine, they can't keep him. He belongs to you."

The road tucks up again and for a little while follows the slow S-curves of a muddy brown river. We go over a noisy two-lane bridge, and there is the abandoned mill that must have given rise to the little mill houses. There is a millpond behind the brick factory, a spill of river water sliding over the lip. The maple and oak trees on the far side are reflected in the water; I'm sure that in a few weeks it will be a dazzling display of color, but right now it's just a pretty image. And then I remember what the guy in the coffee shop said. It's still a pretty image, but I look away.

I'm on a mission and we keep moving, hunting down the next series of signs that will lead us to the road called Old Path.

They still haven't called me back. It's enough to make me think crazy thoughts.

"Right on Creighton Road." I'm down to the last two turns of this complicated backcountry drive. "Quarter mile, right on Owen Farm Road." We're passing pastures and woodlots, a state park, and empty farm stands. We pass the only commercial building we've seen, a manufacturing plant, but I can't tell what they manufacture.

We're finally on Cemetery Road. We pass the cemetery, one stone pillar flaking white paint and the other scraped to the brick. And just beyond, there it is: Old Path Road. My stomach leaps with excitement. I'm within minutes of getting Mack back.

CHAPTER 51

They take the Cutlass because Buddy can sit between them. As they pass the cemetery, for once he doesn't whine, but instead flops down and puts his head in Alice's lap. She strokes his ears gently, thoughtfully, not saying anything to Ed, too much needing to be said.

They take the Pike, then get off on Interstate 91, heading north. Ed seems to have a plan, so Alice watches the scenery go by and lets him be in charge. It takes too much energy even to wonder where they're going. Ed exits at Northampton, asks her if she wants to stop for lunch. She shakes her head no. They continue through town slowly, dodging a constant gauntlet of collegians crossing the wide main street.

It is too much like losing Stacy, and that is a blasphemous thought. How can losing a child in any way be equated to giving up a dog? But the sorrow is there, the same taste of loss. The same weighted limbs and difficulty keeping the breath in her body. She shouldn't have allowed herself to want Buddy. She should have pushed him away. She should have kept Ed away. But Buddy has joined them back together. After being broken shards, cutting each other with every glance, the sense of being cup and saucer again has been good. If Buddy goes, when Buddy goes, what will become of that newly repaired bond?

Their route takes them through the Smith College campus and beyond, past Cooley Dickinson Hospital, until they enter Florence and Alice realizes where they are going—to Look Park. It has been years since they visited the park with its little zoo and the miniature train that circles around it. They spent many a summer Sunday at Look Park, swimming and walking the trails, picnicking on a basket stuffed with their favorite picnic food—cold chicken and potato salad, Jell-O salad, and, at Stacy's request, Ring Dings for dessert. They'd visit the zoo twice, once to say hello and once to say goodbye. A dime bought a handful of feed for the goats. Once one of the goats knocked Stacy down, but she got up, dusted herself off, and announced that the goat was sorry and wouldn't do it again, then asked if she could have more feed.

"Do you remember how Stacy would always call out 'Look! Park!' when we saw the gates?" Ed signals to get in line at the entrance. There are hundreds of cars; even for a spectacular September Sunday, that seems like a lot.

"I remember. She never got tired of the joke."

Ahead of them is a van hauling a small trailer holding a big wicker basket. "Hey, Alice, I think I know what's going on."

"I think you're right."

"The balloon festival. We always promised Stacy that we'd let her go up in the tether ride, just as soon as she got big enough to see over the edge of the basket."

"How come we never did that?"

"Got busy with other things, forgot about it. I don't think we've been here since she was eleven."

They are talking about Stacy. They almost never speak of her. Only the strangled admission of missing her on those days when the grief rises like the immutable tide. Never like this, conversationally.

Ed finds a parking spot on the edge of the field and they sit for a few minutes, watching the balloonists set up. Each group has what seems like acres of silk stretched out on the ground. Oranges, yellows, black, and lime green—the hues are like a giant's spilled paint box. Ed squares his ball cap on his head. "Come on."

Buddy trots along beside Alice, obviously excited to be in a new place. He keeps looking at her to make sure she's there, then puts his nose to the ground to sniff up the myriad scents of new people, dogs, and dropped hot dogs. Ed leads them to a booth advertising tether rides.

"Really, Ed?"

Ed wraps an arm around her shoulders, squeezing her close. "Yes, really. We always said we would, and now we are."

"We said we'd take Stacy."

"And we are."

"What do you mean?"

"We have to believe that she is always with us. Wherever we are, whenever we speak of her, or don't speak of her, she's still with us. She's here because we remember her being here. We'll take her with us on that promised balloon ride because we will both be thinking of her."

Buddy is enjoying himself immensely. This place is laden with new scents. He's greeted two dogs, both very interested in him. Nice guys, also leash-restricted, but not discouraged from saying hi. Buddy thinks that maybe this is a dance place. Even though it is outside, the people and the dogs here all have that special excitement that emanates from people and dogs doing fun things. Alice and Ed are slipping him treats as they wander around. They are touching, and the worry that Alice showed earlier has subsided, although he can still smell it. They stand still for a long time as one of the objects on the ground begins to move. Buddy growls, but the people don't seem afraid, so he stands quietly as they ooh and aah as the thing slowly grows huge, making a constant roar. It is finally upright and a stranger takes Buddy's leash out of Alice's hand. Unbelievably, Ed and Alice climb into the object, which isn't a car and isn't a truck, but it roars with a breathy violence that makes him think of Artie. Buddy locks eyes on Alice, who calls out to him, "Be a good boy."

Gradually, Ed and Alice rise into the air, so high above him that he can't see them anymore. At once, the sense of being lost descends on him and he whines softly, all the while keeping his eyes on the balloon.

Ed and Alice didn't tell him down-stay. Didn't tell him to be quiet. They handed his leash to this stranger and left him. He can't see them, can't smell them, and can't hear them. He is surrounded by these objects with their noise, by strangers and confusion. The nervousness and fear that living with Alice and Ed has made go away suddenly grip him and he can only bark, a sharp volley of panic.

CHAPTER 52

We pull up in front of a raised ranch with a two-bay garage. One of the garage doors is open and the bay empty. Now I'm sure that they've run off with my dog. I jump out of the Camry almost before Mitch has come to a stop. I run to the front door, jabbing my finger at the bell over and over. I can hear the chime ringing like Big Ben in miniature. Failing to get anyone's attention, I risk being arrested as an intruder and go into the garage. I bang on the metal door that leads into the house. I try the knob, but, not surprisingly, the door is locked. They may not care about the contents of their garage, but they do lock their doors. I press an ear against it to see if I can hear Mack barking at the sound of my voice.

Mitch catches up with me as I run to the back of the house. "Justine, wait. Calm down."

"You calm down! I want my dog." I scramble up the steps to the deck and grab the handle of the slider. Locked. Cupping my hands around my face, I peer into their living room. Dog toys litter the space—stuffies and squeakies. A chew bone and a fleece pad lie on the couch. But no dog. If Mack was in there, he'd be frantic with excitement. I step back from the window.

Mitch calls up to me. "Justine. This is Jennifer. She's the Parmalees' neighbor." Mitch is still at the bottom of the stairs, and with him is a young woman, staring up at me like I have two heads.

"Why don't you come down and we'll talk." Jennifer is wearing pink scrubs and white clogs and her tone is pure charge nurse.

"All right." I'm not going to let this stranger prevent me from claiming my dog, but I won't misbehave. "My name is Justine Meade. I saw the Parmalees' ad for a lost dog in the paper. He's mine. I just want him back."

"Buddy's yours, then?"

"Buddy? No. Mack, short for Maksim. Are you going to ask me to prove ownership?"

"I'm not. They might." Jennifer sits down on the second step. "He's been good for them."

"That's the second time someone has said that. I heard about their loss. I'm not unsympathetic, but he's my dog."

"How'd you hear about Stacy?"

Mitch chimes in. "The coffee shop. We stopped for directions."

"Small town. Everybody not only knows everyone else's business but then makes it their business to talk about it." Jennifer gets up. "Come on over to my house for coffee. I don't know where they've gone, but I have Alice's cell phone number. I'll call them."

For the first time since pulling into the driveway, I begin to feel less anxious. Maybe for the first time since Artie left me in Ohio, I can relax. The Parmalees will come home, I will be reunited with Mack, and the whole

ugly episode will be over. I will thank them profusely.
Now I wish that I could give them a reward, but I can't,
not really. I'll send them something from Seattle, a year's
worth of coffee maybe. A Christmas card from Mack
and me every year.

Jennifer has her back to me as she fiddles with the
coffeemaker. "This is going to be very hard on them, on
Alice especially. They've been shadow people ever since
Stacy died, and Buddy—I'm sorry, Mack—has been a
godsend. Even the fact that they're out for a Sunday drive
is a big deal. I guess you must have just missed them."

"I called this morning. When did they leave?"

Jennifer doesn't move for a moment. "A hour, maybe
two. What time did you call?"

"Mitch? What time was it?"

"Eight, maybe quarter past."

"I called and they left." The panic bubbles in my gut.
"They've taken my dog."

"They wouldn't do that. Maybe it's something else,
not a drive."

"Please, just call them now."

Jennifer fishes her cell phone out of her purse, thumbs
a number, waits. "Voice mail. Alice must have her phone
off."

It is a déjà vu moment. "Try again, please." Does everyone who has my dog keep their phones off?

Jennifer leaves a message. She speaks so quietly, I
don't really hear what she says.

"They've doted on him. Ed brings home a new toy
practically every day, and he and the dog go to Lil's every morning."

"I know. The waitress told us. She slips him bacon."
I sip at the coffee I don't want. Mitch is drumming the
table, but when I look at him, he stops.

"Alice is taking him to class to learn how to be a therapy dog." Jennifer spoons a little sugar in her coffee, stirs it gently. "He's a real nice dog. I just . . ."

"What?"

"I don't want to see them regress. Alice is smiling again for the first time in seven years."

Seven years. My child has been gone seven years, too. "Well, I've had him for years, not days. I know how wonderful he is, but they can't be as attached as I am."

"No. Of course not." She taps her spoon against the mug. "Let me call again."

"Thank you." I know about loss. I know about not knowing if your child is safe. But, thank God, I don't know about losing a child to death. I can't imagine how painful that is. A mother's worst nightmare—trumping anything I have suffered.

Jennifer makes the phone call, the look on her face enough to tell me Alice hasn't picked up. She disappears for a minute, coming back holding something. "I'd like you to see this."

It is a small framed picture, a wallet-size school photograph of a girl with blond hair and blue eyes, braces glinting against the photographer's flash. She has a big smile on her face, but her eyes are not smiling. It's as if the photographer said, "Say cheese," and she did, but there is no happiness behind it. It is more of a grimace.

"Stacy?"

"Yes. Her last school picture. She died seven months later."

I stare at the face of an innocent young girl. "Why do you think she did it?"

"No one knows. Alice blamed Ed, because he insisted that they take the psychiatrist's advice and medicate Stacy for her depression. But we don't know why she was depressed in the first place. They did their best with her, and it wasn't easy, them being older parents, but they gave her everything. They loved her entirely."

"So even having love doesn't guarantee happiness."

Mitch takes the little picture out of my hand. "Shit happens. Sometimes you survive it; sometimes you don't."

He's a survivor. And so am I.

CHAPTER 53

The balloon rises to the sky, a perfect azure blue sky without a trace of cloud. Alice grips the edge of the basket and looks directly down as the balloon slowly achieves its maximum tethered height. Buddy is standing with his nose pointed skyward. He is a tiny dot on the ground, hardly discernible as a dog; land-bound and diminished.

The propane engine roars intermittently, keeping them aloft. The vivid orange-and-blue zigzags of the balloon itself gently swell above their heads, so that the view is 360 degrees around them, but not above.

Ed puts his arms around her, leaning against her back, his chin on her head. "We aren't going to give him back." He has his lips close to her ear so that she can hear him against the roar.

Alice sighs, glad to feel herself surrounded by her husband. "Yes, we are."

She'd missed Jen's call, coming as it did while she was fumbling for dollars in her pocket to pay for lunch.

After listening to the voice message, she shut the phone off. Just a few more minutes, a half hour of being Buddy's family.

As slowly as they ascended, Ed and Alice in their beautiful balloon descend, the tethered balloon reeled in so gently so that the landing is barely significant. In between blasts of the furnace, they can hear Buddy, frantic at their disappearance. He is leaping and barking, fighting against the leash being held by the balloonist's assistant. As they get closer, they see the panic in his eyes, the fear that he has been abandoned.

Ed takes the leash from the assistant and says, "What's the matter, boy? Did you think we'd vanished into thin air?" Ed is kneeling, his face buried in the dog's ruff. "We aren't going anywhere. Don't you worry, fella."

Alice has her cell phone out. It's not fair to keep this dog from his rightful owner any longer.

Ed is still on his knees. Alice reaches out and presses her fingers against him. "Jen? It's Alice." Alice keeps her hand on Ed's back as she listens. "Tell them we'll be home in a couple of hours." Alice snaps her phone shut. "Buddy's owner is with Jen. They're waiting for us."

Ed doesn't speak, and she keeps her hand on him as he gets to his feet. The dog keeps his herd-dog eyes on their faces, looking from one to the other.

Back in the car, Alice fastens her seat belt. "It's all right, Ed. Really." She gathers Buddy up close to her. "We have no choice in the matter." She can imagine the anguish this woman, this Justine, has been enduring. She knows something about loss, oh yes, she does. The feeling is fresh inside her, building up to a deadweight. But this time, she won't blame Ed.

They make their way out of the park and back through Northampton. Ed takes the slower route home, skip-

ping the highway and the Pike, making it a true Sunday
drive through a countryside just beginning to show color.
Buddy is between them, snoozing contentedly, happy to
be back in the car with them.

"Ed, do you think we stop so I can water the mums"—
then Alice says something that she's never uttered before—"on Stacy's grave?"

Ed is silent for half a mile. He strokes Buddy's side,
curling his fingers into the fur. "Sure."

Buddy keeps his head in Alice's lap, but his back feet
are across Ed's. He sighs, happy not to be lost. Reunited
with Ed and Alice, riding in their car, going somewhere,
going home. Alice tickles the inside of his ear; Ed plays
with his feet when he's not gripping the wheel. They are
talking quietly, not sadly, but with a little inflection that
tells Buddy they aren't fully content. One word keeps
coming out of their mouths, each time with a reverential
softness: *she*. "When she . . ." "She used to . . ." "Did she
ever . . ." "Do you remember how she . . ."

He dozes and has a running dream, waking himself
up with twitching. The car has slowed and he feels it
making a sharp turn. Sitting up, Buddy yawns broadly.
He knows where he is, but it's the first time Ed has ever
driven all the way up to the place where Alice likes to
go when she brings him here. Usually, Ed stays at the
entrance, Buddy's down-stay place. And usually, Alice
doesn't let him out of the car.

CHAPTER 54

Ed shuts the car off and the engine ticks a few times before anyone moves. "Okay, let's get those chrysanthemums watered." He isn't looking at Alice, because he knows that he can't possibly deserve the look on her face. "Where are the watering cans?"

"Over there." Alice climbs out of the Cutlass, letting Buddy jump out behind her. For once, she doesn't grab his leash.

Ed comes back from the cemetery shed with a can. "Why don't you have one of your own? Why use these?"

"Never gave it much thought." Alice lets Ed fill the can, watches like a mother hen as he drains it over the parched mums.

Ed is careful to water the way Alice wants him to, each one of the four golden mums given an equal share of the water. They are tall and quite bushy, almost, but not quite, obscuring the lettering on the headstone. This is the first time he's seen it, and he is surprised that it doesn't hurt as miserably as he thought it might to look at it. For seven years, he's avoided looking at this rock inscribed with the short life of his only child, as if by putting it in the hard writing of stone, the loss would be made tangible. But in the end, it's just a rock. One that his wife has been carefully tending, making sure no lichen sullies it, no flowers go dead in front of it; that all the major holidays are represented with flags or wreathes, daffodils, or chocolate bunnies. It is Alice's place, her last remaining maternal responsibility. In the end, it is just a rock, and the loss is just the same.

Buddy's eyes are on the pillars. He keeps thinking that he should go and sit there, but he can't remember why that is. It's far more comfortable here, where Ed and Alice bend over the plants. He stands and shakes himself vigorously from nose to tail, circles three times on the soft moss-covered space between the stones. He tucks his nose beneath his tail and continues his nap. This is a pleasant place and he can wait until they are ready to take him home.

CHAPTER 55

I am shaken by this story of loss. Shaken mostly because when I examine it beside my own grievances, the Parmalees' loss dwarfs them. I can't get back any of the time I have lost with Tony, but I can do something they will never be able to do: I can call him. I've made it a policy not to bother him, not to impose my maternal neediness on his independence. My calls have purpose. When he calls me, it is usually with equal purpose—a status update, a holiday greeting. We could be former coworkers, not mother and son. I have meticulously nurtured the wound dealt when he left, until it has become a scar. And I sit in the Parmalees' neighbor's house and hold the last school photograph of their lost child and I am filled with regret. No, something more. I feel ashamed.

Mitch sits quietly, watching me. Jennifer has excused herself to finish getting ready for work. The photograph of Stacy is on the table. Abruptly, I pull my phone out of my back pocket and go out onto Jennifer's deck, carefully closing the sliding door behind me.

I just want to hear the sound of his voice.

The phone rings almost four times. Long enough that he can recognize the number and let it go to voice mail. But he doesn't. "Hey, Mom."

"Tony."

Clearly there is something in my voice that warns him. "You okay? What's up?"

He didn't leave me; he left a lousy situation. I have treated him like he chose Anthony over me. He chose a better life, which is all I had ever promised him. An unfulfilled promise.

"I'm fine, but all of this business, you know, with my dad and losing Mack has made me think."

"About what?" Do I imagine that he sounds wary? In our family, grudges are a contact sport.

I am ready to throw in the towel and let my son know, before fate, or God, or luck, decrees that I have run out of time, that I love him. I want to tell my son, a grown man now, that life is too short not to tend to the relationship you care most about. So I just say it. "I love you."

There is a pause, a furry silence between the cell phones.

"And I love you, too, Mom."

We can't impose any longer on the neighbor—she has to report for a shift at the hospital—so I suggest to Mitch that we go find something to do. What I mean is, give Jennifer a head start and then sit in front of the Parmalees' house until they get home. Mitch isn't at all for that. It's a little early for foliage, but we drive around looking at the trees anyway. Then we decide that lunch is a good idea, although I'm too excited and frustrated to do more than move the french fries around on my plate at the lovely little riverside restaurant we find in the next town. I keep my eye on my watch as painfully slow minutes tick away.

"Maybe they're back." I just want to be on Old Path Road. I can't take the chance of not being there when they get home, can't let them think that I'm not coming back for my dog. They'll claim that I deserted him.

"Are you going to eat those?" Mitch nods toward my fries and I am struck with the most perfect déjà vu of my life. Artie's words to me almost exactly.

"Are you going to leave me in the rest room if I take too long?"

Mitch laughs and then pulls a serious face. "No. Never."

I want to say, It's what everyone else does to me. But I don't.

I think Mitch knows he's hit a nerve, because he reaches across the table and strokes a lock of my hair back behind my ear. A tiny gesture of affection and possession, like a mother might do, or a lover.

We climb back into the car and try to find our way back to the Parmalees' house, where I am determined to sit until they reappear with my dog.

"I think you missed it." I twist in my seat and jab my finger at the cockeyed street sign disappearing behind us. We've missed the turn to get back to Old Path Road.

"I think we must have come on Cemetery Road from the wrong direction. I was looking for it on my right." Mitch slows to turn around, using the cemetery driveway. There is a car up ahead of us, in the middle of the road. Mitch throws the car in reverse to back out.

There are exquisite moments in life. When you first see the face of your baby. When a random act means that you meet someone special. When a car stalls and you have a moment to look out the window and see your lost dog.

There he is. Unmistakable. Maksim. My Mack. My dog. He is stretching himself fore and aft, just like he always does after a short nap. Mitch doesn't see what I'm seeing, and I grab his hand, pulling it off the key. "Wait. There he is!" I'm out of the car and running toward Mack.

Buddy stretches out his left hind leg, a little canine balletic flourish at the end of his stretching routine. Ed and Alice are quiet but not sad, and he knows that they'll be getting back into the car in a moment to head home, where he can have a drink of water and another snooze. A car pulls in, but he doesn't know it, and this isn't his property, so Buddy keeps quiet. It is so quiet that the shout startles everyone.

"Mack!"

A voice that he knows. A word that he knows: *Mack!* He always knew Justine would find him here in this down-stay spot. Mack is a blur of silver and black and he rockets toward the sound of his name, launching himself into Justine's arms like a furry ballistic missile.

CHAPTER 56

Justine is not what Ed has expected since hearing her voice on the answering machine. She doesn't have fangs or two heads. She is a reasonably attractive woman who is bawling her eyes out while smothering Buddy in her arms. It is obvious that she loves the dog. Obvious that this reunion is perfectly sweet to her, and doubly bitter for him. Even though Alice has said he must be returned, Ed knows that losing Buddy is excruciating for her. How will she survive another loss? "Don't take him. Please." He is mortified at his need.

"Ed, that's enough. The dog belongs to her. We love him, but we don't own him."

She has the dog in her arms like a baby. He is covering her face with kisses. Behind her, a large man in aviator sunglasses stands at a distance. "I know this is hard, believe me. But Mack belongs with me."

"You have no idea." Ed shoves his hands into his pockets. "You have no idea how hard it is."

"Ed. Stop. This isn't the same." Alice wraps her arms around her middle.

"As what?"

"As losing Stacy. He's a dog. We love him, yes. But we knew this might happen, and we also know that he's going where he belongs. That he will be safe."

Ed yanks his fists out of his pocket and presses them into his eyes. "I don't want to lose you again."

Alice pulls Ed's face down to hers. "You have never lost me. I'm right here." She looks over her shoulder at where Justine and Mitch wait, Buddy still licking Justine's face. "Come back to our house. I have a few things of his you'll want." She lets go of Ed's face. "Give us time to say good-bye."

Buddy is wriggling in Justine's arms and she puts the dog down on the ground but doesn't take the leash. He hits the ground running, barking his sharp little bark, and begins to run around all four of them.

Buddy/Mack wriggles in the ecstatic dance of a happy dog. His Justine did find him, just where he always thought she would. He is very pleased that Alice and Ed thoughtfully hung around today to wait with him for Justine.

But there is something wrong here. Alice and Ed are exuding that grief smell, the aura that never quite goes away but has been neutralized with rides together in the car and holding hands. This scent is fresh and heavier, easily tracked should they disappear.

Mack recognizes that Justine is tense, partly excitement, partly nerves, like a dog that's going for a ride but doesn't know where to. Her posture and Alice's suggest that these females are contending over something.

The people need to be closer together. Justine is standing outside the herd of two that Alice and Ed make up. The man at the distance, who is a stranger, although his scent, even from this space, betokens friend, is also too far away. This arrangement bothers Buddy/Mack, this distance between the people who should be in the same herd because he is responsible for them all.

Buddy/Mack does what good herd dogs do: He begins to eye Justine, fixing his gaze on her until she does what he wants, and she moves a little closer to Ed and Alice. He eyes them. *Stay put, sheep.* He looks back at the stranger and decides that he'll need moving, too. He dashes away from his herd and nips at the man's leg, finding a surprisingly unfleshlike ankle. Still, it works and the man steps forward. A few more nips and he's beside Justine, touching her. Buddy/Mack eyes this for a moment, then judges it a good thing. Then he takes the next step. He begins to circle the herd of four, racing around them, around the headstone, around and around until he is satisfied that he has brought the herd of humans he cares for home.

CHAPTER 57

Give us time to say good-bye. How can I say no to that? How could I not understand the need to have closure? My life is full of times I didn't get a chance to say good-bye. To Tony, to my father, to Mack himself. "I'm sorry; I can't."

"Please." She keeps her hand tight on her husband's arm. "It's not far."

Mack has been running around us, his excitement almost like that of a little kid at Christmas.

We open our car doors at the same time. "Mack, in." Panting from his crazy, happy run, Mack looks at me and then at them. The confusion is clear on his face, his little eyebrows giving him a perplexed expression. A question of loyalty.

"Mack, in." He doesn't obey. It can't be that a few weeks without class has turned my award-winning dog into a slacker. He utters a soft whine, and it hits me: Mack needs to say good-bye too.

* * *

"It's the right thing to do, Justine." Mitch pats my knee.

"So why do I feel like a villain here? Mack is my dog, my companion. I do understand how they could get attached, but really, folks, enough is enough."

The Cutlass pulls ahead and we follow. It is too easy to read the lettering on the headstone where they were standing when we arrived. The chrysanthemums are beautiful, but they don't obscure their daughter's name. And the brevity of her life.

"It'll be okay. They're grown-ups." Mitch covers my hand and I bunch my fingers together so that we don't end up holding hands. "Besides, from what you've told me about Mack, you can certainly understand their feelings."

All I understand is that I have Mack fur on my vest and he's in another car, disappearing into a garage bay.

Inside, Alice grabs a grocery bag and starts putting in dog food, Frontline, heartworm pills, three stuffed bears, four squeaky toys, and a bowl decorated with tiny hydrants. She moves quickly, as if the touch of each object burns.

"Really, you don't have to give all this to me."

"What do I want with it?" Her voice has that glottal thickness to it of a woman on the verge of tears. "Ed, will you see what's in the living room?" She sets the bag on the floor, as if the weight of it is too much.

Ed comes back with another chew toy. "This is all I can find." Alice takes it out of his hand and adds it to the plastic bag.

Mack shoves his nose in the bag and hauls out a stuffie, which he begins to thrust at me. I know this game, a gentle tug-of-war, and I grab the end of the toy, pulling hard against his resistance. When I let go, Mack doesn't continue the game with me, but shoves it into Alice's hand. She tugs back, but her eyes are on me. Mack lets go and Alice clutches the toy like a baby.

Mitch stands close by and Mack is sniffing him all over, trying to figure out who this new man is.

We're getting to an awkward moment, and I just want to be gone. "Thank you for all you've done."

"He should go out before you go. Ed, can you take him?"

Ed counters with "You should."

"Both of you, go, take him. We'll wait here." Mitch holds my shoulder, as if he thinks I'm going to chase after them down the back steps.

I really don't want to stand here making small talk with someone whose heart I am clearly breaking, but in the end, Ed and Mitch go out back with Mack. I realize that Alice needs to say something to me.

"He's a wonderful dog. You tell him that for us every day." Alice is a woman who has shed tears in public and is unashamed of shedding them now.

"I will." The dreamed-about joy of this reunion is absent. I am happy and sorry at the same time.

"When we lost our daughter, Ed and I, well, we grew apart. Having Buddy—Mack—has . . ." She pauses, collecting her thoughts. She keeps her eyes on the faceless teddy bear, stroking it. "Helped."

I am not a demonstrative woman, but I hug Alice. We hug each other.

Mack comes bounding back in, tail wagging, overjoyed to see me still here. But there is something different. He seems as overjoyed to see Alice as to see me. As much as I have been frantic over his whereabouts, imagining in my darkest moments the absolute worst, Mack has been with good people.

Mack moves from Alice to Ed, sniffs at Mitch, wags

his tail. And then dashes back to me, where he throws himself bodily against my legs, as if asking me to dance.

I send my dog back to the Parmalees so they can give him one last hug.

"You be a good boy. You're going home now." They keep saying the same words over and over, echoing each other, grasping his muzzle and kissing it. "We love you. Don't forget us." Mack gently licks Alice's face in what can only be farewell. Not vigorously like he does when he's excited, but one careful touch, with his ears cast back and his eyes holding hers. He's licked away her tears.

EPILOGUE

I bury my nose in Mack's fur, inhaling his familiar doggy scent, relishing the feel of his body in my arms. I can't imagine how the Parmalees must feel. Oh yes, I can. It's how I felt when Artie drove away with him. I felt that way when Anthony called to tell me Tony wanted to stay with him permanently, effectively ending my life as a single mom. I felt that way when my father married Adele. I felt that way every time some man made promises that he couldn't keep. Bereft. Grief-stricken. Alone.

Mitch is beside me, his fingers dancing on the steering wheel as a violin concerto blasts out of the speakers. He isn't drumming; he's fingering an imaginary violin. Then his right hand leaves the wheel and strokes Mack, coming to rest against my cheek. I lean into it. He smells of soap, his fingertips hardened by years of violin playing.

I'm going to be making changes again. Once more, I'll uproot myself and begin again. My voyage isn't over, but at least I know what I've been pursuing all these years; my particular white whale is forgiveness. I have forgiven my father, or maybe it's more accurate to say that knowing he did love me has allowed me to let go of the past. I have been forgiven, and that's a sweeter thing.

We are almost to Route 84 on our way to Brooklyn, where Anthony, Mary, and Tony are waiting for us with a Marcone's Grill dinner and a place to sleep. After that, I may say good-bye to Mitch, or I may not. We haven't talked about next steps. My duffel is in his trunk. My dog is in my arms, and wherever I end my voyage, with Mitch or not, my Mack, my dancing dog, will be always be with me.

Ed spots the dog first. It's a little forlorn, its shaggy coat a little unkempt. This one has eyes that match, a deep brown, and he's black, with rusty brown on his muzzle and a full white ruff. Sitting alone in the chain-link run, he greets them with a soft whine and a full body shake. He pokes one paw at the wire and then sits quietly.

It feels like the dog's eyes are on him, waiting for him.

"Go ahead." Alice is beside him, encouraging him.

"You're sure?" Ed doesn't mean about this particular shelter dog, but about doing this at all, taking him on.

"Never more so." Alice takes Ed's hand. "Let's take him home."

Ed nods; he cannot speak for the feeling that he has been graced by an angel, blessing him with a second chance.

ACKNOWLEDGMENTS

From conception to delivery—thank you Andrea Cirillo, Annelise Robey, Jane Rotrosen, and, as always, my superlative editor, Jennifer Enderlin. I could never have done this without your guidance, patience, persistence, and razor-sharp insights. This excellent collaboration is what makes a good book potentially a great one.

Thanks, too, for the wonderful support of the entire St. Martin's team: Monica Katz, Joan Higgins, and Paul Hochman, who keep me comfortable with the twenty-first-century way of book promotion; Stephen Lee, John Murphy, Matthew Shear, Kerry Nordling, Anne Marie Tallberg, Carol Edwards, and Ervin Serrano.

For insights into the world of cross-country trucking, I am grateful to Charlie Tucy.

Finally, I couldn't do this without the love and support of my husband, David. Nor would I want to.